A midnight lover beckons.
The moonlit terror begins...

Someone in the House
Barbara Michaels

"Barbara Michaels' thrillers are always a highly satisfying blend of unearthly terrors and supernatural suppositions."

—*Publishers Weekly*

"Michaels has a fine downright way with the supernatural. Good firm style and many picturesque twists."

—*San Francisco Chronicle*

"A master of the modern Gothic novel."

—*Library Journal*

"With Barbara Michaels, you always get a great story."

—*Ocala Star-Banner*

"Miss Michaels is a specialist. When the seances get going and the ghosts walk (and talk), even nonbelievers take notice."

—*New York Times*

"We are not normally disposed to read Gothic novels . . . but when Michaels turns her talents to the genre, we admit to being hooked!"

—*Denver Post*

"This author never fails to entertain!"

—*Cleveland Plain Dealer*

Berkley books by Barbara Michaels

AMMIE, COME HOME

BE BURIED IN THE RAIN

THE CRYING CHILD

THE DARK ON THE OTHER SIDE

THE SEA KING'S DAUGHTER

SEARCH THE SHADOWS

SHATTERED SILK

SOMEONE IN THE HOUSE

WINGS OF THE FALCON

BARBARA MICHAELS
SOMEONE IN THE HOUSE

BERKLEY BOOKS, NEW YORK

This Berkley book contains the complete
text of the original hardcover edition.
It has been completely reset in a typeface
designed for easy reading and was printed
from new film.

SOMEONE IN THE HOUSE

A Berkley Book / published by arrangement with
Dodd, Mead & Company

PRINTING HISTORY
Dodd, Mead edition published 1981
Berkley edition / June 1989

All rights reserved.
Copyrights © 1981 by Barbara Michaels.
This book may not be reproduced in whole or in part,
by mimeograph or any other means, without permission.
For information address: Dodd, Mead & Company,
79 Madison Avenue, New York, New York 10016.

ISBN: 0-425-11389-2

A BERKLEY BOOK ®TM 757,375
Berkley Books are published by The Berkley Publishing Group,
200 Madison Avenue, New York, New York 10016.
The name "BERKLEY" and the "B" logo
are trademarks belonging to Berkley Publishing Corporation.

PRINTED IN THE UNITED STATES OF AMERICA

10 9 8 7 6 5 4 3 2 1

Chapter One

GOD ONLY KNOWS how it all began. After all the searching and seeking, the rational debate and wild, intuitive guessing. I'm not sure we really arrived at the truth. If there is such a thing as truth. We poor humans are so imprisoned in narrow boundaries of space and time, so confined by five meager senses. We are like ants, running frantically back and forth on meaningless errands that consume our years, taking a few square inches of earth for a universe.

Father Stephen would say that God had nothing to do with it. In the early centuries of the Church he'd have been excommunicated for the error of Manichaeism. That's one of your classic, recognized heresies—the idea that the powers of good and evil are equal in strength, waging an unending war for the salvation or damnation of the world. His God is an aristocratic, bearded old gentleman in a nightshirt, and the Other One is a cross between Milton's lofty, tormented dark spirit and a Hallowe'en devil with horns, tail, and pitchfork.

Father Stephen believes that he and the old gentleman in the nightshirt won this fight. Bea agrees with his general premise, but takes a little of the credit to herself. Roger thinks he won, by strictly logical, rational methods. Me? I got away. That's not victory, that's strategic retreat. He who fights and runs away . . . But I won't be back to fight another day. At least not on that battlefield.

If I didn't exactly lose, I certainly didn't win. My adversary is still there, undefeated, strong as ever. The winter storms have come and gone, and the house still stands. It has endured worse—fires and floods, siege and invasion, enemies internal and external—for a thousand years; and I have no doubt it will still be standing a thousand years from now, when the slender silver ships pierce the sky on their journeys to the stars. Who will be living in it then, I wonder? Descendants of man, if there are any left, or buggy-eyed monsters from far-off worlds, alien aesthetes who admire the quaint architecture of the ancient humans? Be sure of one thing: if there is a sentient creature alive in that distant age, it will protect the house. The house will survive. It has its defenses, and its Guardians.

II

Joe left for Europe on Friday the thirteenth. He didn't have to; he picked that date deliberately. Joe likes to throw rocks at the goddess of fortune.

That's why I remember the date. On Thursday the twelfth I was in my inconveniently tiny kitchen mincing and chopping and braising and doing a lot of other things that do not ordinarily constitute my preparations for a meal. I should not have been cooking. I should have been correcting final exams. Some of my unfortunate students were pacing the halls outside my office, wondering—with good reason—whether or not they had passed. To delay their knowledge of their fate for even a day was sheer sadism. I knew that, because I was not too far away from my own student days. I was also, as Joe frequently pointed out, a simple, sentimental schnook. Why should I feel pangs of conscience about the lazy slobs who hadn't bothered to finish papers or study for exams? I did have pangs of conscience. But I fought them down and went on mincing, braising, and so on. This was Joe's farewell dinner and it had to be special.

Joe had suggested we go out—with me paying. Well, that was fair enough; it was *his* farewell dinner. We didn't eat out much. We were both paying off educational loans, and our combined salaries were less than that of a marginally competent insurance salesman.

My reason for vetoing the suggestion was not because I grudged spending the money. My argument ran along these lines: you'll be tired, you'll have a hundred last-minute chores to finish, you won't feel like getting dressed up—and wait till you see how well I can cook, when I put my mind to it. That last was the real reason, though I didn't recognize it then: "Look at me, I can do anything. Won't you miss me when I'm not around?"

We had been together for about six months. They had been good months. Even the fights were entertaining. There were a lot of fights, because Joe was an unreformed male chauvinist, and he kept stepping on my tender feminist toes. Rationally he had to agree with my insistence that we share the domestic chores. My academic load was as heavy as his, my prospects were as good. There was no reason why he should expect to march into the apartment every evening, throw himself into a chair and ask, "What's for dinner?" There was no reason why he should assume I would pick up his socks and do his laundry.

The first time he asked what was for dinner I handed him a pound of raw hamburger and said, "That's for dinner. Let me know when it's ready." I never really won the laundry issue. After a while it seemed simpler to scoop up all the dirty clothes when I went to the laundromat.

It's amazing how many little problems come up when people live together, in wedlock or out of it. Things you never think about in the raptures of first love—things so trivial they shouldn't matter. We fought about how often to clean the apartment, and who would clean it; we fought about scrubbing toilets, and about how much beer can legitimately occupy shelf space in the refrigerator, to the exclusion of less entertaining staples; we fought about our friends, and whether or not to lie to our families about our relationship; and of course we fought about whether we should get married. Sometimes he favored the idea, sometimes I did—but we never agreed.

Strange as it may seem, it was fun at the time. Joe had a quick temper and the sensitivity of a slug, but he never sulked. Our fights ended in laughter, after one or the other of us had recognized the basic absurdity of the issue, or in a loving and tempestuous reconciliation. That was Joe's strong point—tempestuous reconciliations. He made love with a blend of tenderness and toughness that swept me off my size-nine sneakers. His worst fault—or so it seemed to me then—was his complete lack of interest in anything but science. Music bored him; the visual arts were just ways of filling up empty spaces—he couldn't see any real difference between Raphael and Norman Rockwell; and as for my field . . . He told me early in our relationship that he hadn't read a work of fiction since his sophomore year in high school. Poetry? Oh, yeah, there was one poem he used to like: "A bunch of the boys were whooping it up. . . ." I had dreamed of a lover whom I could address in passionate iambic pentameters—Millay or Wylie, if not the Bard himself. But Joe had other good qualities.

We had only been sharing the apartment for a couple of months when Joe heard that his grant for the following summer had been approved. That evening he burst in waving the letter and grinning from ear to ear. I knew what the news was before he told me. We had discussed the grant, and prayed for it, but we had never really expected he would get it.

And—I realized, as my stomach dropped down into my shoes—I hadn't wanted him to get it.

I tried to emulate his enthusiasm, bubble over with congratulations, jump with joy. I guess I was too stunned to bubble or jump high enough. Joe made a snide remark, I snapped back—and we were at it again, hurling verbal missiles at each other. The final insult was when he accused me of being jealous and wanting to keep him tied to my apron strings. I never wore aprons.

The fight ended in embraces and apologies. Joe got himself a beer and we sat on the couch and talked.

"I'll miss you, too," he said, not looking at me.

"I know," I mumbled. "I'm sorry, Joe, I really am. I know what a wonderful deal this is. My God, there must have been five hundred applicants. I'm just a fool."

"Quit apologizing," said Joe. "Love is never having to say—"

"Oh, shut up."

"No, listen. I've just had one of my greater ideas. Come with me."

"What?" I stared at him.

"Come with me. We'll scrounge the money somehow—borrow it, if we have to. Hell, Anne, with you helping me I can get through twice as much work. I was wondering how I was going to accomplish everything in only three months. This is a terrific solution."

It was not exactly the most romantic way of putting the matter; but although this sour thought passed through my mind, I suppressed it. We weren't talking about romance, we were talking about two adult people with career aspirations trying to work out a reasonable solution.

"It's a lousy idea," I said. "Are you suggesting I give up my summer project and play secretary to you? Go farther in debt for the dubious pleasure of watching you work twelve hours a day while I run back and forth taking notes and fetching coffee?"

Joe's nostrils flared and his face reddened. "I am suggesting a way in which we can be together this summer. I thought that was important to you."

"It is. I guess," I said, staring thoughtfully at my clasped hands, "the question is, how important is it to me?"

"That's right."

"I'll think about it."

I thought about it. For the next week I thought about very little else.

Three months isn't much time to donate freely to

someone you love. However, the decision involved bigger issues. If I went with Joe it wouldn't be a free gift of love, it would be concession and surrender. He didn't compromise. I could go his way or not go at all, and that was how it would always be. The choice was mine, not just on this one issue, but for as long as we were together. Did I want to spend my life married to Joe, cooking and cleaning and having babies and typing his papers for him, with rewards like "And finally, I dedicate this book to my wife, who typed the manuscript and made a number of valuable suggestions"? Or did I want to type my own manuscripts and write my own patronizing dedications?

Less vital, but nonetheless important, was the fact that my summer plans involved someone else. Kevin Blacklock was a friend and a colleague. Like me, he was an English instructor; like me, he was poor and ambitious. We had been working on a book. A high school English text doesn't do a lot for one's academic prestige, but it was work we both enjoyed and we hoped to make a little money out of it. We worked well together; at least we had, until Joe moved into my apartment and my life. I had not seen much of Kevin in the past months. He had accepted my repetitive apologies with amiable goodwill, remarking finally, with the smile that was one of his most attractive features, "I understand, Annie; I've been there myself. Forget the book for a while. We'll go at it again next summer."

You can't help but be fond of a man like that. And you can't leave him up the creek without a collaborator when he's been so nice.

I tried to make myself believe my sense of responsibility to Kevin guided my final decision.

When I told Joe I wasn't going with him, he just shrugged. "It's up to you," he said.

The decision having been made, I stopped worrying about it. Sure I did. I changed my mind five times a week until finally it was too late to get reservations. Life was hectic that last month. In addition to the usual end-of-term work, I caught flu and went around in an antihistamine fog for days. Joe was even busier than I, but as the day of our parting neared, he succumbed to a certain degree of sentiment, and we had a couple of really marvelous weeks. Hence the gourmet dinner, the last night, the final moments . . . How romantic.

It was romantic, at first. I had gone all out—flowers on the table, candles, champagne icing in a cooler I had concocted from the bottom of a double boiler. The total effect was pretty impressive.

I was not so impressive. I don't *think* my name was ever intended to be a bad joke—though I sometimes wonder why any woman would call a scrawny, red-headed infant Anne. My hair isn't auburn or red-gold, it's pure carrot color and it curls up into tight, wiry curls when the weather is damp. When I was the same size as the repulsive kid in the comic strip, my figure looked just like hers. As I got older, the basic shape didn't change much, it just elongated. The crowning blow was when I learned I had to wear glasses. On that muggy May day, with four pots boiling on the stove, steam kept clouding the lenses so that my eyes looked like big blank circles.

Joe was late, so I had time to defog the glasses. There wasn't much I could do about my hair. He didn't seem to mind. He raved about the meal, as well he might have. The atmosphere was thoroughly domestic. After dinner Joe stretched out on the couch, with his head on my lap, and grumbled jokingly about how full he was.

This was not the first occasion on which I had vaguely sensed that domesticity and passion may be incompatible. I was tired. Six hours in a steaming kitchen had taken all the starch out of me. Piled up in the sink, awaiting my attentions, were all the pots and pans and dishes I owned. I could hardly ask Joe to help wash up, not on his last night, but I could see them in my mind's eye, like a great swaying pyramid of grease, and the prospect only added to my monumental fatigue.

However, when Joe started making the usual overtures my interest awoke. It really did. My state of mind cannot account for what happened.

Suddenly, shockingly, I was submerged in a drowning tide of despair. Every negative emotion I had ever experienced melded and magnified into a great enveloping cloud. I was blind and groping in the dark, my mouth wry with the bitter taste of fear, my ears deafened by my own cries of pain. In subjective time it only lasted for a few seconds. When I came out of it I was clutching Joe with clawed fingers and my face was sticky with streaming tears.

My tender lover pulled himself to a sitting position and gave me a hard shove. I saw his face through a distorting film of water; it wore a look of pop-eyed consternation. His eyes rolled toward the door, as if seeking the nearest exit. Then his mouth set in a straight, ugly line and he lifted his hand.

"Don't," I gasped. "I'm all right. I . . . please don't, Joe. Give me a minute."

Joe slid back to the extreme end of the couch and

watched stonily while I searched my disheveled person for a handkerchief. Of course I possessed no such thing. After a moment Joe got up and came back with a box of tissues. He did not sit down again. He stood watching while I mopped my face and my sweating palms and fumbled to find my glasses. I felt a little less naked and defenseless when I had them on.

Like a gentlemanly fighter awaiting his opponent's recovery, Joe judged I was ready to resume the match. "What the hell is the matter with you?" he demanded.

"Nothing . . . now." I pressed my hands to my head. "It's gone. My God, it was awful. I felt so frightened, so . . ."

And there I stopped—I, with my supposed gift of moderate eloquence, I who was steeped in the accumulated wit and beauty of the long English literary tradition. I could think of no words that would describe that experience.

"Do you know what you said?" Joe asked. "Do you know what you did?"

Dumbly I shook my head. The words I wanted still eluded me; I could see them fluttering in the darkness of my mind like bright moths, escaping the net with which I tried to trap them.

"You kept saying, 'Don't go, please don't leave me,'" Joe said.

I found words—the wrong words—stinging wasps, not pretty butterflies. "How very touching," I said.

"Oh, yeah? This is touching too." With a gesture worthy of Milady baring her branded shoulder, Joe pulled his shirt back. Bloody punctures spotted his chest.

"I don't know what came over me," I said feebly.

Joe sat down on the edge of the couch. He watched

me like a man facing a dangerous animal, alert for the slightest sign of menace; but mingled with his apprehension was an unmistakable air of complacency.

"I didn't realize you cared that much," he said. "Why didn't you say so before? You were so damned calm about it—"

"I don't care that much."

I might have put it more tactfully, but at the moment I was too worried about my own state of mind to care about Joe's. I was remembering stories about amnesiacs and people who suffer from epilepsy —people with blank spots in their lives and no recollection of what they might have done during the missing moments.

"Maybe you ought to see a doctor," Joe said.

I had been thinking that myself. The fact that Joe suggested it made me want to do the opposite.

"You're the one who needs a doctor," I said, with a weak laugh. "You had better put some iodine on those scratches."

"Yeah, sure. Listen, Anne—seriously—I mean— maybe you ought to get somebody to stay with you. I mean—"

"I know what you mean."

"Damn it, you don't! I mean, if you think I'm implying—"

"Well, what are you implying?"

A few more inane exchanges of this sort and we were shouting at each other. The quarrel developed along the old familiar lines, and it ended as our quarrels usually did. But it wasn't the same. I couldn't blame Joe for holding back, nor was I my usual responsive self. To put it bluntly, we were both afraid —afraid that the whining, clawing thing would return.

I awoke from heavy, too-brief sleep to find that the room was gray with dawn and that Joe was no longer beside me. Sounds of emphatic splashing from the bathroom assured me of his whereabouts, so I dragged myself out of bed and went to make coffee. When I got my turn in the bathroom and contemplated my face in the mirror, I saw that my eyes were sunk deep in their sockets and almost as expressionless as those of my namesake.

Joe never needed much sleep, and the fact that we had made it through the night without another outburst had restored his equanimity. I was too sodden with sleeplessness and disgust to regard his irritating cheerfulness with anything stronger than lethargy. I fed him breakfast, making scrambled eggs in the last clean pan in the house, and drank three cups of coffee. Thus fortified, I hoped I could make it to the airport and back.

We had borrowed a car from one of my friends, so we could be alone together till the last possible moment. The drive passed in almost total silence. We were an hour early, but Joe wouldn't let me wait.

"I hate standing around in airports saying the same stupid things over and over," he said gruffly. "Get the hell out. I'll be seeing you."

"Right," I said.

Awkwardly Joe put his arms around me and kissed me. He missed my mouth by a couple of inches. Before I could respond or return the embrace, he turned me around and gave me a little shove. I took two or three staggering steps before I regained my balance. When I looked back, he was striding toward the gate.

I went out and sat in the car. Planes kept landing

and taking off. Finally a big silver monster lifted up, in a roar of jets, and I decided arbitrarily that it must be Joe's plane. I watched it circle and soar until it was only a speck in the sky. The air was already warm and sticky. It was going to be another hot day.

III

I could have gone back to bed, but I knew I wouldn't sleep. I had two nasty jobs ahead of me, so I chose what seemed like the least nasty. At least I could sit down while I read exam papers.

An hour later I was still staring at the first sentence of the first paper. It read, "John Keats was born in 1792." Even the date was wrong. I was afraid if I picked up my red pencil to correct the date, I would start scribbling vituperative comments, so I just sat there, wondering how any college freshman could start an essay with "So-and-so was born . . ." Joe's plane was nearing the coast by now. It was a good day for flying, not a cloud in the sky.

The knock at my office door came as a welcome relief. Even a student would have looked good to me then—except perhaps the imbecile who had written that exam. "Come in," I said.

It wasn't a student, it was Kevin, my abandoned collaborator and good buddy. He stood in the doorway, all six-plus feet of him, smiling. In his hand was a paper cup.

"Coffee?" he asked.

"Bless you."

"I won't stay. I just thought—"

"Stay. I can't face these damn exams right now;

maybe a conversation with someone who knows how to speak and write English will make me feel better."

Kevin sat down in the student's chair beside my desk. "Joe get off all right?"

"Uh-huh."

Kevin nodded and looked at me sympathetically. With friendly dispassion, I thought to myself that he really was one of the best-looking men of my acquaintance, if you like the long, lean, aesthetic type— and who doesn't? His thick dark hair curled around his ears and waved poetically across his high intellectual forehead. He had fantastic cheekbones, with the little hollows underneath that are supposed to bring out the maternal instinct in all womanly women. His nose was thin, with narrow nostrils that would be incapable of flaring; his sensitive mouth looked equally incapable of shaping cruel words. Despite the delicacy of his features, there was nothing effeminate about him. He was a good tennis player and swimmer; his body was as neatly modeled as his face, and when he moved, susceptible female students forgot what they had meant to ask him.

I started to feel better.

"He's going to have a wonderful summer and get a lot done," I said briskly. "So will we, right?"

Kevin's long lashes (the man doesn't have an ugly feature) fluttered and fell. "That's what I came to tell you, Anne. I hate to be the bearer of bad news, after . . . It's bad news for me, in a way, but maybe it won't be for you; you could join Joe—"

"Oh, no," I said, in tones of heartfelt woe. I had not realized until that moment how much I had counted on our summer project. Without it I had nothing to hang on to. I might even be weak-minded enough to chase after Joe. And that would be worse than deciding to go with him in the first place.

Kevin sat in silence, his mouth twisted in a rueful grimace. "I'm sorry," he said, after a while.

"What happened?"

"It's my parents. You remember I told you about them winning all that money?"

"What money?"

Kevin's big beautiful brown eyes lifted to meet mine. He looked surprised; then he smiled.

"You were thinking about something more important at the time, I guess."

"Wait a minute, I do remember." Disarmed, as always, by his humility, I felt ashamed, and was able to dredge up the recollection of that conversation, months before. "The state lottery, wasn't it?"

"That's right. Half a million dollars."

"My God! That much?"

"Maybe I didn't mention the amount. Of course a lot of it went in taxes. But that's only the half of it. You know what they say about money begetting money? I don't understand how Dad did it—I'm a financial moron myself—but apparently all he needed was a stake. He's manipulated his winnings into a fortune, in less than a year. He didn't tell me about it till a few weeks ago, and honest to God, Anne, when he gave me the grand total I had to sit down."

"I'm so glad for them." The sentiment was as sincere as such statements ever can be; Kevin's parents, of whom he spoke often and fondly, sounded like nice people. "But what's the problem?"

"The problem is that they just bought a house," Kevin said. He was smiling with warm amusement, as he always did when he mentioned his parents. "I couldn't believe it. They sold the old house in Fort Wayne after I left, because they said it was too big for the two of them; and now they are the proud owners of a ten-bedroom manor house. Mother said she knew it was crazy, but she fell in love with it at first sight."

"That kind of craziness I can sympathize with. Why shouldn't they have a good time with their money?"

"Exactly." Kevin beamed at me. "I haven't seen the place myself, but it sounds fantastic. The trouble is, they don't want to leave it empty this summer when they go to Europe."

I laughed. My amusement was genuine; Kevin's mother and dad sounded like my kind of people, even if they had ruined my summer. "They really are living it up, aren't they? I can see why they don't want to take a chance on burglars and vandals; and I suppose you feel obligated to volunteer, right?"

"They've never asked much of me," Kevin said. "It isn't just the house, it's the family pets. Belle is a pretty old dog, she isn't happy without one of the family around, and one of the cats has this medical problem—"

"How many pets do you have?" I asked, half amused and half exasperated. I didn't mind (much) being supplanted by a sweet old mom and dad, but a senile dog and a cat with prostate trouble . . .

"Only four. Two dogs and two cats. Unless Mother has taken in more. She does that."

Kevin was looking so noble and serious and guilty that any decent person would have patted him on the head and told him not to worry. I couldn't oblige, I was too depressed. I wanted to put my head down on the desk and howl.

"I was thinking," Kevin said hesitantly.

"Good for you."

"I figured you would go to Europe with Joe."

"You figured wrong."

"Well. Then maybe you might consider . . . No, probably you wouldn't."

"We'll never know until you ask, Kevin."

"We don't have to work here. There's a good library at the house, I'm told, and plenty of room . . ."

I can't say that the suggestion took me by surprise. It was such an obvious solution that it had occurred to me immediately, and I had assumed that Kevin was using his parents' request as an excuse to cancel our summer plans. I wouldn't have blamed him. Unless his father made some disastrous miscalculation in his financial manipulations, little Kevin, the only child, wasn't going to be interested in three-digit royalties. Apparently he wasn't trying to weasel out of our deal after all, but I could see, by his furrowed brow, that something was bugging him; so instead of shouting "I accept," I waited to see what he would say next.

He said, "But maybe Joe wouldn't like it."

My jaw dropped. The people in the department sometimes joked about Kevin's old-fashioned manners and antique notions of polite behavior; there were even rumors that he never kissed on a first date. I had laughed at this bon mot, but had never taken it seriously. Now I wondered, but only for an instant. There was another, more plausible explanation for his outrageous remark.

"Joe has nothing to do with it," I exclaimed. "Honestly, Kevin, how chauvinist can you be?"

"I didn't mean—"

"I'm sick and tired of men telling me they didn't mean what they said!" That was unfair—Kevin had no way of knowing this was one of Joe's less attractive habits. "What is it really? Would your parents object if they heard I was living in the same house? Would the neighbors burn crosses on the lawn?" Kevin's mouth opened, but I didn't give him time to answer; I had worked myself into a steaming rage. "Because if that's the reason, I can live with it, but if you really think that I go when Joe says go, and come when Joe says come, then you and Joe can both take your notions of masculine supremacy and—"

Kevin fell forward, out of his chair. On his hands and knees, he banged his forehead twice against the floor.

"Will that prove an acceptable substitute to what you were about to suggest?" he asked meekly.

"Get up, you idiot," I said, laughing.

He did so. "I'm sorry, Anne."

"Okay."

Kevin shook his head. "It's the damnedest thing, how these subconscious preconceptions linger; I never suspected I was thinking that way, but you're right, it was a stupid, dumb idea. Will you come?"

"Certainly."

"Great."

Solemnly we shook hands across the desk.

Chapter Two

TWO WEEKS LATER I was hopelessly lost in Pennsylvania. The taxi driver was lost too. The sun was sinking in the west, the numbers on the meter had reached a total that froze the blood in my veins, and there was nothing to be seen but rolling hills, a stretch of rutted road, and two bored black-and-white cows.

"We must have taken a wrong turn at the last intersection," I said.

"You said turn right," the taxi driver remarked tightly.

"I was wrong. We'd better go back and try the other direction."

The taxi driver was an elderly gentleman. The noun is well deserved; if he had not been a gentleman he would have kicked me out of his cab long before. In eloquent silence he turned around and we went back the way we had come. The cows watched disinterestedly.

It was my fault. Kevin had given me detailed directions before he left campus. I don't know whether I misplaced them while I was packing to go home, or while I was packing to leave home. All I know is that when I got in the taxi, at the bus station in Pittsfield, they were gone.

I turned the contents of my purse out onto the seat of the cab. I found a recipe for cocktail dip, three old shopping lists, and some notes for a lecture on Byron. I did not find Kevin's directions.

The taxi driver watched with an air of fatherly patience. The meter was running.

"Oh, well," I said. "I know approximately where it is. Ten miles northwest. The name of the road is Green Valley. Or maybe Green Haven."

It wasn't Green Haven. There was no such road. Green Valley Road had two farmhouses and a tavern named Josie's Place.

By that time I was sitting up front with the driver, looking at his map. I had told him the life story of Kevin's parents—their poor but honest beginnings, their recent affluence, their purchase of the house. He was very interested, but the tale conveyed no clue to him.

"I don't get many calls out to the country," he explained apologetically. (At that stage he was still apologetic.) "And if these folks are newcomers, well, see, I wouldn't even know the name."

"But you must know the house," I argued. "It's a historic home, or something of the sort."

"Miss, every damned house in the county is on the historic register," said the driver. "If you just knew what it looked like, or its name, or something about it . . ."

Which I didn't.

We finally got lucky. A country store, at a cross-roads, had a gas pump, shelves of dry goods and canned goods, and a sharp-eyed little old lady who had lived in the area for all of her seventy years.

"You must mean the Karnovsky place," she said. "I did hear as it was sold to some folks from out west. You go down to the next intersection and hang a right . . ."

Her directions took us into a region so different from the farmlands we had been traversing that I could hardly believe we were in the same county. It was an area of big estates, and not nouveau riche, either. For the most part the houses were invisible, but the wrought-iron gates and stone gateposts, some with heraldic animals perched on top, indicated the quality of what lay beyond the trees and hedges. A few miles farther on and we reached another crossroads, around which clustered, not a town or a wide spot in the road, but a genuine Old World village. It was tiny—a dozen pretty old houses, a surprisingly large church, and a general store. The latter was not at all like the establishment run by the old lady who had given us directions. Instead of a sagging front porch with splintery wooden steps, it had a long stone facade with tubs of geraniums flanking the door. Instead of decals advertising beer and bread and cattle feed, it had a carved wooden signboard.

After passing through the village, we soon came upon the high stone wall the old lady had mentioned. It went on and on and on before we reached the gate. A bronze plaque on the left-hand pillar said "Grayhaven."

The taxi driver refrained from commenting on this example of confused thinking. He turned off the highway and came to a sudden halt. The iron gates were closed.

I had developed a not entirely unreasonable annoyance with Kevin, who might have offered to meet me at the bus station, damn him. I was prepared to climb the wall, seek out the house, and tell him what I thought of him, but these heroic measures proved to be unnecessary. The gates were not locked. We proceeded for another mile along a driveway walled in by trees and bushes. An abrupt turn brought us out of the leafy tunnel and gave me my first sight of Grayhaven.

The other day, when I was looking through some papers, I found a snapshot of the house. I burned it, which is not easy in an all-electric apartment. If I wanted to remember its appearance, which I do not, I would not need reminders. Every detail of the place is clear in my mind.

It lay in a green cup of valley, surrounded on all sides by wooded slopes. Behind it, terraced gardens rose in measured steps toward the trees. The plan of the house itself was square, four wings built around a central courtyard. The irregular roofline showed numerous stages of building, but the dominant feature was a massive gatehouse, castellated, battlemented, crenellated, and what have you. Sir Walter Scott would have loved it.

I rubbed my eyes. I have never been abroad, but I am an armchair traveler of the most fanatical type. I had seen photographs, engravings, even other people's slides. What I saw now was a medieval English manor house, perfect in every detail.

The driver's exclamation assured me that I was not dreaming.

"Criminy," he said. "Sure is big, isn't it?"

"Sure is."

We proceeded at a respectful twenty miles an hour along the road that descended in gentle curves. I could understand why the taxi driver was unfamiliar with this area. The owners of country estates don't need taxis; they would own three or four cars apiece, and maybe a helicopter. If they had car trouble, they just threw the blasted thing away and bought a new one.

The closer we got to the house, the more I doubted my eyes. Space warp, I thought; we drove through some sort of science-fiction gadget at the gate, and we are now in southern England, and maybe in another century. The taxi came to a stop before the gatehouse. It had been incorporated into a later wing, Elizabethan or early Tudor. The only door visible on this side of the house was a mammoth arched portal in the gatehouse itself. It was not difficult to identify this as the principal entrance—one could hardly demean such a structure by calling it a front door. I would not have been surprised to see a couple of lackeys dressed in knee breeches rush out to greet us.

Nobody rushed out. After the driver had switched off the engine, the silence of rural peace descended. The door, built of blackened oak planks, remained uncompromisingly closed.

I looked at the driver. He took his cap off and scratched his head.

"Looks like there's nobody home. You sure this is the right place, miss?"

I was not at all sure. It was hard for me to picture Kevin in this ambience. It was hard for me to picture anyone I knew in this ambience.

Then, from the shrubs along the driveway, came an incongruous figure, that of a shaggy, fat, ambiguous dog, clearly the result of some act of canine miscegenation. White hairs ringed its muzzle, which was of inordinate length. The muzzle opened; two rusty barks issued forth. Then, as if the effort had been too much for the animal, it collapsed onto the grass and lay there watching us.

"Belle?" I said, wondering why my illogical brain could forget the name of Kevin's house and retain that of his dog.

The dog's raggedy ears twitched when I spoke the name. Another rusty bark confirmed my identification.

"It's the right place," I said. "Look, it's late and I already owe you a month's pay; why don't you start unloading my stuff? I'll see if I can rouse my friend."

No doorbell was visible. In the center of the panel was a knocker, platter-shaped and two feet in diameter. Using both hands, I lifted the thing and let it thud back into place. I did this twice more before my muscles protested. The sound produced no result, not even from Belle, who had closed her eyes and dropped off to sleep.

The driver had unloaded my things—one bag of clothes, three of books and papers. He accepted the bills I handed him and scratched his head again.

"I don't like to leave you here, miss, if nobody's home."

I reassured him, if not myself, and he left. It seemed highly possible that Kevin had forgotten I was to arrive that day. I felt sure he would not leave the old dog unattended for any great length of time, but if he had gone out he might not be back till midnight.

Retreating a few steps, I shaded my eyes and looked up. The gatehouse was one story higher than the rest of the wing whose center it formed. Its windows were small squares, deeply imbedded in the thick walls. But the sunlight was still bright; as I stared I saw something move behind the highest window. A pale circle that might have been a face pressed itself against the glass.

The idea that someone was in the house and had refused to answer the door made me even angrier than I already was. I went back to the door. I would have kicked it if I had been wearing regular shoes, but the bare, dusty toes protruding from my sandals gave me pause. Moved more by exasperation than by an expectation of finding the door unlocked, I seized the iron handle and twisted it.

It turned, sweetly and smoothly. The door swung open. Before me was a vast open expanse of dully shining floor, framed by paneled walls hung with paintings and tapestries—and a tall form, trotting quickly toward me.

Kevin was wearing jeans and a blue T-shirt streaked with paint. His feet were bare, and as he came toward me, smiling broadly, a pattern of dusty prints marked his path. He should have looked howlingly out of place in that elegant, baronial hall, but he didn't; even the grubby footprints seemed appropriate, marking his right to be there.

He gave me a quick, brotherly hug. "Hey, good to see you. Have any trouble finding the place?"

"I lost your directions," I admitted. "And I've been banging on the door for hours. Where the hell were you?"

"Honest Injun, I didn't hear you."

"I'll bet you were asleep."

Kevin's protestations were so heartfelt and his pleasure at seeing me so genuine that I got over being miffed. We carried my luggage inside, and then he said, "Want to see your room first, or have a drink?"

"I could use a little something. I've been on the road

since seven this morning." I spoke absently; now that
my eyes had adjusted to the lesser degree of light
inside, I was increasingly awed. The hallway must
have been forty feet long, bisecting this wing of the
house. At the far end a double stair lifted toward a
central landing. Between the two wings of the stairs an
open doorway showed part of the central court—
flagstones, a fountain, hanging pots of flowers.

"This way." Kevin took my arm.

By the time we reached the library I really did need
a drink. It was in the west wing; to reach it we passed
through a dining room with mullioned windows and
tapestry-hung walls, a parlor lined with cupboards
holding Delft pottery, and the Great Hall, which had a
medieval timbered roof and one of those stone fireplaces big enough to roast an ox. By comparison the
library was almost cozy. Walls covered with books
always make me feel at home. There were two levels of
bookcases, the upper gallery being reached by a spiral
iron staircase. The room was large enough to contain
several big tables, couches, and chairs without looking
crowded. Double doors opened onto another part of
the central courtyard. Deep leather chairs and low
tables faced the fireplace, with its carved stone
overmantel.

When Kevin asked me what I wanted to drink I
collapsed into a chair and waved my hand distract-
edly.

"Anything, I don't care. Good heavens, my boy, I've
never seen a place like this—except in museums,
where they have whole rooms taken from castles and
manor houses. The place can't be genuine, it's four
hundred years earlier than the first settlements in
America. Did some eccentric millionaire reproduce
his ancestral mansion, or what?"

Kevin handed me a glass and took a chair opposite mine. A table between us was covered with books, papers, glasses, coffee cups, and plates. Obviously this was where Kevin spent much of his time. I was pleased to see such evidences of scholarly industry.

"You get points for the eccentric millionaire," he said, "but this place is no reproduction. It's authentic, from the topmost chimney pot to the stones in the cellar. Rudolf Karnovsky found it in Warwickshire, back in the twenties, and moved the whole kit and caboodle to Pennsylvania."

"It wasn't his ancestral home, then?"

"He was an emigrant from somewhere in central Europe," Kevin said, smiling. "Rumor has it that he arrived on Ellis Island with a pocket handkerchief and a mind full of guile, and very little else. He was fifteen. Thirty years later he was one of the richest men in America—which is pretty impressive when you consider that his peers had names like Carnegie and Rockefeller. Of course those were the good old days; no nasty taxes, no unfair antitrust laws."

"So he bought himself some roots and the stones to anchor them in. Fantastic."

"It wasn't so unusual. Hearst did something similar at Sans Souci, if you remember. He spent over a million dollars a year for fifty years, buying not only ceilings and mantels and paneling from European châteaus, but whole medieval castles and monasteries."

"Yes, I've read about that."

Kevin hardly waited for me to finish the sentence. His eyes shining, he went on. "I'll bet you don't realize how many castles were actually built in the United States. One of the most elaborate was in Pennsylvania, just outside Philadelphia. It was modeled after

Alnwick Castle in England, and was over two hundred feet long. Then there was Palmer Castle in Chicago, and Dar Island Castle in the Thousand Islands region, and Lambert Castle in Paterson, New Jersey—"

If I hadn't interrupted he might have gone on for hours. "I didn't realize you knew so much about the subject."

"I've been doing some reading," Kevin indicated the books on the table; they were not lit books after all, but bore such titles as *American Castles* and *The Gothic Revival in America.* A vague, undefined feeling of discomfort passed through me when I realized this, but my interest in what Kevin was saying made me forget it.

"The craze was at its peak during the 1890's," he continued. "But there was a castle-type house built in western Pennsylvania as early as 1843, and Hammond Castle, in Massachusetts, wasn't begun till 1925. It incorporated sections of actual buildings brought here from Europe, not to mention a reproduction of the Rose Window at Rheims Cathedral. The only thing that differentiated our friend Rudolf from other eccentric millionaires was that he had better taste; instead of using bits and pieces, he bought the whole house and everything in it."

"You don't mean every stick of furniture in the place is medieval," I said skeptically.

"No, of course not. The family from whom Rudolf bought the place was hard up; they had sold most of the remaining antiques. But the library was virtually intact. There were also family portraits and odds and ends, things that had more sentimental than commercial value."

"Well, I am speechless."

"Not you," Kevin said, grinning.

"Almost speechless. I love it, Kevin."

"You ain't seen nothing yet. How about a tour?"

I didn't want a tour. My simple mind can only absorb small amounts of wonder; that's why I never spend more than an hour at a time in a museum. If I had been allowed to follow my own inclinations I would have preferred to soak up the treasures in small sips, getting to know them gradually. Also, I was starved, having had nothing since breakfast except a stale sandwich somewhere between Philadelphia and Pittsfield. Before I could voice these sentiments, Kevin took my hand and pulled me up out of my chair.

I got to know the place later, only too well; but I can still recall the daze of confusion that followed that first inspection. There were a music room and two parlors, large and small, and a kitchen that had one small island of modernity—electric stove, refrigerator, and so on—lost in a vast stone-floored expanse of quaintness; there were bedrooms with four-poster beds and embroidered hangings and names like The White Room and Queen Mary's Chamber. There were also bathrooms, which I was happy to see, having wondered whether antiquarian types worry about such things. I don't know why I wondered, because the house showed other signs of continual remodeling and modernization. The bathrooms were the sort of thing Queen Victoria might have designed, but in their way they were rather divine, with fireplaces and marble tubs. One tub was either a good copy, or a genuine Roman sarcophagus, with carved reliefs of cherubs and nymphs.

By the time we finished admiring the bathrooms it

was almost dark, and Kevin reluctantly admitted that we had better wait till morning before touring the grounds. "Why don't we have a drink in the courtyard while our dinner cooks?" he suggested.

"What are we having?" I asked. The immaculate rooms had suggested that the house must be supplied with invisible servants, or old-style serfs who popped out of hidden doors in the paneling to scrub and dust as soon as we left. I allowed myself to hope that the same unseen servitors had prepared a pasty of peacock's tongues to be followed by syllabub and grog.

"TV dinners," Kevin said. "Would you rather have fried chicken, or spaghetti and meatballs?"

II

I had spaghetti and meatballs. By means of plantings of boxwood and shrubs, one side of the central courtyard had been formed into an enclosed patio area, adjoining the kitchen. I sat at a table there, with my aching feet up on another chair, and watched through the open doorway while Kevin went through the arduous labor of peeling the foil off the dinners. The household animals had congregated, and been fed; when Kevin came out to join me, they followed: Belle, pacing with slow arthritic strides, a younger dog, part Irish Setter, which had apparently spent the day in a bramble patch, and three cats of varying sizes and shapes. One was a meek-looking tabby tomcat who obviously went in terror of cat number two, a long-haired beauty who outweighed him by at least ten pounds. Kevin indicated the third, a minuscule creature with ears much too large for its pointed face.

"Mom's latest acquisition. Somebody dumped it at the gate. The clods are always abandoning unwanted animals. I suppose they think the poor things can fend for themselves out in the country. Most of them die horrible deaths, of course."

"But not the ones that meet your mother," I said, trying to pet the kitten. It spat at me and backed off, its fur bristling.

"Bad girl, Pettibone," said Kevin.

"I don't blame her for being suspicious of humans."

"She had a bad time, all right. She was skin and bone when Belle brought her in."

"Belle?"

The old dog cocked a lazy eye at me when her name was mentioned.

"Belle is worse than Mother," Kevin said. "She's always bringing strays home. She must be part retriever; she never hurts anything, just fetches it. We've had rabbits, groundhogs, and once an extremely irritated skunk. Took two weeks, and a couple of gallons of tomato juice, to get Belle fit for human society."

One of the other cats, the long-haired gray-and-white one, jumped onto my lap. It weighed almost twenty pounds. My knees sagged, and the cat dug in all its claws to keep from falling.

"That's Tabitha," Kevin said. "Chow hound and sex maniac."

"She likes me," I said, as Tabitha rubbed her head against my chest, leaving a patch of gray hair.

"I wish I could tell you that is a compliment. However, Tabitha likes everybody. She has no discrimination whatever."

Tabitha squirmed and purred as I tickled her under the chin. One of the reasons for her affection became apparent when my TV dinner was delivered; I had to fight her for every meatball.

The long summer twilight deepened; the crenellated roofs and pointed towers of Grayhaven were sharp black silhouettes against the soft blue of the sky. I sat back in my chair with a sigh.

"It's the most peaceful place. I can see why your parents fell in love with it, even though it is impractical."

"Not all that impractical," Kevin said quickly. "It seems outlandishly large at first, but there are only ten bedrooms."

"Plus a Great Hall, a music room—and did you mention a chapel?"

"Most of the rooms are closed off unless the folks give a party."

"I'm on your side," I said, a little surprised at the sharpness of his tone. "It's their house and they can do what they like. The only thing that worries me is the amount of housekeeping. I fully expected to do some cleaning, that's only fair. But I can't do justice to this place, Kevin, especially if we hope to get any work done on the book."

"No problem. A cleaning team comes out a couple of times a week."

"No live-in servants?"

"I think Mom has some people lined up for when they get back," Kevin said vaguely. "She offered to get somebody for us, but I told her never mind; I figured you wouldn't want a lot of people around, getting in our way."

A few hours earlier I would have told him he had figured right. I do find it hard to concentrate when people are scuttling in and out, running vacuum cleaners and grabbing dirty cups out of my hand. That's why I can't work at home. But now that I had seen the house I would have welcomed servants, scuttling or not.

I was brooding about this when Kevin added non-chalantly, "Besides, Aunt Bea will be here tomorrow."

"Who?"

"My mother's sister. Her divorce was final last month, and she's at loose ends, after thirty years of marriage. She was pleased to come and help out."

As one of my favorite writers must have said somewhere, the direst forebodings pressed upon my heart. Aunt Bea, struggling with the pangs of single-ness, would be worse than a gaggle of maids. She would have carefully tinted hair poufed up around her face—unless she had fallen prey to melancholy, and let it fall in gray wisps. She would be comfortably rounded or tightly corseted, depending, again, on her state of mind. And she would talk, interminably, on all sorts of boring subjects, ending up with Harry, or whatever his name was. How his decision to leave her had taken her completely by surprise, how she never imagined there could be another woman, how she had fought to keep her home.

All this flashed through my mind with formidable and depressing completeness. Because I had to say something, and because I could not force my lips to shape exclamations of rapture, I asked politely, "What happened, after thirty years? Or should I ask?"

"I don't know," Kevin admitted. "All she told Mom was that Uncle Harry (aha, I thought) had gone into male menopause and didn't look as if he was ever coming out. There's a rumor going through the family that he hit her."

"How awful," I said, visualizing the frail old lady cowering on the floor nursing her black eye and begging Harry not to hit her again.

"Whereupon," Kevin continued, "she gave him a karate chop to the Adam's apple, and a right to the jaw, and walked out."

My mental image underwent an abrupt metamorphosis, the frail little lady ballooning into a formidable matriarch with iron-gray waves and a forty-five-inch bust. I found this image more sympathetic than the first (let him have it again, Aunt Bea!) but did not suppose I would find it any easier to live with.

I relapsed into moody silence while Kevin rhapsodized about Aunt Bea's cornbread and angel-food cake, her needlepoint and her quilts, her skill at storytelling and at Snakes and Ladders. But it was hard to remain glum; the silken warmth of the air, the splendor of the night sky over the battlements, the purring cats and snoring dogs—the general air of comfort was too pervasive to be resisted. I finally made a sound that Kevin recognized as a yawn.

"You must be bushed," he said. "Want to hit the sack?"

"I guess I will." I rose, accompanied by Tabitha, who was stuck like a limpet to my shirt front.

"You know where everything is," Kevin said lazily.

"If I don't, I'll look for it." The cat licked my chin. "What do I do with this?" I asked.

"She'll sleep with you if you let her. But watch out, she hogs the covers."

"Thanks for the warning. Well—good night."

"You don't get nervous at night, or anything, do you?"

"What do you mean by 'anything'?"

Kevin laughed. "Well, I'm always open to seduction. Feel free. Actually, for once that wasn't what I had in mind; it just occurred to me that my room is some distance from yours, so if you're the type that hears burglars or sees ghosts you might want to move into my wing of the house. Mother thought you would prefer that room, but it is rather isolated."

"I do not hear burglars or ghosts. And I'm tired enough to sleep soundly. Don't call me; I'll call you."

"Whatever you say," Kevin murmured.

I found my room without any difficulty, though manipulating the light switches with my arms full of twenty pounds of cat was not so easy. When we reached the bedroom Tabitha unhooked her claws and jumped onto the bed.

When Kevin had shown me where I was to sleep I'd been a little disappointed. I would have preferred the older part of the house, where his room was located. According to Kevin, that portion dated from the fifteenth century, which I could well believe; its thick walls and narrow, tortuous passageways appealed to that childish streak of mystery and romance that is buried, more or less deeply, in all of us. I had said something about ghosts—maybe Kevin hadn't realized I was joking, though he had let out a whoop of laughter and replied that he only wished there were some.

At any rate, I couldn't find fault with my room, which was in the Queen Anne part of the house. I appreciated Kevin's mother's thoughtfulness in selecting it for me, even if I did suspect that her real motive had been to put me at a discreet distance from her son. Like the corresponding downstairs rooms, this one had been decorated in 1745, and the molded plasterwork on the overmantel and ceiling was delicately lovely—swags of pastel vines and roses against a white background. The canopied ceiling of the bay window overhanging the garden must have been added at the same time. Someone had put bowls of fresh flowers on the dresser and on the table beside the ivory velvet chaise longue. I deduced, cleverly, that the cleaning team had been there that day, and that Mrs. Blacklock had left explicit instructions. There was even a good light for reading in bed.

I rummaged around in my suitcase till I found the book I had been reading, and climbed into the bed. It was big, double-sized, with a frilly canopy, but the damned cat had gone to sleep smack in the middle of it, and I had to shove her to one side before I could stretch out. Halfway through the chapter I found that the volume was slipping out of my hands, so I turned out the light.

The dark of a summer night, silvered by moon and stars, is not black; it is the most beautiful shade of velvety blue. The breeze that touched my face smelled like roses. I watched the pale translucence of the muslin curtains twist and lift, like dancers without bones, ghost dancers. Kevin's suggestion that I might be afraid struck me as the funniest thing I had heard in months. I started to laugh but fell asleep before I could produce more than a chuckle.

Chapter Three

THE CAT WOKE ME next morning, standing on my stomach and pushing her cold nose into my face. She was so fat her four paws felt as if they were digging into me clear down to my backbone.

I let her out and considered the possibility of another hour's sleep; but it was too gorgeous a morning to waste in sodden slumber. My window faced east. Dawn was a filmy curtain of rose and azure above the dark-green hills. When I made my way to the kitchen I was joined by the entire animal population making peremptory noises. I had no idea where Kevin kept their food, so I opened the door and urged them out. Belle was the last to leave; her sigh and reproachful look assured me that I had disappointed her.

It was midmorning before Kevin appeared, rubbing his eyes and yawning. I greeted him with the condescension early risers feel for slugabeds. Coffee restored him to relative coherence and affability.

"I am a night person," he announced. "I hope that isn't going to be a problem."

"I am normally a night person too. But it was so pretty this morning, I couldn't stay in bed. We'll work out a schedule, don't worry."

"I suppose you've been outside," Kevin said. "I wanted to show you the gardens."

"I like seeing things myself. The grounds are beautiful. I've never seen so many roses. And I met the gardeners—Mr. Marsden and his assistant, Jim something—"

"There's another one," Kevin said. "I think his name is Mike."

"Three gardeners? How often do they come?"

"Every day, I guess."

I blinked. My mother has a cleaning lady—so-called—one day a week; she weeds her own petunias. But of course those acres of flower beds and velvet lawn and exotic trees must require a lot of work, especially during the summer. I was to have a series of shocks like that for the first week or so; it is hard for the bourgeoisie to realize how the other one-tenth of one percent lives.

"So," I said, seeing that Kevin's eyes were showing signs of intelligence, "what do we do today?"

Kevin looked at his watch. "Is it that late? Damn, I've got to meet Aunt Bea at the airport in a few hours."

With only a few hours to spare, there didn't seem to be much point in starting work on the book. Kevin suggested a game of tennis. (There was also a squash court and a swimming pool.) I went down to ignoble defeat in straight sets. After lunch—ham sandwiches and canned soup—Kevin left. Aunt Bea was getting a lot more consideration than I had rated; but my mood was so mellow I didn't even drop a hint to that effect.

Big white puffy thunderheads were building up in the sky. The air was warm and sticky. I felt good, though. Perhaps because I do it so seldom, exercising always gives me a feeling of virtue.

There didn't seem to be any point in working on the book. I went to the kitchen. Kevin had made an incredible mess with a few glasses and TV-dinner trays. He hadn't washed the animals' food bowls either. When I got through, the kitchen was spotless. Might as well let Aunt Bea start out with a good impression of me, I thought.

I wandered out into the courtyard with a book of crossword puzzles that I had found in the library, but instead of opening it I just sat, hands folded, staring peacefully at the sky. I couldn't remember when I had felt so relaxed. It had been a hard year, what with one thing and another. I had worked like a dog. I deserved a rest.

When I opened my eyes again, the puffy white clouds were developing dark edges and the sunlight was gone. I crossed the courtyard and went out through the covered arch that led to the gardens. The sun blazed out in its last defiance as I emerged from under the shadow of the arch, and the roses in the neat beds glowed like gems—rubies and garnets, pearl and rose quartz, golden topaz. Then the sun blinked out behind the mass of clouds that were boiling over the rim of the hills. Lightning split the liver-colored belly of the sky. I counted automatically. One thousand, two thousand, three thousand . . . before I heard a bellow of distant celestial rage. It was coming on fast, and it was going to be a good one. So far the sheltering hills had kept the rising wind from reaching me; it was uncanny to watch the branches high above genuflect and writhe under the lash of the air, while I stood in a little pool of calm.

I wished Kevin would get back, not so much because I was concerned about his getting caught in the storm, but because I would have enjoyed some company. I am afraid of thunderstorms. When I'm alone I get in bed and pull the covers over my head. I started back to the house with every intention of doing just that. The sight of the patio furniture distracted me. The frames were wrought iron, but the bright cushions would get soaked unless I did something about them. I dragged them into the kitchen. As I carried the last one in, a drop of rain smacked down onto the flagstones, leaving a spot the size of a quarter.

A cat went whizzing past me through the kitchen door. It moved so fast I couldn't see which one it was. "Belle!" I called, scanning the darkening courtyard anxiously. A bark from the kitchen replied. Belle, no dumbbell even if she was slow and old, had long since sought shelter.

What about the rest of the animals? And the windows—mine I knew were open, some of the others probably were too. I went racing through the house, calling as I went. The only animal who responded was Amy, the part-Irish Setter. She hadn't realized anyone was home. When she heard my voice she galloped to meet me and tried to persuade me to pick her up. She followed me as I went from room to room, getting under my feet and moaning.

A quick check assured me that the windows were all closed except for the ones in the rooms we had used—kitchen, library, bedrooms. I finished my rounds in Kevin's room, which had long French doors opening onto a balcony that ran along past all the bedrooms in that wing. The rail was crenellated and high enough to be useful in a siege. I could picture Kevin shooting arrows through the slits. He would look sensational in a tunic and tights.

If I had been an admirer of thunderstorms, this one would have been worthy of attention. From Kevin's windows I could see out across the swimming pool as far as the northern hills. The treetops twisted like creatures in torment, and the gray-black clouds might have been heavenly cattle stampeded by the silver whip of the lightning.

When I turned from the window the room was so dark I could hardly make out the shapes of the furniture. I switched on every light I could find as I hurried along the hall and down the stairs. Candles, I thought busily. If the power fails I'll need candles.

I was also worried about the big-eared scrap of a kitten. Did it have sense enough to come in out of the rain? The other animals were inside; I had seen both cats during my check of the house, and there was no question about Amy's whereabouts; she was still stepping on my heels as I walked. I went to the kitchen and opened the back door. A ruffled ball of fur rolled in, squeaking angrily. I scooped it up—I could hold it in one cupped hand—and to my pleased surprise it began to purr.

"I got here as soon as I could," I said.

It didn't like thunderstorms either. It attached itself to my shoulder and clung, while I searched for candles and found them in a cupboard above the sink. I made myself a cup of coffee and sat down at the kitchen table, a solid slab of wood five feet long and six inches thick, with the kitten on my lap.

With a certain smugness I wondered how I could

have gotten into such a panic about the storm. There was nothing to be afraid of. The house was secure, its inhabitants were safe inside; candles on the table, matches beside them, I was prepared for any emergency. The house was like a fortress. The walls were thick, the windows tight; except for the night-dark skies and the flashes of lightning I would not have known a storm was shaking the outside air. Even the thunder, now close overhead, was diminished by the thickness of the ancient stone.

Reassured, the kitten climbed down my pants leg and headed for its food dish. I thought I heard a door close, somewhere off in the other wing. Kevin must be back—just in time. The rain was still only an intermittent spattering, but the torrent wouldn't hold off much longer. I got up and went to the front door.

There was no one in the entrance hall. When I swung the heavy door back, no living form was visible, only silvery threads of rain that rapidly wove themselves into a thickening veil.

I stood there looking out. It occurred to me that I could not possibly have heard the sound of this door opening and closing. It was too far from the kitchen. A door somewhere else in the house—closer to me? The thought might have been frightening. It was not; I considered it and dismissed it almost in the same moment. Perhaps it had not been a sound at all, but only a sense of presence and of companionship. I had the feeling still, so strongly that I turned and scanned the brightly lighted hall.

No burglars, no ghosts—only the house itself, solid, secure, sheltering; so strong it had a presence of its own. Smiling a little at my fancies, I turned back to the door and saw the car lights appear at the top of the ridge.

II

Aunt Bea, in the flesh, destroyed my fantasies about dear old aunts. She must have been in her fifties, and she looked it, but in the nicest way. A little thick around the middle, a little gray around the ears—"I need to do my roots" was the way she put it—and no attempt to conceal the lines around her mouth and eyes. They were lines of laughter; when she smiled they fell into their proper places like pieces of a puzzle.

If I had had any feelings of self-consciousness at meeting her they would have been dispelled by her manner and by the necessary informality demanded by the weather. As she and Kevin came running in through the rain, the lights flickered and went out.

"Hello," Bea said, laughing. "I would shake your hand if I could find it. Help!"

The lights promptly went on and Bea broke into another peal of laughter. "That's service for you. Quick, Anne, take my hand before they go out again."

"I've got candles," I said, taking the hand she extended.

"Where?" Kevin asked, as the lights died once and for all.

"In the kitchen."

"Smart girl." This sarcastic comment was followed by a thud and a curse as Kevin tripped over something.

We made it to the kitchen, groping and laughing and banging into furniture along the way. The water in the kettle was still hot, so I made tea, and Bea and I sat with our elbows on the table and a candle dripping into a saucer while Kevin went out and started the emergency generator. I might have known there

would be something like that, but even if I had known
I would not have had the faintest idea how to operate
it.

The lights went on; Kevin returned, dripping. I paid
him no heed. Already I felt as if I had known Bea for
years, and I was fascinated by her animated description of how her marriage had collapsed, after so many
years. It was a very funny story. If I hadn't been so
entertained I might have been suspicious of her
excessively casual account, and wondered why she
was confiding so readily in a stranger.

After a long sedate career as a CPA, good old Harry
had suddenly found God and joined a group known as
"The Elect of the Second Coming." Celibacy being a
desideratum, if not a requirement of this cult, Harry
had sought a divorce, which by then, his wife was
happy to give him. She had not been so happy about
his handing over their life savings to the Elect. "At
least I saved the house," she concluded cheerfully. "It
was in both our names, and Harry couldn't sell
without my signature. Kevin, darling, you're soaked!
Go up and change this minute, before you catch
cold."

I could hardly apologize to Bea for what I had been
thinking about her without admitting what I had been
thinking about her, so I said a silent "mea culpa." She
was certainly entitled to a few months of recuperation
and reorganization after Harry's astonishing performance. Now that I had met her, I felt sure she would
be an asset instead of a liability. This impression was
confirmed when she sneered at Kevin's tentative offer
of a TV dinner (lasagna or turkey?) and began rummaging in the larder.

There wasn't much in the larder except TV dinners.
I knew, because I had looked. Bea produced a deli-

cious meal from odds and ends, and refused my offer to wash the dishes.

"You're not to touch the housework," she said firmly. "The book is more important. Kevin told me all about it. I expect to be mentioned in the foreword, of course."

We spent the evening in the library, with the rain hissing against the windows and the animals sprawled on the rug in abandoned poses. It was like a family. Bea produced an enormous piece of needlework that would one day be a rug—"Harry tried to sell it, too, but nobody would buy it." We talked. I don't remember what we talked about—nothing in particular— but we laughed a lot. I remember that. We laughed a lot.

III

Next day Bea and I went grocery shopping. She tried to persuade me to stay home and work, but it didn't seem fair to ask her to tackle such a monumental job alone. Usually I hate grocery shopping, but with Bea it was fun. We had lunch in Pittsfield and did a little browsing around. When we passed a needlework shop Bea had to look in, just for a minute, and I bought a needlepoint pillow with a picture of a Chinese lady on it. Bea helped me pick out the yarn and promised to show me how to do it. I worked on it that evening and got quite a bit done—all the lady's skirt and part of her umbrella.

When Bea said she thought she would turn in, I got up too. I was halfway through *Forever Amber,* which I had never read, and I was curious to find out what she was going to think of next. It would be comfortable reading in my nice soft bed, propped up on ruffled pillows, with Tabitha sprawled across my feet.

"By the way," Bea said, struggling to squash her acres of canvas into a huge shopping bag, "you may not have noticed that tomorrow is Sunday. I suppose both you young creatures are heathens?"

"Druid," said Kevin, stretched out in his chair. "Reformed."

"I'm afraid . . ." I began.

"My dear girl, I'm not trying to convert you," Bea exclaimed. "I merely wanted to establish my claim to the car tomorrow morning."

"There are three cars," Kevin said. "And a pickup truck."

"I don't think the truck would be suitable," Bea said seriously.

I stayed up till late finishing *Forever Amber*. Bea had already left by the time I got downstairs next morning. The air had a Sunday feel to it and the garden was pure Italian cinquecento—heavenly blue skies, dark-green cypresses, porcelain roses. It was delightful being out in the garden alone, without some gardener popping out from behind a bush; I got a basket and some clippers from the garden shed and cut off the dead roses. Then I picked a bunch for the house. They were so opulent I couldn't resist adding flower after flower to the sheaf in my basket. I was arranging them in a crystal vase when Bea came back, looking very sweet and demure in a blue linen suit with a white bow under her chin.

"How was the service?" I asked politely. Kevin came in just in time to hear the question and the response.

"Wonderful. Father Stephen is an inspired speaker. He looks the way I've always imagined Saint Francis would look: fully cognizant of and sympathetic with human weakness, but with a touch of the divine."

I was a little startled by this rhapsodic description, and by the glow in Bea's eyes; it was a mood I had not seen and would not have expected. I was also surprised by the title she had given the minister.

"Is he—are you—Catholic?"

"Episcopalian," Bea said. "I mean, the church is; I'm ecumenical."

"Uncritical," Kevin said, smiling. "Undiscriminating. Susceptible to any smooth-talking, good-looking—"

"That's one way of putting it," Bea said calmly. "I have always selected my church, not by denomination, but by the character of the pastor. Father Stephen is uniquely gifted."

"Clever of you to have found that out after only one sermon," Kevin said. I frowned at him. I am no church-goer, but I don't believe in making fun of other people's sincere beliefs.

Bea seemed to be used to Kevin's teasing. "One sermon is enough," she said. "But Father Stephen has a fine reputation locally. I talked to several people after the service, and they praised him to the skies. It was nice to meet some of our neighbors."

"Neighbors?" I repeated, recalling the empty acres that surrounded us.

"Well, they are the closest ones we have. I've been invited to dinner tomorrow night. They asked you, too, but I told them I would have to check—that you were very busy and had no time for social activities."

I cringed mentally when she said that; I had certainly come here to work, but so far my accomplishments were nil.

Kevin appeared untroubled by guilt. "I wouldn't

mind meeting the neighbors," he said, "but I'm not sure they would like to meet me. Do they understand that Anne and I aren't married or even engaged? I'll bet they think the worst."

"Nonsense," Bea said. "You young people always think anyone over forty is a hopeless old fogy. People take this kind of thing quite for granted today—even when there is anything to be taken for granted, which in this case there is not. Besides you are being chaperoned by your Aunt Bea."

Kevin burst out laughing. I didn't join him until I saw the twinkle in Bea's eye.

So next night we went out to dinner. The house was one of the ones whose gateposts I had admired on the day of my arrival. Heraldic griffins perched atop the stone pillars, paws (or do griffins have hooves?) lifted in majestic warning. The house was a lovely old Georgian mansion built of soft red brick and filled with handsome antiques. The host, Dr. Garst, was a surgeon. His wife was considerably younger than he, with the overly slim figure and haggard face that indicate a fanatical preoccupation with the beauty-youth cult.

There were a couple of sticky moments during the meal, when the subject turned to politics. Our host and hostess were dyed-in-the-wool reactionaries, and Kevin's views, not to mention my own, were not exactly conservative. However, I learned long ago, after a series of screaming matches with my father, that rational argument is impossible with such people, so by adroitly changing the subject from socialized medicine to local history, and from the iniquities of income tax to horticulture, I managed to keep our host from accusing Kevin of being a communist.

Most of the other guests were of the same social

class and age group as Dr. and Mrs. Garst—nice but dull. Two were different.

Father Stephen was one of these. I could understand why Bea had fallen for him, in the most ecumenical sense. If I had been casting a romantic old-fashioned film I would have picked him to play the kindly parish priest. He was an extremely handsome man, with a head of thick white hair and a trim body, and he exuded that aura of warmth that the best priests, doctors, and psychiatrists have. He was also a witty and intelligent conversationalist. He and Kevin got together and started discussing the metaphysical poets, and Kevin lost the pained smile that was his unfailing sign of boredom.

I didn't have much opportunity that evening to talk with Roger O'Neill, the only other person in the group who attracted me. He spent most of the time making eyes at Bea, who was looking particularly pretty. I liked his face. It was one of those homely-amiable faces, with a lumpy nose and a wide mouth that curved up in a perpetual smile. But there was a quirk at the corner of the smile that kept it from being saccharine; every now and then his left eyebrow would shift, parallel to the quirk, which gave him a pleasantly cynical look. I guessed he was in his late fifties or early sixties, and he let it all hang out—his stomach, his jowls, and his bald spot.

When Father Stephen was drawn away by one of the women—another fan, from her adoring look—Kevin was left with Dr. Garst's niece, who had dogged his footsteps all evening. She was the only other young person in the group, and I felt sure that one of the reasons we had been invited was that the Garsts hoped we would be playmates for Leila.

Leila had other ideas. She wanted to play, all right,

but not with me. She looked at Kevin the way a dieter looks at a chocolate sundae. Apparently she had decided to charm him with the wit and gaiety of her conversation; her smile never relaxed, and her lips never stopped moving. It wasn't long before Kevin's answering smile took on the stiffness I knew so well.

I made my way toward Bea, who was still talking to Roger O'Neill. I had to jog her elbow before either of them noticed I was there. I said I thought we ought to be going home, adding, mendaciously, that Kevin and I still had work to do.

"You mean you and Kevin are bored," said Roger. He had a deep, gravelly voice, and nasalized his final *r*'s, like Humphrey Bogart. "I can't say I blame you. Mrs. Jones here and I are the only people in the room worth talking to."

Bea blushed prettily. "I hope we won't be thought rude—"

"No, no. The good Father and I usually take off about this time; as soon as he leaves the rest of them start drinking seriously, and bitching about the state of the world."

O'Neill insisted on walking us to our car. He lingered even after Kevin had started the engine, his head halfway in the car window, his eyes fixed on Bea.

"I'm going to stand here till you invite me over," he said. "Tea, lunch, breakfast, dinner, drinks—I don't care which, so long as it's soon. How about tomorrow?"

Bea's laugh was a little breathless. "Why, Mr. O'Neill—"

"Roger."

"Roger—I would be delighted to see you anytime, but these young people—"

"I won't bother them. You're the one I want to see."

"Me, or the house? You told me that was your primary interest," Bea said demurely.

"That was before I met you. Tomorrow, about five? We'll go out to dinner. Just the two of us."

Without waiting for an answer he walked away.

"Well!" said Kevin. "Who's chaperoning who around here?"

"Whom, you mean," Bea said. "And you an English teacher."

IV

Roger arrived at four forty-five. Bea was still upstairs primping; she had been very blasé and worldly when Kevin kidded her about her conquest, but she had started her toilette at three o'clock. I opened the door for Roger and took him out to the courtyard, where Kevin joined us and offered him a drink. He accepted tonic with a slice of lime.

"I pickled my liver for twenty years in the service of my country," he explained. "Gave the stuff up when I retired. I didn't need it any longer."

Bea had told us he had been in the Foreign Service. I started to make conversation about his interesting posts abroad, but Roger didn't respond. He had not been joking when he said he was interested in the house; his comments showed not only interest, but considerable knowledge of architectural history.

"You've really never seen the place?" I asked.

"I've only lived in the area for a few years," Roger said. "When I came here the house was owned by old Miss Marion Karnovsky. The only person she consented to see was Father Stephen."

"How about a tour, then?" Kevin suggested.

As we entered the hall, Bea made her appearance, descending the staircase with the aplomb of an actress. The sunset light from the window on the landing gave her a reddish-bronze halo (the roots had received attention that morning) and softened the lines in her face. She looked attractive enough to distract Roger from his architectural interests, and Kevin had to prod us into continuing the house tour.

However, Roger's interest revived as we proceeded. He even asked to see the cellars, which I had never visited. I had assumed, if I thought about the subject at all, that they were the usual subterranean excavations, native to the hills of Pennsylvania. One look at the massive stonework told me that Rudolf had been pedantically thorough. From the topmost chimney pot to the cellar floors, Kevin had said, and Kevin had not exaggerated.

Like the rest of the house, the cellars had been electrified, but the glow of a dozen bulbs could not dispel the somber atmosphere of a region that resembled a church crypt rather than a storage area for old furniture and wine. No one spoke as we followed Kevin from room to room. It was a relief to come upon objects as modern and mundane as a furnace and hot-water heater.

We were in a room on the north side of the cellar when I happened to look down. What I saw made me squat, ungracefully, for a closer inspection. The carving was almost effaced by time and traffic, but the remaining letters and the squared-off dimensions made the function of this stone uncomfortably clear. Without stopping to think, I stepped off it.

"It's a tombstone," I squeaked.

"Here's another one," Roger said, indicating the stone next to the one I had abandoned. "And another . . . I suppose this room is directly under the chapel?"

"Right," Kevin said.

"Kevin," I said. My voice sounded higher and thinner than usual. "Kevin—how much did—*how far down did Rudolf dig?*"

Kevin laughed. The room had too many echoes; a dim, maniacal titter underscored his next few words. "I wondered about that too. I suppose there are documents somewhere that would tell us; I haven't found them, though."

I've been tempted, since I started writing this, to turn it into a ghost story, full of the gruesome descriptions that sell so well these days. A bloated corpse . . . a ghost or two . . . some puddles of gore . . . Kevin as a psychotic killer chasing me with an antique broadsword . . . who knows, I might even get a movie offer. But it wasn't like that, not ever. Even that strange subterranean chamber failed to induce waves of chilly horror. My impression of discomfort was quite natural, the result of the somber physical surroundings and the conventional blend of respect and repugnance in the presence of the dead. But when Kevin turned toward the next door along the dank, stone-floored passageway, I informed him I had seen enough of the nether regions. Bea supported me, pointing out that it was getting late.

"Okay, we'll go up, but you've got to see the chapel," Kevin insisted. "Just a quick look. I know Roger will be interested. The vaulting is remarkably good." His air of proud proprietorship was rather funny, in a man who called himself a left-wing socialist.

Since it was not one of the rooms in daily use, the chapel was not on the regular schedule of the cleaning team, who had quite enough to do without such additions. When Kevin opened the door, dust motes danced in the light streaming in through a high arched window over the altar.

There were half a dozen pews, each ornately carved, each with cushions and kneelers of faded needlepoint. From the absences of crucifixes and other such accoutrements I deduced that the most recent services performed there had been Protestant. Originally, however, the chapel had been consecrated to the Church of Rome. The fan vaulting that carved the ceiling in a delicate tracery was clearly late-fifteenth century. Though on a miniature scale, it resembled the work in the chapel of Henry the Seventh at Westminster Abbey. The tall pointed windows were of the same period. Those on the side of the chapel were boarded up. This had been done by the previous owner, who feared the rare early stained glass might be vandalized.

"Sorry it's so dark," Kevin apologized. "This is the only room in the house that has never been electrified."

Quietly and without self-consciousness Bea took a seat in one of the back pews. She sat with bowed head and folded hands while the rest of us inspected what we could see of the chapel. The only part of it not in shadow was the altar itself, which was illumined by sunlight from the window above it.

I am always uneasy in a church, never quite sure what is proper. While I hung back, Roger, who clearly suffered no such qualms, mounted the shallow steps that led up to the altar. It was only a slab of stone, resting on two supports. A gold-embroidered crimson cloth covered all but the extreme ends and hung down to the floor in front. Roger pulled this up and stooped to look underneath. There was something almost rude about the gesture, like peeking under the skirts of Mother Church.

"Interesting," Roger said. "What is this, Kevin?"

He hadn't asked me, but I went to look anyway. Under the altar table was a stone slab some three feet wide by two feet high. It appeared to be marble, veined with streaks of rusty brown, but there were no visible carvings or inscriptions.

"A holy relic, maybe," Kevin said, faint amusement coloring his voice. "A stone from the Holy Sepulcher, or the Temple?"

"Hardly." Roger's reply to this joking suggestion was prompt and vigorous. "They didn't make much use of marble in the Holy Land before Roman times. Unless I miss my guess, this is Italian marble— possibly Greek."

I assumed he knew what he was talking about; he had, after all, spent many years of his professional service in the eastern Mediterranean. What I failed to understand was his interest in a plain, unmarked Stone. He actually dropped to his hands and knees and poked his head under the altar, touching and peering at the stone. Finally he rose, reluctantly, and glanced at his watch.

"I'm forgetting the time," he said. "I made a reservation for seven thirty. I guess we'd better go."

Yet he was the last to leave the chapel. He paused in the doorway for one final look, a slight frown wrinkling his high forehead.

If I had asked him then . . . No, I'm not going to lapse into trite "had I but known" clichés, or torment myself with guilt. It would not have made the slightest difference, in the end.

Chapter Four

REREADING what I have written so far, I am tempted to destroy it and start again. It seems so misleading, in the light of what I know now. Yet it is an accurate description, not only of what happened, but of the mood of those early days—peaceful, contented, idyllic. It would be even more misleading to imply that those sunlit days were shadowed by the slightest foreboding.

However, there had been moments, such as my feelings in the crypt, and my sense, on the day of the thunderstorm, that there was someone in the house. Such moments recurred in the days that followed Roger's intrusion into our little society. I call it an intrusion because I know Kevin felt it as such. From the start there was a kind of wariness between them—not that of enemies, but of persons who know that one day, under certain circumstances, they may come to be enemies. Roger actually spent very little time with me and Kevin. He picked Bea up and they went out, to lunch, to dinner, on long drives. Occasionally she spent the evening with him and came back with enthusiastic descriptions of his pleasant house. He had one of the restored eighteenth-century cottages in the village.

Kevin and I never went to his house. I don't believe I ever had any sense of not being welcome, but there was never time. I had too many other things to do. The garden was an increasing source of fascination. Old Mr. Marsden finally, with great condescension, allowed me to help with the weeding. I had my needlepoint and my crossword puzzles. Kevin and I played tennis almost every morning and swam every afternoon. I developed a good tan, and some of the flabbiness that even a skinny frame acquires over a long, sedentary winter changed into firm muscle. I actually did a little work on the book—preliminary things, arranging material, and so on. There didn't seem to be any hurry . . .

But there were moments. Times when I would suddenly look up from my needlework with a sense that someone was leaning over the back of my chair, watching with friendly, approving interest; times when the branches of the shrub whose roots I was weeding would stir, as if someone had brushed past it. And there were the dreams.

I had the first one the night following our visit to the chapel. I couldn't remember any of the details; struggling back to consciousness I knew only that I had dreamed, and that the dream had not been pleasant.

It all came on so gradually. But I can pinpoint the exact day when I realized that the serpent had entered Paradise—or rather, when I saw the shimmer of iridescent scales under the flowers and knew it had been there all along.

I awoke that morning with a grinding, bone-jarring start, as I had sometimes awakened from dreams of flying and falling. I had dreamed again. This time I remembered a little.

I had dreamed about Joe. Remember Joe? I had not given him much thought myself, at least not much conscious thought. Since arriving at Grayhaven I had received one miserable postcard from him. Joe's minuscule handwriting, which looks so neat and is so difficult to decipher, covered only half the space available for a message and seemed to concern itself chiefly with the amount of research he had accomplished. It concluded, "Write, dammit. Joe."

I had no intention of writing. Joe was no more than an irritating memory, an episode long past. If I had stopped to think about it I would have marveled at the ease with which I had shoved Joe into a dark closet in my mind and slammed the door.

Now I did stop to think about it. It was another beautiful day. From my comfortable bed I could see sunlight and blue skies and hear the birds singing. A muted purr in the background told me that Bob, or Mike, or someone of that ilk, was mowing the lawn. I might have pondered all the pleasant things I meant to do that day—tennis, swimming, finishing my crossword puzzle and the Chinese lady's background of pale-turquoise wool. But something was pounding on the door of that locked closet in my mind.

Joe wasn't the first man with whom I had fancied myself desperately in love, but I had never gotten so deeply involved as I had with him. Every other love affair had ended in pain and regret and long weeks of suffering. How could I have forgotten him so easily? And why the devil was he struggling out of his prison now, to haunt me? The dream was already fading. All

I could recall was a feeling of danger and a frantic, desperate struggle to do something, or reach some place, before it was too late. I had seen Joe's face, distorted by anger or fear, his mouth wide open, screaming.

It was no use. I couldn't recapture it, and I wasn't sure I wanted to. Like a big comfortable feather bolster, the thought of the hours ahead embraced me. Father Stephen was coming to tea. That would be nice.

Yet some nagging prickle of discomfort must have jabbed at me, because as soon as I had finished breakfast—a meal at which we fended for ourselves, since our schedules varied so—I went to the library instead of to the rose garden.

We usually spent our evenings in this room. Despite its size, it was more livable than the formal reception rooms. Bea had taken over a little parlor for her own use, but by tacit consent this was left to her; sometimes she entertained people Kevin and I did not care to see, and we felt she was entitled to her hours of privacy.

Chairs in a semicircle around the hearth and the big table before them were mute witnesses to our hours together. Bea's needlepoint and mine—I had two projects going now, the second a more complicated pillow—my crossword-puzzle book, a scattering of animal hairs on the hearthrug. Kevin and I had each taken one of the big library tables as a desk, covering the gilt-stamped leather tops with blotters to protect them against ink stains. At first glance the desk-tables looked impressive witnesses to our labors, covered with books and papers and writing implements, including Kevin's portable typewriter. Something impelled me to run my finger over the surface of the typewriter. The cleaning team had been told to leave this room alone unless we specifically requested their attentions. A little pile of fine white dust followed the path of my finger.

A closer look at the books on Kevin's desk showed me that few had anything to do with literature, and those few were at the bottoms of the piles of volumes on medieval history and architecture. I turned to my own desk. When I looked through my notes, my sense of disquiet increased. I had not accomplished much since . . . Had I really been at Grayhaven for three weeks?

At that moment Kevin's voice calling my name reminded me that I was late for tennis. I replaced *Studies in Contemporary Literature* on my blotter and hurried out.

II

We usually met for lunch in the kitchen, which was one of the pleasantest rooms in the house, with its beamed ceiling and big fireplace. Bea had placed pots of scarlet geraniums on the wide windowsills and gay woven mats on the table. After we had finished Kevin murmured, "I'll be in my room, if anybody wants me," and wandered out. I had heard him say that before; for the first time I wondered what he did during those early-afternoon hours. Surely he didn't need to nap. He was looking very fit, better than I had ever seen him.

I had acquired the habit of helping Bea with the lunch dishes. Her protests were, by now, purely mechanical—another part of the routine. Today, however, she was not her usual chatty self, and I noticed that she avoided my eyes. I was about to ask her what was wrong when she said, in a rapid, rather prim voice, "I thought you might like to know that I am going to change rooms this afternoon."

"Really? Something wrong with yours?"

"It is next to Kevin's, you know."

"I know."

"We share the balcony."

"Yes."

"These warm summer nights . . . I leave the French doors open."

"I hope you do," I said, wondering. "What's the matter—does Kevin snore?"

Bea's face was half turned away as she concentrated with unnecessary attention on the cup she was washing. I saw a wave of dull, ugly red move up from her neck over her cheek. She blushed easily and prettily, but this was not her normal pink flush of pleasure; it was embarrassment, raw and uncomfortable. She turned completely away from me and spoke in a quick monotone.

"I'm not making judgments or condemning you; you are both adults, it's entirely your affair. I guess I'm more conventional than I thought. Kevin is like my son, I've watched him grow up, and most mothers would find it uncomfortable to actually hear . . ."

I should have seen what she was driving at long before I did. The idea had been so far from my mind that it penetrated slowly. I started to laugh, then

hastily checked myself. It was no laughing matter to
Bea.

"Bea, believe me, Kevin and I are not . . ." I
dismissed the first verb that came to mind and tried to
find a euphemism that would not increase Bea's
embarrassment. "We are not sleeping together. You
know I would have no hesitation about admitting it if
we were."

"No, you wouldn't." Bea's voice was more normal,
with a touch of wry humor. She turned. The angry red
had subsided, but her cheeks were still flushed. "Forgive me. I'm ashamed of thinking . . ."

She spoke as if she had falsely accused me of
murder, or embezzling the life savings of little old
ladies. I had to remind myself that to her generation
the accusation was almost as bad! And indeed, it
would have been thoughtless of us, knowing Bea's
attitude, to carry on an affair so close to her when
there were a dozen unoccupied rooms in the house,
and acres of grounds. I thought of making love with
Kevin on the billiard table, or the hearthrug in the
library, or in the potting shed, and had to stifle
another laugh.

"Forget it," I said magnanimously. "The only thing
that surprises me is how you could have supposed
Kevin and I had that kind of relationship. Even with
our depraved generation, sexual intimacy usually implies a certain degree of emotional involvement.
Kevin treats me like a sister."

Bea's eyes were still troubled. "I did think of that,
Anne. I was disappointed, because I had begun to
hope that you two . . . But that really is none of my
business."

"I can assure you that if we do decide to—uh—get

more friendly, we'll do it in private," I said. "You don't have to change rooms."

"You don't understand." Another wave of red suffused her face. "I hear things. I can't help hearing them. Anne, if it isn't you, who is it?"

The words hit me like a slap in the face—especially the word "who." She wasn't referring to an ambiguous collection of noises—a "what." With deliberate intent she had chosen a personal pronoun.

A number of explanations flashed through my mind. None of them made any sense because I did not have enough data. I thought of asking Bea to describe what she had heard and dismissed the idea immediately; her tongue would never be able to form the right words. Nor could I be sure that her description would be accurate. How could I know what neuroses or sexual hangups vexed Bea's subconscious mind?

"Who?" I repeated. "Damn it, Bea, what are we talking about—vampires, or succubi? I can't see Kevin smuggling some local charmer into his room, even if he knew any. Is there some girl on the cleaning team? . . ."

I knew the suggestion was absurd even before Bea's emphatic shake of the head denied it. The cleaning team consisted of men and unglamorous middle-aged women. Dr. Garst's niece had called a few times, but Kevin had consistently refused her invitations and ignored her broad hints about how she hated to swim alone.

"Then he must be talking in his sleep," I said, after we had canvassed the possibilities. "It may be as simple as that."

Bea's mouth set in a stubborn line. "If he is," she said, "he's using two different voices."

III

After Kevin had finished his nap—or whatever—and gone to the pool, Bea and I made the transfer—her things to my room, mine to hers. She wasn't enthusiastic about the latter part of the program, but I managed to convince her that I was not motivated by idle curiosity or perversity. It would have been easier to convince her if I had told her I had been worried about Kevin anyway, but I couldn't do that. It would have been vicious to mar the new serenity of Bea's life, so welcome after months of unhappiness, with vague forebodings. They seemed unfounded and irrational even to me.

The most logical explanation for the sounds Bea had heard was that she had imagined them, or blown up some harmless noises into something sinister. I wouldn't know about that until I had heard, or not heard, for myself. But I didn't really believe that was the explanation. If I had, I wouldn't have gone to the trouble of moving into a position where I could spy on Kevin. I was uncomfortable with the idea, but I was even more uncomfortable about certain other things. Bea's revelation had been like a beam of light shining into dark corners, showing the true shapes of the shadowy objects that lurked there.

It was almost impossible for me to get Kevin to do any work on our book, which was, after all, the reason for my being there. He always had some graceful excuse, some other pressing chore. His disinclination, I told myself, accounted for my own failure to concentrate on what I was supposed to be doing. "There isn't any point starting work now." How many times had one of us said that, how often had I thought it—and then proceeded to waste hours playing with one of the many entrancing toys available?

Not only was Kevin not working on the book, he was spending great amounts of time on other research; and all that research somehow centered around the house.

I would have felt like a fool mentioning this sort of thing to Bea as evidence of a dramatic change in Kevin. It was all so harmless and so understandable. Why should Kevin slave at dull work when he no longer needed the money? Why shouldn't he be fascinated by the beautiful old house and its history? But one of the qualities I had always admired in Kevin was his honesty, with others and with himself. He was wasting my time. If he had decided to abandon the project we had been working on for almost a year, he would have told me so, flat out.

Kevin didn't seem like the same eager, idealistic man I had met eighteen months earlier at a political rally on campus. It was one of those cases of a local jury freeing some character who had, quite by accident, of course, shot and killed a young black man who had been a friend of his daughter. Kevin had banged me on the head with the sign he was carrying —really by accident—and had offered to buy me a beer by way of apology. Sitting with his elbows on the table, ignoring the puddle that soaked into the sleeve of his faded shirt, he had talked nonstop, first about the case, then, after discovering that we were in the same field, about his ideas for a really good, really useful textbook. The picture was as clear in my mind as a photograph. Next to it I placed Kevin as he looked now—tanned and fit in tennis whites, or drinking brandy in his manorial library after dinner.

Physically he looked a hundred percent better. But I missed the sallow, shabby man whose hair always needed cutting and whose shirts never had all their buttons.

There was another thing, but I had a hard time admitting it to myself; it made me sound so stupid. All the same, in those early days, before Joe came on the scene like a bomb exploding, I had begun to think that Kevin might be getting interested in other parts of me besides my brilliant brain. I suppose it is obvious that I am not particularly secure about my physical attractiveness. I was even less secure then, and there were so many other women in Kevin's life—women with straight, shining hair and perfect white teeth and pneumatic Playboy-bunny bodies and twenty-twenty vision. But now I had the advantage of proximity. So why not the billiard table, or the hearthrug in the library? Why hadn't the thought occurred to me, if not to Kevin? There must be something wrong with me—or with him.

If I had only pursued this thought, I might have reached the truth sooner. (But I have already admitted that I don't know whether there is such a thing as truth, haven't I?) I knew something was amiss, but I knew it through instinct, not logic, and in my attempt to find a logical excuse for my concern, I picked Kevin as the fall guy. I'm all right, Jack, it can't be me.

We finished moving my things, and Bea, looking grave, went off to make goodies for tea. Father Stephen was going to get the full treatment—watercress sandwiches and little frosted cookies, and, for all I knew, scones and clotted cream. I decided I would join the party after I had had my swim. Bea's cooking was too good to pass up.

But before I went to the pool I walked out onto the balcony. Standing behind those breast-high battlements I could imagine myself a lady of high degree, watching from her tower window for the return of her lover from the Crusades or some equally romantic and useless enterprise. The sun was warm on my face. A perfumed breeze blew locks of hair across my cheek. I could almost feel the weight of one of those high, horned headdresses pressing my hair down.

Out of the corner of my eye I saw that the doors leading to Kevin's room were ajar. I wandered casually along the balcony, head held high, wondering how the hell women had kept those medieval monstrosities from falling off. Did they have hatpins?

Playing medieval lady was a silly little game that distracted my mind from my real intention—to invade Kevin's room in the hope of finding some clue as to what was ailing him. It came as something of a shock when the first thing I saw was a painting of a medieval lady in long trailing robes and a horned headdress.

The picture, framed in hideous gold Victorian curlicues, hung on the wall to my left. It was not very large, only about two feet square, and even at first glance I realized that it was an appallingly bad painting. Certainly it was no priceless ancestral portrait from the fourteenth or fifteenth century. The young woman's rounded face and the soft folds of her robe did not in the least resemble the stiff, hieratic style of the Middle Ages. I was reminded instead of William Morris and Burne-Jones, and the late-Victorian interest in pseudo-medieval subjects made popular by Sir Walter Scott. This painting was not even a good imitation of a second-rate painter; it was clearly the work of an unskilled amateur, perhaps one of the gentlemanly dilettantes of a more leisured age.

I was standing just inside the French doors, and shame kept me from advancing any farther. As I had expected, my survey of the room showed nothing unusual. Perhaps if I searched the drawers and closets. The idea made my cheeks burn. Like the rat I was, I scuttled out.

Yet as I stripped and changed into my swimsuit, something nagged at me like a burr under my pants. That portrait—it had not been in Kevin's room the first time I visited it, on my initial tour of the house. I would have remembered it because of the frame, which was almost the only completely tacky object in the house. In fact, I had seen it somewhere before—in one of the other rooms, never mind which one; the point was that Kevin had seen fit to move it. He was the only one who could have done so. Bea wouldn't rearrange his room, and the members of the cleaning team surely did not indulge in interior decoration. Why had he chosen to hang an ugly thing like that on his wall—and on the wall opposite his bed?

IV

Later that afternoon I told Kevin I had changed rooms with Bea. He received this news with a shrug and announced that he planned to join us for tea. Father Stephen had said something the other evening about Donne that he wanted to pursue. Besides— quoting Henri IV—if Paris was worth a Mass, Bea's cookies were worth a sermon.

The tea was sensational. Father Stephen wasn't bad

either. This was the first chance I had had to talk with him at length, and I could understand why his parishioners thought so highly of him. Without wishing to denigrate the man's undoubted charisma, his appearance didn't do him any harm. He resembled that magnificent Holbein portrait of Sir Thomas More—the visual embodiment of intelligence and integrity—except that he was even better looking. He had a way of turning to the person who was speaking with a look of intense concentration, as if nothing else on earth mattered to him at that particular moment. I had an impression, however, that it would not be comfortable to offend him or his principles—that the gentle mouth could harden and the mild gray eyes flash fire.

There were no demonstrations of fire and brimstone that afternoon; he obviously enjoyed the company, the food, and most of the conversation. He and Kevin talked about Donne. All very interesting, of course, but the metaphysical poets are not my bag—all that about white rings of eternity and mistress's breasts that really aren't breasts but something to do with the Church.

Bea and I couldn't have gotten a word in edgewise even if we had wanted to contribute. After a while Father Stephen decided it was time to change the subject and give us a chance.

"What a pleasure it is to see this beautiful old home being restored to the state it deserves," he said, with an appreciative glance around the room. "I am looking forward to having your parents as neighbors, Kevin. I called on them, you know, shortly after they moved in."

"Dad isn't exactly what I would call religious," Kevin said a little awkwardly.

"So he informed me." Father Stephen chuckled. "In the nicest possible way, of course! I'm not the proselytizing type, Kevin. I hope I can say that my friends include people of all faiths, and of none. After all, I consider Roger O'Neill a friend, and," he added, his voice thickening into a caricatured brogue, "and the bhoy is the blackest of heathens, and proud of it, bedad!"

Bea was the only one who didn't smile at this joking indictment. In the same tone I said lightly, "Yes, I can hear him bragging about it. He told us when we first met him that his chief interest was in seeing this house."

Father Stephen laughed and shook his head. "That's Roger. His idea of candor is to paint himself much worse than he is. But of course he would be interested in the house; he's a widely traveled, intelligent man, with a broad background in history and art. I suppose part of the charm of this place is also its previous inaccessibility. The former owner was a recluse. For the last ten or fifteen years I was the only one she invited here."

"The former owner was a woman?" Kevin leaned forward interestedly. "I thought Dad told me he had bought the house from Mr. Karnovsky's estate."

"Mr. Karnovsky passed on forty years ago." Father Stephen's voice was brusque. "The house was inherited by his only surviving daughter, Miss Marion. She lived here alone until her death two years ago."

"Alone, in this big house?" Bea exclaimed. "She must have had servants, friends—"

"No." The answer was so emphatic that we were all silent. After a moment Father Stephen sighed and went on in a quieter voice, "I beg your pardon, Bea.

The truth is, Miss Marion was someone whom I failed, badly. Blaming myself, I snap at my friends."

Bea's transparent face reflected his distress. She would have accepted his rejection of the subject, but Kevin, displaying an uncharacteristic insensitivity, remarked, "So that's why the place was so run down. Dad had a regular army of workmen here before he and Mom left. I suppose the old lady was a miser who didn't want to spend money on the house."

"She didn't have it to spend," Father Stephen said sharply. "Her father was one of the victims of the crash in 1929. He struggled for years to recoup, without success. The house was the only thing he managed to hang on to, the only unencumbered asset he left his daughter. Certainly she loved it and did what she could; I remember once finding her on her hands and knees mending a worn spot in the drawing room curtains. She was almost eighty then."

He stopped abruptly; and Bea began talking about the weather. What a lovely summer it had been so far! She had heard that the farmers were worried about rain, though. How fortunate that the house had its own water system. Had the wells ever run dry?

In thoughtful silence Kevin polished off the rest of the food.

V

We had our usual quiet evening in the library. Superficially it was the same as many other evenings, with long periods of peaceful silence broken occasionally by casual comments, and each of us busy with our own hobby. But something was different that evening, and I knew what it was. Tonight was my night for spying on Kevin. I was sorry now that I had moved into Bea's room. What the hell business was it of mine what Kevin did?

At eleven o'clock, her usual hour, Bea folded her carpet and rose. She yawned. I yawned. She made a laughing remark about the early hours she had been keeping. I countered with a laughing remark about my unusual fatigue, and followed Bea out.

On the upper landing we stopped and looked at one another. "Did you tell him?" Bea whispered.

I didn't need to ask what she meant. "Yes. He wasn't particularly interested."

"Maybe it was my imagination."

"We'll see."

"Call me if . . ."

"If what? We're making mountains out of molehills, to coin a phrase. You can tell I'm an English teacher, can't you?"

My attempt at humor didn't even fool me. Bea's face remained serious. "Anne, I'm not sure this was a good idea. Why don't you move back into the new wing? There's a nice room next to mine."

If this was meant to be reassuring, it had the reverse effect. I had suspected before, and now I was sure: the sounds she had heard from Kevin's room had not only embarrassed Bea, they had frightened her. And I had removed the only rational explanation for them.

"Don't be silly. Nothing is going to happen. Sleep well."

She didn't return the sentiment. I knew she was standing there watching me anxiously as I turned into the corridor leading to the old wing.

After switching on the lights in my room I stood in

the doorway looking the place over. Bea's behavior had set my nerves tingling. If I had seen the slightest abnormality, the least little thing that didn't look right . . .

But of course I didn't. The rooms in this part of the house lacked the charm of my former bedroom, with its high ceiling, big windows, and delicate plasterwork, but they had another kind of appeal, which was partly that of sheer age. The furniture in this room was heavy and the decor subdued—mostly browns and tans, with touches of dark blue. The French windows and the balcony were obviously later additions, an attempt to admit light and air without destroying the medieval appearance. The most impressive piece of furniture was the bed, whose russet velvet curtains hung from a high canopy. It was a winter room, which would be at its best when flames leaped on the hearth and woke the rich red tints in the massive mahogany furniture. On a snowy night the velvet bed hangings would enclose a sleeper in warmth, and muffle the wails of the winter wind—a box within a box, safe and secure.

All at once Bea's ominous hints seemed absurd, the inventions of a woman no longer young, who had just seen thirty years of her life crumble around her. The scars weren't visible, she hid them well; too well, perhaps? Pain must be exposed, anger openly expressed, if they are to heal.

I was so smug it makes me squirm to think about it. I even told myself that starting next day I would encourage Bea to talk about her troubles. It would be so good for her.

Among the newer books in the library were several shelves of detective stories, including a complete

collection of Agatha Christie, which I was devouring.
I had never realized what soothing late-night reading
they provided. The formalized mayhem and the routine procession of suspects, interrogated in the most
suave manner by the amateur detective, were so far
removed from the brutalities of real crime that they
had no deleterious effect on the nerves.

I finished *And Then There Were None,* and picked
up *The Hollow.* It had been years since I read a
mystery story or a popular novel; nothing lighter than
Thomas Hardy had met my critical eye since I turned
to the solemnities of Literature with a capital *L.* I felt
a little embarrassed at wallowing in crime now, that
was why I had smuggled a stack of Christies to my
room. Literature they emphatically were not. Slick
superficial style, cardboard characters, improbable
plot devices. So why, O critic, are you enjoying them
so much?

By the time I was halfway through *The Hollow* I
knew I couldn't go to sleep till I found out who done
it. I didn't hear Kevin come upstairs, the walls were
too thick, but I was aware of his presence in his room
because sounds were audible through the open window. The high balustrade of the balcony must have
acted as an acoustical funnel, magnifying and project-
ing the smallest noise.

I finished my book and turned out the light. Kevin
had apparently gone to bed. There was no sound from
his room. I would have preferred to follow his example, but something—a combination of curiosity and
duty—got me out of bed. I went on little cat feet to the
window and drew the curtains back.

The moon was down, but the night was not dark.

For reasons of security a number of outside lights were left burning, so that the heavy mass of the house seemed to squat in a shimmering pool of brightness. A spectral blue glow to my left betokened the presence of the swimming pool. Somehow the lights made the house seem more vulnerable instead of less so. I could see why Kevin's parents had not wanted to leave it unoccupied.

I thought of Kevin smuggling some woman across the lighted lawns and in through one of the spotlighted windows. He would have to turn off the burglar alarm, and remember to turn it on again after she left. Since Bea had arrived, we had been meticulous about this; conscious of her responsibilities, she had insisted that Kevin pull the master switch when he locked up for the night. She was usually the one to turn it off, since she was the first one down in the morning, so she would notice any omission in the routine. The idea was obviously absurd—insanely complicated, and also unnecessary. If Kevin wanted to dally with a local nymph, there were easier ways. I pictured Dr. Garst's niece, who had a behind like a bushel basket, crawling along the bushes and climbing the vines to Kevin's balcony, Romeo and Juliet in reverse. I was contemplating this captivating image when I heard the noise.

I probably would not have heard it if I had been tucked in bed where I belonged. The doors in that house didn't creak. All I caught was the double click as the knob turned and went back. I assured myself that Kevin had probably gone downstairs for a snack or a book. Then the other noises began, and my neat, substantial structure of common sense fell in ruins.

I won't describe them in detail. But Bea's imagination had not been overactive; there was no way, no way at all, that the sounds could have been anything except what she had assumed them to be.

And there were two voices.

Even in the murmurs of soft loving the girl's tones were distinct and exquisite, like pianissimo singing. Girl, not woman; the timbre was as light as a child's. Now I knew why Bea had used the words she had chosen. There was someone there, a person, a "who." It wasn't just her voice, it was a sense of presence.

Not until sighs and soft breathing succeeded the ecstatic culmination did I realize that I was clutching a fold of the curtains in a sticky hand and that my own breathing was faster than normal. Poor Bea. I had done her an injustice and I shared her shame. Not because what I had heard disgusted me—it didn't, it was beautiful—but because I was playing voyeur, or whatever the equivalent may be for someone who listens.

Finally—and how sickeningly bedroom farce it sounds—I heard the bedsprings creak. Belatedly realizing what this signified, I sped across the room and with infinite care opened my door just wide enough to peer out.

The lights in the hall were always left on at night. They were soft and shaded, just enough glow to prevent accidents and deter burglars. At first I saw nothing except a curve of narrow hallway, fading into darkness toward its end. Then Kevin's door opened.

He was naked, and his body was so beautiful that I caught my breath. One of the marble statues of classical Greece, the Doryphorus come to life— glowing brown flesh instead of white stone, glistening with a faint sheen of perspiration, as the bodies of the athletes had gleamed with oil. He was half turned away from me. His weight rested on one foot; one arm hung at his side, the other was raised, the hand extended, as if it touched something I could not see. The pose was like that of Polyclitus' classic statue, but his face had not the remote calm of the Lance-bearer. His lips were curved in a soft, closed smile, and his eyes were focused on something . . . something close to him, a few inches shorter, a few inches away.

I saw nothing. But I knew when the something moved away. Kevin's eyes followed it; his body turned like a compass needle seeking the north.

In the shadows of the passageway a faint glow appeared. "Shape without form, shade without color; Paralyzed force, gesture without motion. . . ." But it was moving, slowly, drifting toward the dark. Then the vague outlines shifted and solidified. Misty-white, twisting like a wisp of fog, surmounted by a golden shimmer. In another moment it would have been recognizable. I didn't wait. Smoothly and silently I closed the door. Smoothly and silently I crossed the room. I managed to get into bed before I started to shiver, all over, chilled to the bone in the warm air of that summer night.

Chapter Five

BEA HAD A DATE to go sightseeing with Roger next day. They intended to leave early.

I remembered that when I awoke, with profound thanksgiving. I had five or six hours to figure out what I was going to tell her.

It may seem ridiculous that after seeing the whole sensible world turn topsy-turvy I should be chiefly concerned with what I was going to say to Bea. But that was the crux of the matter. I might have talked myself into believing nothing unusual had happened if I had been the only one involved. Psychoanalysis and modern skepticism have provided us with a variety of comfortable cop-outs and assured us that practically everything is normal. Just offhand I could have come up with several neat explanations for those two voices I *thought* I had heard.

But Bea had heard them too.

If she was suffering from frustration and messed-up hormones, then so was I. Glib phrases like "collective hallucination" and "mass hypnosis" made slippery patterns in my mind. I had no doubt—such is the comfortable stupidity of the smug at heart—that something of the sort accounted for my final fantasy. The gestures of a skilled mime can create a world of people and objects for his audience; how much more effective the behavior of a man who really believes in what he thinks he sees? So intense was Kevin's belief in his dream lover that he had hypnotized me into believing too. If I had stood there watching for a few more seconds, I would have seen her clear—white robes, golden hair.

I talked myself into believing this rubbish without too much difficulty, but it still left me with a problem: Kevin. I didn't know much about abnormal psychology, but I had the impression that few sexual aberrations are considered sick these days. Perhaps making love to an imaginary partner was just one of those pleasant little variants that would make a psychiatrist shrug tolerantly. But opening the door for an invisible woman? Talking to her—and answering back? Kevin's voice was a deep baritone shading to bass. He could never have mimicked that soft soprano consciously.

My unpleasant meditations were interrupted by a knock at the door and a voice yelling my name. It was Kevin's voice—the bass-baritone—and such was my state of nerves that I actually screamed out loud. Kevin promptly flung the door open.

"What the hell—" He broke off, staring at the spectacle I presented, bolt upright in bed, eyeballs bulging, both hands clutching the sheet under my chin.

"You look," said Kevin, "like Clarissa Harlowe waiting to be ravished. Have no fear, fair virgin, you are safe from me. What's the matter—nightmare?"

"Yes. I mean, no. I mean . . ."

Kevin was dressed for tennis. He sat down on the foot of the bed and studied me critically. I managed not to shrink back.

"You scared me, yelling like that," he said. "I thought you'd hurt yourself. Or seen a mouse."

"I do not scream when I see a mouse. I was—er—asleep. You startled me."

"Oh. Sorry. You hardly ever sleep this late. I started to wonder whether you had OD'd, or something."

"Funny," I said.

"Want to play tennis?"

"For God's sake, I haven't even had my coffee. How can you make such obscene suggestions?"

Kevin grinned. "My dear girl, if you think that is an obscene suggestion, wait till you hear my excerpts from the Restoration dramatists." A puzzled expression came over his face. "What are you doing in here? You weren't in your room, and Bea's things were in there, so I cleverly deduced you had switched rooms. How come?"

My experience of the previous night was rapidly taking on the insubstantiality of a nightmare. Surely this man was not the one I had seen transfigured and entranced. His blunt question gave me an opening, but I chose my words with care.

"I told you yesterday," I said. "Don't you remember?"

"Oh, yeah, so you did. I was thinking of something else at the time. Whose idea was it?"

"Bea's."

Kevin's face fell. I could have laughed out loud. I had damaged his precious male ego. His reaction was so blessedly normal I was sorry I hadn't let him hang on to his delusions.

"Oh," he said.

"Apparently you snore."

"I do not!"

"Well, you make noises. Peculiar noises."

"I've never had any complaints before."

His expression had changed from hurt pride to outrage. He couldn't be acting. It was obvious that he had not the slightest recollection of what had happened. Was that a good sign or a bad sign? I had no idea.

I promised to join him at the tennis court as soon as I had had some breakfast. When I got there he was banging balls against the backboard, still sulking over my multiple insults. The game restored his good humor—he beat me badly, as he usually did—but it reduced me to a lump of sweating protoplasm. The weather was savagely hot and humid, and by the time we finished playing, clouds were mounting up behind the hills.

By early afternoon the air was like a Turkish bath, but the rain still held off. My physical discomfort was only exceeded by my mental confusion. My brain felt like pea soup. I decided to have a swim. The tepid water felt good, but it didn't help my thinking. I was floating on my back in a state of utter mindlessness when Kevin appeared. He stood poised for a moment on the edge of the pool, arms over his head, before he dived, splitting the water as cleanly as a knife. It was beautiful to watch. Suspecting that his next move would be to grab my ankle or my arm and pull me under, I started swimming with more speed than grace.

I had noticed—what red-blooded female wouldn't? —that Kevin had a good body. When he was stripped for swimming, practically all of it was visible; the previous night I had seen very little more of him than

I had seen many times before. Why, then, had I been
struck all in a heap, like a teenage groupie? There had
been something different about him—or about me.
The cause, dear Anne, is in thyself, that thou art crazy.

When the first roll of thunder echoed from behind
the trees I scrambled out of the pool, followed by
Kevin's jeers.

"Swimming pools are dangerous in thunderstorms," I yelled at the sleek dark head that lay atop
the smooth water like a reminder of the French
Revolution. Kevin opened his mouth to reply, forgot
to tread water, and sank. Laughing, I ran in to change.

I now understand something about human nature I
couldn't comprehend before—why people who have
been wiped out and almost killed by a volcano or
some other natural disaster move right back to the
same place after they have cleaned up the debris. They
do it because they don't believe it will happen again.
They didn't believe it would happen in the first place.
Oh, sure, Vesuvius blows up every now and then—it
can happen—but it will not happen to them. Human
beings have an astonishing capacity to ignore what
they don't want to believe. Here I was alone in the
house with a man who entertained imaginary ladies in
the middle of the night; and twelve hours after I had
watched the performance I had convinced myself I
must have been dreaming.

He was so normal! In spite of his snide remarks he
was not far behind when I fled the pool. Together we
went through the now-familiar routine of securing the
house against the storm, closing windows, collecting
the animals. Together we settled in the library, Kevin
with a can of beer, I with a glass of iced coffee. We
joked about poor Amy, who was trying to climb into

Kevin's chair with him. I stroked Pettibone, who had settled on my lap and was purring vehemently.

"She likes me," I said.

"Cats purr when they are nervous," Kevin said. "She's probably afraid of the storm."

"Thanks a lot."

The skies outside were night-dark. Kevin switched on the lamp beside his chair and reached for a book. It was a handsome volume elaborately bound in brown calf, with tooled gold decorations.

"What are you reading?" I asked lazily.

"This? It's a history of the Mandevilles—the family that owned the house back in England."

"The name sounds familiar."

"Wasn't to me. They weren't anybody in particular; in fact, they were a dull lot."

"Then why are you reading it?"

"Damned if I know," Kevin said cheerfully. "I guess I keep hoping I'll discover some florid Victorian scandal."

"The real identity of Jack the Ripper?" I suggested. "The name of the mistress of Prince Albert?"

"I didn't know he had a mistress."

"He must have. Nobody could be that pure and loyal to a boring woman like Queen Victoria without breaking out sometimes."

"Well, if he did, she wasn't a Mandeville. They didn't do anything interesting."

"I take it they were the ones our friend Rudolf bought the house from."

"Right. There were no male heirs left in 1925; both the sons had been killed in World War I." Kevin tossed the book aside. "I'll have to go farther back," he said, as if to himself.

"Back? To what?"

"The people who owned the house before the Mandevilles. They only lived in it for a few generations—bought it in the early nineteenth century from a family named Leventhorpe."

"So?"

"Well, it's just that . . ." Kevin eyed me warily. "If you laugh, I'll put toads in your bed."

"I won't laugh."

"A place like this—it's like a trust, you know? I'm the last, or the latest, of a long line of people who have lived here, looked to the house for shelter, kept it going, you might say. It gives a person a sense of continuity that's rare in this day and age. I mean, some of the stones in these walls are over five hundred years old."

"No, they aren't, they're five million years old—or however long ago it was when the earth was formed out of hot gases. It's like searching for ancestors," I went on scornfully. "We're all descended from somebody. It doesn't make any difference to me whether that somebody was Julius Caesar or one of his slaves."

His eyes brilliant, Kevin leaned forward, ready to pursue the argument. A cannonball of thunder burst overhead. The kitten and I both jumped.

"Scared?" Kevin asked.

"I don't like storms."

"Want to sit on my lap? I'd rather have you than Amy."

The look in his eyes told me that he meant what he said—and more than he said. I might have accepted the invitation, but was prevented by the slam of the front door and voices in the hall.

They came in laughing, as if at a joke neither Kevin

nor I had heard. Bea's hands pushed dampened tendrils of hair away from her face. Roger shook himself like a big dog. They were not holding hands or touching, but the minute I saw Bea's face I knew something had happened between them—nothing to be formalized as yet by words to others, nor perhaps even to themselves, but something as visible as a smile, as palpable as an embrace.

Roger accepted a chair and a glass of tonic. We talked about where they had been, and how they had just missed the storm. After a feeble pretense at resistance, Roger accepted an invitation to dinner. He went to the kitchen with Bea; and I did not volunteer my services. As soon as they had left the room, Kevin began rummaging through the papers on the table, as if in search of something. Seeing he was disinclined for conversation, or for anything else, I picked up my crossword puzzle. The kitten purred, the rain thrummed against the window. My eyelids drooped.

II

That little nap served me in good stead. When I slipped out of my room at about one A.M., I was wide awake.

There was only one practical means of entrance into Kevin's bedroom. The balcony was too high, the wall too sheer for anyone to climb up that way. Besides, I had heard his door open and close; I had seen him say farewell, good night, thanks a lot, to . . . a real flesh-and-blood female? Perhaps my eyes had deceived me. Some trick of the light, some trick of my mind, half-asleep, half-dreaming? Tonight I was alert and forewarned. If anyone or anything visible visited Kevin, I would see her, coming and going.

I had managed to avoid a confrontation with Bea. Her new state of euphoria and Roger's presence—he stayed till after eleven—distracted her from awkward questions. Once, when we were clearing the table, she had turned to me with raised eyebrows and a murmur of "About last night—" I cut her off. "It's okay. We'll talk tomorrow, but don't worry." Roger came in then and carried her off to her sitting room, so she didn't have time to pursue the matter.

I went to my room early, partly to avoid Bea and partly to give myself time to arrange my ambush. Later, sitting in the dark with my door slightly ajar, I heard Kevin come upstairs. I gave him half an hour to brush his teeth and settle down. Then I transferred myself to the spot I had selected, a small alcove near the stairway end of the passage. It had been cut out of the stone of the walls, which were three feet thick in this part of the house. A small window at the back of it gave enough light during the day to encourage a miniature forest of potted plants, from among whose boughs a marble nymph peeked coyly out. There was just enough room for me between the wall and the pedestal of the statue, if I shifted some of the plants.

I had to sit with my knees drawn up, and after an indeterminate amount of time had passed I realized I had not anticipated the incredible discomforts of the spying profession. My bottom ached, cramps tied knots in my legs, and my brain went numb with boredom.

I know quite a bit of poetry by heart. I repeated all of it, including all of *The Wasteland* and the entire second act of *Hamlet*. Then I just sat, feeling my glutei maximi congeal and wishing I had had the sense to get a wristwatch with an illuminated dial. The lights in the corridor were widely spaced, with deep pools of shadow between. The rain had diminished to a drizzle, but the night sky was still overcast; no moon, no stars brightened my hiding place.

Eventually I dozed off, from boredom rather than fatigue. It was a light, uneasy slumber; the discomfort of my position and the night noises of the house kept jerking me awake. Then I heard a sound that woke me completely—the soft click of a latch.

I had slumped down into the space between the nymph's pedestal and the back wall of the alcove. Gingerly I slid forward, painfully I transferred my weight onto my aching knees; cautiously I peered out.

I have tried several times to describe what I saw, but on those occasions I was under a certain emotional strain. This is my first attempt to set it down in cold black and white.

Kevin's door was open. He stood in the doorway. The room behind him was dark. The doorframe concealed part of his body, which was in profile to me. His arms were extended, his hands slightly curved and facing one another, as if he touched something lightly. His lips parted. A murmur of sound reached me, but no distinct words. Then his hands dropped. For a few seconds he stood still. Then, moving slowly, like a swimmer under water, he withdrew into his room. The door closed.

The figure was clearly visible by then. Its outlines were blurred, like a foggy vapor, but the shape was definitely human. The lower limbs were concealed by the long trailing garment that covered the entire body, so that it seemed to glide instead of walk. It passed from shadow into light, and the glow of the lamp reflected from the silver-gilt substance that covered its head and trailed down its back—hair or some kind of hood; I could not be sure.

To describe my feelings would be unscientific. I will try to confine myself to what I did. I started on the multiplication table. I got to three times four before I had to stop because I couldn't think of the answer. I took a fold of skin between thumb and forefinger, and pinched, hard. The marks were still there next day.

The golden gleam was that of hair, silky locks that streamed below the thing's waist. There were arms, in long, full sleeves, slightly extended, as if it needed to balance itself. It was fully formed now, except at the lowest part of the long garment, which trailed off into misty wisps like fog, several inches above the floor. I could see the hall carpet under it. And I could see, from the pattern on the carpet, that it had stopped moving.

A ripple passed over it, like the tensing of muscles. It knew I was there. Through some sense beyond the normal five it had felt my presence. I knew that as surely as if it had cried out or pointed an accusing finger. I tried to stand up. My legs ached. I felt the pain, just as I was fully cognizant of my other sensations and my physical surroundings. It was not the pain that kept me from moving.

With a sudden snakelike twist, horribly unlike its earlier slow drifting, the thing whirled around. For a split second I saw the face Kevin had seen—a smiling, dimpled girl's face, softly rounded. Then the features melted like those of a wax doll over a flame. The dainty nose became a dripping blob, the cheeks sagged into shapelessness around an empty hole of a mouth.

In the shifting mass I caught flashes, fleeting and hideously incomplete, of other features taking shape and instantly dissolving—an acquiline nose, a protruding high curve of heavy cheekbones, lips that squeezed themselves into an animal-like snout before they blurred into doughy chaos. The writhing, waxen mass was still trying to shape itself when the figure made a lurching movement forward—toward me.

I must have gotten to my feet, though I don't remember doing so. All I remember is a yielding and a ponderous movement and a dark mass looming over me. A thunderclap exploded six inches from my ear, and the dark enveloped me.

III

I awoke to find myself in Kevin's arms. I started to scream.

He took two long steps and dumped me onto a soft-hard surface that yielded to my weight. I bounced.

"She's hysterical," he said. "Shall I slap her?"

"Certainly not." Bea pushed him aside and sat down on the edge of the bed. Her face was ashen. "Anne, it's me. Are you all right? What happened?"

Something froze my tongue. It wasn't bravado or strength of will, it was the sight of Kevin standing by the bed, his eyebrows drawn together in a frown. He was wearing pajama bottoms—out of deference to Bea, I supposed—and one hand was raised to his cheek.

"You tell me what happened," I said feebly. "I don't remember."

"Thank God." Bea's body sagged forward. "I mean —thank God you can talk. I was afraid of concussion. That statue couldn't have missed you by more than six inches. It was criminal carelessness to leave it just standing on the pedestal, it ought to have been anchored."

"I hope I didn't break it," I mumbled.

Bea laughed unsteadily. "My dear child, it's marble, and weighs over two hundred pounds. You are the one who might have been broken. Are you sure? . . ." Her hands fluttered toward me.

I rubbed my forehead. "I must have hit my head when I fell. It's a little sore, but there's no blood."

"Thanks to that Orphan Annie mop of yours," Kevin said. His stern look had relaxed. He lowered his hand to display an angry red spot on his cheekbone. "You hit me, you dirty rat. I shouldn't have grabbed you up so suddenly. You must have had quite a shock seeing that statue topple toward you."

"It was a shock, all right," I said.

"I'm still shaking." Kevin gave an exaggerated shudder. "That damn thing hit the floor with a crash like a howitzer; I was out in the hall before I woke up completely. And seeing you lying there, with the statue practically on top of you. . . . Don't do it again, okay?"

He patted my arm. I bit my lip and managed not to cry out or recoil. His touch made my skin crawl.

Bea saw my reaction. Her eyes narrowed. "Go back to bed, Kevin. She's not hurt."

"Sure you don't want me to call a doctor? Okay, then. If you change your mind, don't hesitate to wake me."

After he had gone, Bea ran her hands methodically over me, ending with my head. When I winced she parted my hair and looked closely.

"It's not even bleeding. You were very fortunate, Anne—physically, at least. What happened?"

Her eyes begged for a reassuring lie. I tried to oblige.

"I went down to get a book. I must have tripped and fallen against—"

"No." Bea sighed. "I'd like to believe it. But I saw your eyes when Kevin touched you. It has something to do with the sounds I heard, doesn't it? Why didn't you tell me before?"

"There was nothing to tell. Nothing definite."

"Did Kevin hurt you? Attack you?"

Her face was drawn with anxiety. I let out a harsh croak of laughter.

"No, honey, Kevin is not a rapist. I wish it were that simple."

"Tell me, then. I have to know, Anne."

"I'm not sure I can describe it. But I'll try."

My narrative was by no means as precise or smooth as the one I have written. Yet I think my halts and hesitations were even more convincing. Bea listened without interrupting. There was something steadying about her stillness and gravity.

"I thought it was coming toward me," I ended. "That broke my paralysis. I must have lurched to my feet and grabbed at the statue to steady myself. I was numb from sitting so long."

Bea nodded. "That makes sense. Unless . . ."

My mind was so stretched by the uncanny that it was more receptive than normal. I seemed to catch the thought straight from her mind.

"You mean—it—pushed the statue, trying to mash me? You don't have to scare me any more, Bea; I'm already gibbering."

"I'm not trying to scare you." Bea smiled faintly. Her face had a Madonnalike calm as she sat, hands quiet in her lap. "I'm trying to keep an open mind. I'm sure the idea is as repugnant to you as it is to me, but we've got to face the possibility that what we are dealing with is . . ."

"Ghosts," I said. The word came out like a vulgarity.

"This is a very old house."

"I know, I know. But damn it, Bea, I'd rather believe I was sick in the head and hallucinating. And if you quote *Hamlet* to me, I may call you a bad name."

"Horatio, wasn't it? Anne, would you like a cup of tea?"

I had to laugh. "What I really want is a drink, but I don't think that would be a good idea. Go ahead and make the tea, if you want some; I can't quite visualize us calmly discussing ghosts over a cup of tea, but—"

"I don't intend to discuss it now. You've had enough for tonight. You need to rest. What are your plans for tomorrow?"

"I may drive to Pittsfield and try to locate a good shrink."

Bea frowned. "I suppose joking about a shock is the way your generation handles it."

I had not been joking. Before I could tell her so she went on, "I'm meeting Roger for lunch. You had better join us. He will want to hear an eyewitness account."

"Roger? You're going to tell him?"

"Why not? We need advice."

I could think of a number of reasons why not, but the decision was not up to me. I had no copyright on the "ghost"; in fact, the problem was Bea's. Kevin was her nephew, the house belonged to her sister and brother. She had no need to consult me.

"I just don't like running to some man, like a couple of helpless little females," I muttered.

"Believe me, I'm not in the habit of doing that either," Bea said dryly. "My ex-husband was a leaner, not a rock. Roger is an intelligent man, rational and skeptical. Too skeptical, in my opinion, but that quality may be what we need just now."

I couldn't argue with that. In fact, the more I thought about it, the better Roger seemed. Feeling as he did about Bea, he wouldn't dismiss her ideas as menopausal fancies. He was a sophisticated man who had been around—and he was an atheist, or close to it. He wouldn't mumble about troubled spirits or suggest solving the problem by prayer.

"That's settled, then," Bea said. "Now try to sleep. I'll just stretch out in the big chair over there."

"You don't have to do that. I'm not nervous now."

She didn't argue, she just smiled and sat down, wrapping the skirts of her robe around her. It was nice to have her there, even if she didn't resemble the conventional little old gray-haired mom. In a surprisingly short time I felt my eyelids getting heavy. As I drifted off, I thought it was strange that I felt so comfortable. I ought to have been afraid.

Chapter Six

THE OLD STONE INN, five miles west of us, was one of Bea and Roger's favorite restaurants. The exterior was charming—weathered stone and dark shutters, shaded by tall old trees. I thought they had gone a little overboard on heavy beams and quaint carvings when they restored the interior; the room was so dark I could hardly see where I was going.

That was the least of my worries. I was absurdly self-conscious at the idea of telling my story to Roger. My state of confusion had not been alleviated by seeing Kevin that morning, all tanned and bright-eyed and cheerful and full of concern for me. He had even let me off playing tennis. There was only one thing. I couldn't stand the idea of his touching me. When he put out his hands I saw those same hands caressing a melting, twisting horror.

The hostess led us to the table where Roger was waiting. I don't think he saw me at first. Rising, he took the hand Bea extended, and they just stood there looking at each other. It was rather sweet.

I had wondered how Bea would lead up to the subject we wanted to discuss. There was no need. No sooner had we taken our seats than Roger said quietly, "What is it, Bea? Something wrong?"

"How did you know?" I exclaimed.

Roger made an impatient gesture. "I'll always know when Bea is upset. Want to tell me about it?"

"It's very simple," I said. "Either Kevin is losing his mind, or I am."

"It isn't that simple," Bea said. "I heard what you heard, Anne."

"I'm tempted to shake you both," Roger exclaimed. "These dire hints and allusions—" He broke off as the waitress approached to take our order. When she had left he put both elbows on the table and looked at Bea. "Go on," he said.

Roger's eyebrows were a performance in themselves. They rose and fell, tilted and wriggled, as Bea spoke. I half expected Roger would laugh, or smile knowingly, at some of her phrases; they were so primly euphemistic. But he remained grave, and when she paused he went unerringly to the main point.

"The second voice. Not falsetto or—"

"It was a woman's voice," Bea said. "No, a girl's voice. Very young, very light."

"Beautiful," I added. "Musical."

"Go on."

Bea told him about our decision to change rooms. Then she nodded at me.

The words flowed more easily than I had expected they would. Roger was a good listener. By the time I finished, his eyebrows had soared up to his former hairline, but there was neither mockery nor disbelief in his expression.

He turned to the food that was being placed in front of us, remarking only, "Not a bad place to take a break." When we were alone again he shoved his plate back and restored his elbows to the table.

"All right," he said briskly. "Let's get the dirty work over with. Try not to lose your temper, Anne; I have to say these things, to clear the air. You have never been subject to epilepsy, fainting fits, delusions or hallucinations? Have you ever consulted a psychiatrist? Is there a history of mental illness in your family? Do you at the present time take drugs of any kind? Have you in the past ever used LSD, peyote, or any of the other hallucinogens? Are you now or have you ever been a member of any organization dedicated to the proposition that the spirits of the dead can be contacted by the living, for any purpose whatsoever?"

I was angry when he began. By the time he finished I was laughing, and shaking my head like a robot.

"I'm serious, dammit," Roger said. "I don't know you. I like you, but I don't know anything about you. I assume that, like most of your contemporaries, you have played around with grass—come on, don't be cute with me, I'm sure you have. Unless you were loopy to begin with, it is unlikely that a couple of reefers would send you into that kind of a tailspin, even if you were smoking at the time."

"Really, Roger," Bea said indignantly.

Roger's face relaxed into a fond smile as he turned to her. "Just checking, honey. Don't you see that in a case like this we have to lean over backward to be rational?" His mouth split wider, into a blissful grin. "God, this is wonderful! It's so good I'm afraid to believe it. But if it works out—"

"What are you talking about?" I demanded.

Roger was still gloating. "A real, genuine, honest-to-God manifestation. I never hoped to see one. The SPR will give me a medal."

The initials meant nothing to me, but Bea recognized them. The bewilderment on her face changed to hostile suspicion. "I hope I misunderstand you, Roger. You would never be contemptible enough to publicize our personal problems, would you?"

"Darling." Roger grabbed her hand. "Sweetheart, forgive me. That was a lousy, stinking thing to say. I got carried away. If you knew how many years. . . . Naturally my chief consideration is your well-being. Say you forgive me, or I'll slit my wrists with the steak knife."

Bea's lips quivered. "You're making a spectacle of yourself," she whispered, trying to free her hand. "People are staring."

"Then tell me you—"

"I forgive you. Roger, let go of my hand."

Instead Roger put his hand, and Bea's, under the table. Without taking his eyes from her face he said, "Wipe that smirk off your face, Anne. I know it must be amusing to see the old folks making fools of themselves—"

"I think it's beautiful," I said.

"You're a nice girl." Roger grinned at me. "To show my genuine regard for you, I will now proceed to deliver a well-organized, methodical lecture. Ready for it?"

"I have a feeling I'm going to get it whether I'm ready or not," I said.

"Go on, Roger," Bea said.

"I'm sure most of these theories have already occurred to you. I just want to make sure we haven't overlooked anything. First, we have the possibility that the two of you imagined the whole thing—or rather, that you misinterpreted what you heard. Of course that theory implies that Bea is a frustrated, neurotic female and that Anne's not only equally neurotic but idiotically susceptible to suggestion. I don't believe that. Do you?"

"Hardly," Bea said.

"Second: Kevin is the one suffering from delusions. You say, and I will take your word for it, that he appears to have no conscious recollection of what he does and says during his midnight—shall we call them 'encounters'? This theory still leaves Anne looking feebleminded; it assumes her visual hallucinations were induced by Kevin's actions. I don't believe that either."

"Thanks," I said.

"De nada. Third, and most probable: what you heard was real; what you saw was really there. There is something in the house, some psychic force, that manifests itself under certain as yet undefined circumstances. Kevin sees it as a beautiful, desirable woman. This force may work directly on the auditory, tactile, and visual centers of the brain, or it may take on physical form, palpable enough to give Kevin . . ."

He glanced at Bea.

"I understand," she said quickly. "That's very interesting, Roger, but you are omitting a fourth and, to me, much more plausible interpretation."

Roger let out a long, pensive sigh. "I was afraid you were going to bring that up."

"She's right," I said. "If we are going to consider your psychic force, you have to consider—well—a ghost."

"The word is not the one I would use," Bea said. "It is too loaded with negative connotations, some humorous, some merely silly. I would rather put it this way. You said, Roger, there was 'something in the house.' Why not 'someone in the house'?"

I started. Bea glanced at me. "You've felt it too, haven't you?"

"Yes," I said reluctantly.

"A presence," Bea went on. "Call it a soul or a spirit; it is personalized, it has identity. Why not, Roger? Every one of the world's great religions, and most of the pagan cults, accept the separateness and the survival of a spiritual body apart from the flesh."

"Your Church isn't crazy about the idea," Roger said. "Organized religion has been the strongest opponent of spiritualism and psychic research."

"Because spiritualism is a dangerous, unlicensed interference in matters that ought to be left to those trained to deal with them." Bea was very much in earnest. Leaning toward Roger, she tried to hold his gaze. His eyes dropped, avoiding hers.

"It's too damned—what is the word I want?—too childish! You know the classic ghost stories—they're all like something Dickens or Thackeray might have written, the plot devices neatly worked out to make sure the characters, living and dead, survive happily ever after. You say you have a sense of presence—of someone in the house. That's a common phenomenon. I don't know what the psychological term may be, but I've felt it myself when I was relaxed or absorbed in something. Let me ask you this, Anne: did you have any such impression last night?"

"I meant to ask you that," Bea said. "There is a mistaken impression that such entities must be malevolent or hostile. And that blasted statue did come close to hitting you. I couldn't help wondering . . . Well, Anne?"

I had to think about it. "I don't know," I said finally. "It was so monstrous-looking, so messy. I've often wondered how humans will feel if and when they encounter an alien race that is benevolent but utterly dreadful-looking. The mere strangeness of appearance can cause us to recoil, even if—"

"Cut out the philosophy," Roger said rudely. "I see what you mean, and so does Bea. What you felt was horror of the unfamiliar and unexpected, right? No specific threat."

"I guess so," I said; but I had an uneasy feeling that I was being led.

"But that proves my point," Roger exclaimed. "The forces I am hypothesizing are neutral by nature; they don't possess or project emotions."

"It also supports my hypothesis," Bea said firmly. "An earthbound spirit, bewildered and confused—"

"Bull."

Bea scowled at him. "I intend to consult Father Stephen. Roger, if you swear at me again, I'll leave."

"Sweetheart, I would never swear at you. But why the hell do you have to drag him into this?"

"He is trained to deal with spiritual problems."

"Look here, he's a friend of mine; I like the guy. He's reasonable and intelligent—on all subjects but one. The mere mention of the Holy Ghost sends him into airy flights of fancy. Damn it, Bea, he'll try to exorcise it!"

"That might not be a bad idea," I said. "Maybe a little exercise is what it needs. A long walk every morning, a swim in the afternoon." My feeble attempt at humor got the response it deserved. Both of them turned outraged stares onto me. "All right, so it wasn't funny," I said. "Roger, your diagnosis is neat and logical, but I don't care all that much what the cursed thing *is;* I want to know what to *do* about it. Have you any practical suggestions?"

"I have one." Roger's voice was deadly serious. "Move out of that room. Right away."

"I thought you said it wasn't dangerous," I said, trying to ignore the icy prickle that ran down my back.

"I never said that. I said it wasn't hostile. That doesn't mean it may not be dangerous. It is. Damned dangerous."

II

We were the last ones to leave the restaurant. When the waitresses started standing around coughing suggestively in chorus, Roger took the hint. We had not by any means finished our argument; it continued to rage as we stood by our respective cars in the almost empty parking lot.

I wasn't an active participant. I just made remarks now and then, taking one side or the other—remarks that both combatants ignored. They finally hammered out a compromise of sorts. Bea agreed to wait till next day before talking to Father Stephen. She also agreed to let Roger carry out an experiment that night.

It seemed to me that the compromise was pretty one-sided, with Bea doing all the giving in. When I mentioned this, Roger swept my comment aside with a gesture of lofty disdain.

"If I had my way, Steve wouldn't be involved at all," he said. "Never mind; hopefully, tonight I will get enough evidence to settle your silly little fears, my darling."

Bea looked as if she were tempted to reply to his endearment with a shorter, pithier epithet, but curiosity overcame her resentment. "What precisely are you planning?" she asked.

"Wait and see." Roger rubbed his hands together and chuckled. "Just play along with me when I turn up this evening. I'll feed you the appropriate cues."

On that unsatisfactory note we parted. It was a good thing I was driving. It gave Bea a chance to vent her feelings, which she did by stamping her feet and clenching her hands.

"Men!" she exclaimed.

"Annoying creatures," I agreed.

The corners of Bea's mouth twitched. She laughed ruefully. "I really like him, Anne."

"I thought you did."

"What do you think of him?"

"I like him too. I'm happy for you, Bea."

"I don't want to act prematurely," Bea said, half to herself. "It would be a mistake to jump into anything too soon."

"That makes sense."

"Can I ask you something?"

"Feel free."

"If I'm out of line say so. But I've wondered, sometimes, why you and Kevin haven't become closer —romantically, I mean. You seem so well suited. Is there someone else?"

"There was. To tell you the truth, I don't know where I stand with Joe—or vice versa. He got a grant to work abroad this summer. Up to the time he left there was a tacit assumption, on my part, at least, that we would get back together again in the fall. The night before he left—"

Bea broke the silence. "Something happened?"

"Yes," I said in a choked voice, remembering my sudden, senseless terror, my clinging and whining. Could that bizarre incident be connected with the thing that haunted Grayhaven? A premonition of danger—or the first sign of incipient mental or physical breakdown?

Seeing my look of consternation, Bea began to murmur apologies.

"It wasn't anything you said," I assured her. "I just remembered something that . . . I'll have to think about it. So far as my relations with Kevin are concerned—" I broke off as a horrible suspicion occurred to me. "Bea! You aren't by any chance thinking that I ought to throw myself at Kevin to get his mind off his imaginary lady?"

"You must have thought of it yourself," Bea said coolly. "You wouldn't have reached that conclusion so quickly if the idea had not passed through your mind."

"I suppose it did. We keep coming back, don't we, to the suspicion—the hope, even—that Kevin is suffering from some kind of sexual psychosis. It would be so much easier to accept than the alternatives. But Bea—even if that were the case, which I don't really believe, I've got better sense than to suppose my questionable charms could cure anything as serious as that. Besides . . ."

"Well?"

My hands clenched on the wheel. "If Kevin made love to me . . . I'd never be sure it was really me he was holding."

That was as far as I could go toward the truth. I couldn't bring myself to tell Bea how I really felt about Kevin. She had not seen his dream girl dissolve into a squirming mass of flesh. What I said was bad enough. She flinched as if I had slapped her.

"I understand," she said.

"I'm sorry if I—"

"Let's stop apologizing to each other, shall we? I

have a feeling we are going to be saying and doing a lot of things that may be misinterpreted. We must take one another's goodwill and good intentions for granted."

It was an excellent suggestion. I only hoped we could live up to it.

Kevin was not in the house when we arrived. It seemed a good time to carry out Roger's idea that I change rooms—an idea with which I was in enthusiastic accord. I selected a room next to Bea's. As I trotted back and forth with armloads of clothes and books, I decided this would be my last move in that house. If my clothes went traveling again, they would go in suitcases and to a considerable distance.

One might well ask why I didn't pack up then and there. I had so many reasons that a psychiatrist would probably have told me that none was the real reason. For one thing, I had nowhere else to go. I had sublet my apartment. The family homestead was swarming with young siblings and their obnoxious friends—I didn't even have a room of my own anymore; I had to share my kid sister's. Also, I didn't like the implication of copping out—of leaving Bea, whom I liked, and Kevin, who was a friend, in the lurch.

There was another reason—the true reason—but I hadn't defined it, or recognized it, then.

It didn't take long to transfer my things. Kevin still had not put in an appearance. I decided to go down to the pool and see if he was there. The idea of a swim was attractive, but I wasn't sure I could stand our old horseplay without having a fit of hysterics.

Kevin was at the pool. I heard him before I saw him. I heard something else that made me go weak at the knees. It was a girl's voice—light, high, laughing.

I stood petrified for a moment, breathing hard, and

then the sounds sorted themselves out. There were several voices, not just two, raised in laughter and shrieks of general joie de vivre.

The pool area was surrounded by an eight-foot fence, as required by local ordinance. Kevin was always careful to lock the gate when we were not swimming. Now it stood open. I approached it warily, ready to retreat.

I was so used to swimming alone with Kevin that at first glance the water seemed full of bodies. There were only four of them, really—Kevin and three females. Another girl was stretched out on a bright beach towel sunning herself. She had untied the straps of her bikini top to avoid nasty white streaks. Her face was hidden in her arm, but I recognized her hips: Dr. Garst's niece.

My knees went weak again, this time with relief. I felt silly. I ought to have anticipated this. As I believe I have mentioned, little Miss Leila had thrown out some very broad hints. Tired of waiting for an invitation that never came, she had simply invited herself, and had brought along some friends.

I sat down at one of the tables scattered along the pool edge. I sat there for several minutes before Kevin saw me. He seemed to be having a jolly time. What man wouldn't with three almost naked females climbing all over him? One in particular caught my eye— and, I thought, had caught Kevin's. She had long blond hair that streamed out artistically in the water or wrapped itself around her face, effectively obscuring that part of her a good deal of the time. The rest of her was under water. I got an impression of a slim, tanned body wearing the skimpiest of black bikinis.

When Kevin spotted me he let out a whoop of welcome and swam toward me. His harem followed like ducklings after mama. He pulled himself out of the water and sat down, shaking his wet head.

"Hi."

"Hi."

"Have a nice lunch?"

"Yes."

"Some people dropped in."

"So I see."

The girls stood in studiedly casual attitudes. The blonde wrung out her hair. Garst's niece sat up. Her bikini top fell off. She grabbed at it, but not very fast.

"You know Leila," Kevin said. "This is Debbie." He indicated the blonde. "Mary Sue, and—er—"

"Er" told me her name. I never saw her again, so there is no reason why that name should encumber these pages, even if I could remember it, which I can't.

"Do you live around here?" I asked, making polite conversation and addressing all three impartially.

"We're staying with Leila," said Mary Sue, or maybe "er."

"My sorority sisters," said Leila.

"How nice," I said.

"We're having a wonderful time," said Mary Sue. "This is beautiful country."

Poor little things; they kept chattering brightly, casting frequent glances at Kevin to see if he was impressed. The only one who didn't talk was Debbie. She had acknowledged the introduction with a smile and then spread herself out on a chaise longue, one slim arm over her eyes. Her face was pretty, in a conventional sort of way—the clean-cut American girl who appears in commercials selling makeup and cameras. She was smarter than the others, I thought, withdrawing instead of hovering. But maybe she knew she had already won the first round. Kevin's eyes kept wandering in her direction.

After I had been polite to the girls I took my swim and then my departure. They stayed for another couple of hours. At least it was that long before Kevin came in. I was in the kitchen peeling potatoes.

"There you are. Just wanted to tell you I won't be here for dinner."

"Oh. Got a date?"

Kevin had never looked more relaxed or more normal. His face wore the cocky grin assumed by the male of the species when he thinks he has made a conquest. "Clever deduction," he said.

"Debbie?"

Kevin's smirk assumed disgusting proportions. I suppose he thought I was jealous. "Rejected and crushed by my first choice, I am on the rebound." He gave me a look of burning passion, clutched his brow, and staggered. It was a devastating imitation of the performance given by the Drama major who had played Hamlet in our spring production.

"She does look like Ophelia," I said maliciously. "All that droopy hair."

"Meow, meow," said Kevin.

He left and I went back to my potatoes, then stopped peeling because I had more than enough already if he wasn't eating with us. It had happened again—a violent swing back to normalcy after all my uneasy surmises and fears. Or was it possible that Kevin knew he had given himself away and was throwing out a smoke screen? If he was, he was giving a better performance than our Hamlet. Admittedly, that is not saying a great deal.

Bea came bustling in, apologizing for being late to

start dinner. I told her Kevin wouldn't be with us and
told her why. Her first reaction was typical aunt.

"Who is the girl?"

"All I know is her name and what she looks like,
and that she is a sorority sister of Dr. Garst's niece."

"Humph," said Bea.

"You said it," I agreed.

Kevin was upstairs for a long time. He looked very
neat and trim when he popped in to say good night to
Bea. He even smelled of one of those ridiculous men's
colognes that are supposed to perform like the best
aphrodisiacs. Bea admired him and straightened his
collar and tweaked at his sleeve. After he had left, with
a swagger in his walk and a whistle on his lips, Bea and
I decided it was too hot to cook. She made a salad
while I fed the animals. A little thing like temperature
didn't interfere with their appetites. I lined up the
food bowls in a row and stepped back to escape the
rush. The kitten elbowed its way in next to the Irish
setter, and for a few minutes there was no sound
except vulgar gulping. Studying the line of furry
rumps, I was struck with an idea.

"Aren't animals supposed to be sensitive to supernatural presences?"

"So I've heard," said Bea, slicing tomatoes.

"This crowd doesn't seem to have been affected."

"That's true," Bea said thoughtfully. "Mention that
to Roger, Anne. It's definitely an argument against his
ridiculous theory."

I thought it didn't do much for her theory either,
but I didn't say so. Roger certainly would.

A row of buzzers on the wall next to the fireplace
was a survival from the days when every house had a
full staff of servants. None was ever used except the
one that was hooked up to the front door. There was a

doorbell; I just hadn't seen it the day of my arrival, since it was unobtrusively buried in the wood. The sound of the bell was so shrill and penetrating it always made me jump. This time Bea jumped too. It gave me a hint of the strain hidden beneath her appearance of calm.

"That can't be Roger, can it?" I asked. "I got the impression he wasn't coming till later."

"He didn't say."

Neither of us moved until the buzzer sounded again.

"It must be Roger," I said. "Anyone else would give the butler time to get to the door."

It was indeed Roger, looking more rumpled than usual. A smear of blue streaked his cheek, like an unfinished attempt at war paint. He was carrying two enormous suitcases.

"Greetings," he said loudly. "Can you take pity on a poor homeless stray? I painted my bedroom this afternoon and forgot the fumes always make me—"

"Kevin isn't here," I said.

"Oh." Roger looked blank.

"Just as well," I went on. "That's the most unconvincing story I ever heard. And those suitcases—I'll bet you don't even own that many clothes."

"Makes no difference," Roger said. "Kevin isn't the inquisitive type. Most men aren't. They have a trusting faith in—"

"Oh, come on in," I said. "What the hell have you got in those bags?"

"My equipment."

"I suppose you haven't eaten," Bea said.

"How could I cook in a place permeated with paint fumes? I'm glad Kevin isn't here; we can talk freely. Where did he go?"

"He'll probably be late," I said. "He's picked up a new lady."

"Indeed." Roger looked interested. "Don't tell me now, wait till I get this stuff out of sight. You did move out of your room, didn't you, Anne?"

"You aren't going to sleep there!" Bea exclaimed in alarm.

"I don't plan to sleep."

"Roger, you said it was dangerous. Please—"

Roger dropped the suitcases with a crash and put his arm around her. "Honey, it isn't dangerous if you take precautions. I know what I'm doing." He turned to me. "What are you staring at, young woman? Don't you smell the stew burning?"

"We are not having stew. But I can take a hint."

I went to the kitchen and sat down. Time passed. I got out some cold cuts and cheese and arranged them artistically on a plate. Roger had eaten half a ton of lasagna for lunch, but I assumed he would not be content to dine solely on tossed salad.

More time passed before they came, their differences apparently resolved. In other words, Roger had overruled Bea. He was beaming and rubbing his hands together. A qualm of foreboding passed through me. It was a game to him, an intellectual challenge. I sincerely hoped he would feel the same way twelve hours from now.

He was serious enough when we sat down to our food, which we took out to the courtyard. Bea mentioned the animals, and he nodded gravely.

"That may be significant. Traditionally animals are supposed to be aware of psychic entities. I'm not sure how much meaning can be attached to this, however. We ought to run some tests."

"What kind of tests?"

"Oh, we could take them into various rooms and watch their behavior. This thing may have a specific focus, some places being more permeated than others."

"The upstairs hall and Kevin's room have to be one focus," I said. "The animals aren't nervous there. Tabitha slept with me . . . Wait a minute, that was in my former room."

"That doesn't mean anything," Bea said. "Cats sleep around."

Roger was in the act of taking a huge bite of his ham-and-cheese sandwich. He started to laugh. The results were disastrous. The Irish setter leaped to its feet and began licking up scraps.

Catching Bea's eye, Roger got laughter and sandwich under control. "It's going to be a long job civilizing me, my dear," he said. "I spent twenty years being the perfect diplomatic gent. Now I've relapsed. Fair warning."

"If you have finished eating," Bea said gently, "there is something I want you to see."

"I'm finished." Roger tossed the rest of his sandwich to the dog.

Bea led us to the library and indicated the chair by the hearth, where we habitually sat in the evening. "You keep talking about evidence, Roger; I've found something that supports my belief."

"Someone in the house," Roger said.

"Someone still in the house," Bea said. I noticed that, like myself, she had glanced involuntarily over her shoulder. "The spirit of someone who once lived here. I've been trying to find a record of a past tragedy or violent death."

The idea had its fascination. If true, it would reduce the apparition to something understandable in human terms, and bind it within the neat artificial construction of a detective story. I had read my share of horror and ghost stories; some are classics of literature. Cathy and her Heathcliffe wandering the foggy moors, Judge Pyncheon, succumbing to the curse of the house of the Seven Gables, Kipling, Stevenson, de la Mare. . . . Writers had made ghosts almost respectable. I felt I could deal with a disturbed spirit, who only needed a few prayers, or a name cleared, or a buried treasure unearthed, to give up haunting and go where it belonged.

Roger was not immune to the notion either. The gleam in his narrowed eyes betrayed that.

"Find anything?" he asked.

"Not yet. But I found something else." Bea indicated the untidy heap of books on Kevin's side of the table. "Kevin is working along the same lines."

"Come on now," Roger began.

"She's right!" I exclaimed. "I should have noticed it myself." I told them what Kevin had said about the Mandevilles, and his odd comment about "going farther back."

"He has gone farther back," Bea said, with a certain grimness. "Look at these."

The books she indicated were a motley lot: some bound in calf, some tattered pamphlets, some only collections of loose papers stuffed into folders and envelopes.

"Wait, let's not go off half-cocked," Roger said. "The fact that Kevin appears to be interested in the history of the house doesn't prove he is looking for a ghost. Hey—this is interesting."

He had been thumbing through one of the books, a heavy quarto volume. The top was studded with paper clips, which was Kevin's untidy way of indicating pages on which he had found material he wanted to refer back to. Roger opened the book to one of these and read aloud.

"'In 1586 came the last and most dangerous of the plots to assassinate the queen and place her imprisoned rival on the throne of England. Anthony Babington, a young Catholic nobleman, had fallen victim to the fatal charm of Mary; he was prepared to risk all to restore her sacred rights. In July he wrote Mary that six noble gentlemen of the court stood ready to kill the queen whenever the chance arose.'"

"Mary Queen of Scots?" I asked.

"Who else? The queen was Elizabeth the First of England. The plot was discovered, of course. It was the last such plot because Elizabeth was finally annoyed enough to sign Mary's death warrant. She was beheaded. The conspirators died less neatly. One of them was Robert Romer, of Grayhaven Manor."

I knew what he meant by "less neatly." Hanged, drawn, and quartered. They took the victims down before they were dead, drew out their bowels, and cut the body in pieces, to be displayed in public as warnings to other enemies. I wondered if Robert Romer had thought the cause worth dying for, in the final moments.

"If he's the one haunting the house, we're in trouble," I said dismally. "We'll never collect his bones to give them burial in holy ground."

"Let's assume it isn't Robert, then." Roger seemed to have forgotten that he had vigorously denied the existence of a specific ghost. "He was the last of his line. This second marked passage tells how the property of the traitors was handed over to various cronies of Elizabeth's. Grayhaven Manor went to someone named Weekes."

"This must be the same Weekes." Bea looked up from the pamphlet she had been perusing. "Anthony Weekes, antiquarian and scholar, 'much in the Queen's favor for his learning.' The pamphlet was printed privately by his grandson; it describes Anthony's restoration of the house and gardens."

Roger tossed the book onto the table and reached for another. "What a mess. Kevin must be a rotten scholar, he's made no attempt to sort this material. You know what we're going to have to do?"

"Make up a chronological list." I nodded. "A sort of genealogy of the house. Roger, that will take forever, and it may not give us what we want to know. We won't find many dramatic deaths like Robert Romer's."

"We've got nothing else to do until Kevin comes home," Bea said. "This may be our only chance to look through the material without rousing his suspicions."

Roger nodded abstractedly. I could see his mind was on something else. "I've just had a horrible thought," he said.

"What?" Bea and I spoke simultaneously.

"Not that kind of horrible thought. It's just struck me that we're treating Kevin like an enemy. Maybe we're overlooking the obvious. If I talked to him—"

"No," I said. Bea shook her head.

"Why the hell not?" Roger demanded. "We'll feel like damned idiots if it turns out there is a simple explanation for this, and that Kevin knew about it all along."

He looked at Bea. She didn't say anything, she just kept on shaking her head. So I said, "You haven't been living with him, Roger. Oh, hell, I can't give you reasons; I just *know*. It would be fatal to tell Kevin the truth. And if you are wondering whether this could be some kind of elaborate joke on his part, forget it. He's not faking."

"Hm. Anyone capable of such a fancy and unpleasant practical joke would be sick in the head anyway," Roger admitted. "It was an idea, though."

"We're wasting time," Bea said. "I'll get paper and pencils. Anne, divide this material into three parts."

There was very little conversation. They were dead serious, and so was I. And it was good to be working again, even on something as crazy as ghost hunting.

It was ten o'clock before Roger closed his book and glanced at his watch.

"Let's compare notes now. I want to get settled upstairs before Kevin comes home. Tell me when you reach a good stopping place."

I was ready then. Bea asked for five more minutes while she finished a chapter. I expected Roger to act as coordinator. Instead he handed me the notes he and Bea had taken.

"You're the trained researcher. See if you can make anything coherent out of this while I rustle up something to drink."

I was surprised to see how much information we had put together. There was little duplication, since we had used different sources. After a time I glanced up to find Bea and Roger looking at me expectantly, and felt the self-consciousness that always attacks me when I have to give a paper or a lecture.

I cleared my throat. "What we've got here is a rough outline of the main events in the history of the house from about 1485 to the present. Architectural additions, remodeling, changes of ownership, plus a few facts about some of the owners, such as Robert Romer, who were involved in well-known historical events. I don't see any diaries or other family papers here, except for that book on the Mandevilles, which Kevin said was not informative."

Bea had dealt with this later material. She nodded agreement. "The author was concerned with proving how noble and dedicated his ancestors were. They died quietly in their beds after exemplary lives, or perished gloriously in battle for England and the king. One or two accidents are mentioned, but no details are given. Is the house really that old, Anne? My material only went back to 1700."

"I divided it chronologically," I explained. "Roger got the earliest part. His notes start with 1485. Does that date have any significance historically, Roger?"

"What do they teach you kids nowadays? Bosworth Field, Richard III killed in battle, crown in the thornbush, end of the Wars of the Roses, beginning of the Tudor dynasty—"

"Oh, right."

"The house is older than that," Roger said. "It was probably a fortified manor, complete with moat and drawbridge. They needed their defenses in those days, there was a dynastic upheaval every few years, with battles and sieges and bloody fighting. People changed their coats so often they wore them out. The family that owned the house at that time was named Lovell; they may have been related to the Lord Lovell who was a supporter of Richard III. Our Lovell, George, fought at Bosworth on Richard's side. He was killed, 'fighting with valor worthy of a better cause,' according to the victors. The manor and lands were given to one John Romer, who happened to be on the winning side."

"And that's where the Romers come in," I said.

"They held the manor for less than a hundred years. When Robert lost his life, not to mention his entrails and other vital organs, the Weekeses took over. They lasted till 1708, when the house was bought by the Leventhorpes. Next came the Mandevilles, then Rudolf, then Kevin's parents. Quite a few changes of possession."

"No more than one would expect," Roger said, "considering the age of the place and the vicissitudes of life. Nor is the survival of the house unique. There are hundreds of stately homes in England—"

"Surely not this old," Bea said, with something of the same defensive pride Kevin had displayed when he spoke of the house.

"Not all of them, of course. But quite a number date back four or five hundred years."

"And in that length of time every old house must have had its share of violent deaths," Bea insisted. "We've already found several. Robert Romer, the Lovell who was killed at Bosworth, the two Mandeville sons in World War I—"

"Admitting that your naive idea is correct, you're on the wrong track," Roger said. "We're looking for a woman."

"You say the house is older than 1485," I said. "How much older?"

Roger looked at me keenly. "You've got something in mind. Don't be coy."

"I'm not. I just this minute remembered. That picture in Kevin's room. The costume is medieval, but the style—"

"That's right," Bea exclaimed eagerly. "It is a woman's portrait. A woman with long fair hair—"

"But it's the wrong period," I said stubbornly.

Roger banged his fist on the table. "What are you talking about? Have you been holding out on me?"

"I don't think it has any relevance. It's the wrong—"

"Period. I know," Roger said resignedly. "I won't ask what you mean by that ambiguous evaluation; I'll look at it myself. Let's put this stuff back the way we found it. I'll take charge of the notes."

When we had restored the books to their original state of disorder, we locked up. Bea scribbled a note for Kevin explaining that Roger was spending the night. Then we went upstairs, trailed by two of the cats and one of the dogs. Belle stayed in the library waiting up for Kevin. She was courteous to all of us, but she really preferred him.

We went first to Kevin's room to show Roger the portrait. After studying it, he shook his head.

"What a daub. I see what you meant about the wrong period, Anne. The costume is medieval, but the style is Late Victorian or Edwardian."

"The costume is wrong," Bea added. "It's a mixture of styles that would never have been worn at the same era—an early-fourteenth-century kirtle and mantle and a Mary Queen of Scots cap, which is inappropriate with her long, unbound hair."

"I didn't know you were an expert on the history of costume," I said admiringly.

"One of my hobbies. The painting may not be very good, but it is of a young woman with long fair hair."

"Bah," said Roger. "Nobody with the slightest rudiments of good taste could admire this catastrophe, much less develop an adolescent romantic crush on it."

"But he moved it," I said. "He brought it in here.

When I arrived it was hanging someplace else, in one of the other bedrooms."

Roger turned away with a shrug. "I fail to see any connection. Where is that kid anyway? Time he was home."

"He may not be back for hours if Debbie comes through as expected," I said. "You're going to have a long boring wait, Roger. Where are you planning to hide?"

"In the same alcove you used. Much more convenient now that the statue is out of the way. It's a neat setup, with the plants as camouflage. Come and see."

Gadgets and machines are our modern religious symbols. Watching something click or tick or turn gives us the same sense of security a medieval peasant felt when he touched a reliquary—a hope that the incoherence of the universe is thereby regulated. I could not help being impressed by Roger's gadgets, which included every tool I had ever seen and a good many I had not seen. His camera was an expensive Japanese model, small in size but absolutely exuding efficiency.

"Infrared film," Roger explained proudly. "It takes a frame every second, automatically. This—" indicating a square black box bristling with knobs and antennas—"measures and records changes in temperature. I'll have to wait till Kevin goes to bed before I set it up; he might notice it. Same with the black thread, which attaches to these cameras. The suction cups enable them to be clamped to the walls."

"So you think your psychic force is solid enough to move a thread," Bea said scornfully.

"We have not eliminated the possibility of human trickery," Roger said. "Wait—" for Bea's lip had curled in protest—"I'm not saying I think Kevin is guilty. But a scientist can't operate on feelings. If anything palpable touches the thread, it will be photographed. If it doesn't trip the thread, I'll catch it with my other camera. There are more sophisticated instruments available, but I don't own them and I didn't have time to borrow them. We can make a start with these."

"What shall we do?" I asked. Bea remained silent, her lower lip protruding mutinously.

Roger looked surprised. "You go to bed, of course. Nothing is going to happen. I don't intend to attack the thing, just take its picture."

I scooped up Tabitha, who had already taken a couple of swipes at Roger's dangling thread, and Bea and I went to our rooms. I got into bed with Tabitha and Agatha. I did not expect I would be able to sleep, but I couldn't decide whether I hoped something would happen—or that it wouldn't.

I had left my door open. The late-night silence was so profound that I heard Kevin when he came home—first the distant rattle of chains and bolts as he locked up, then the creak of one particular stair. After that, silence descended again. I glanced at the clock on my bedside table. It was one A.M. Roger was probably tiptoeing around stringing his threads and putting his cameras in place.

One forty A.M. The murderer was the innocent-looking young girl. Hercule Poirot arrived just in time to keep her from killing again. . . . My chin banged into my chest. Blearily I glanced at the clock. Two ten. I dropped the book onto Tabitha, who moaned but did not move, and let my eyes close.

I was walking along a road—a yellow brick road.

The forms that lined it on either side were not cute little Munchkins, they were human-sized people—or perhaps their statues. The figures were rigid and motionless, frozen in position. I knew some of them. Bea and Roger, Kevin . . . An old, old woman dressed in rusty black, her face a mass of wrinkles. A man in top hat and white tie, a heavy gold watch-chain stretched across his potbelly. I started to move faster. More women, wearing old-fashioned clothes, gowns with bustles and full skirts. A child with wide blue eyes that never blinked—a china-doll child in pantalets, holding a hoop. A tall young man in a gaudy uniform, gilt epaulets, scarlet tunic, a sword at his side. I was running, faster than the fastest Olympic racer, and a voice somewhere was chanting, "Back, farther back, farther . . ." The figures flashed by. I caught glimpses of white faces, rigid as marble, and clothes that belonged in museums or portrait galleries—a gown of forest-green velvet, twenty yards in the skirt; pleated ruffs, wide sleeves bordered with fur, a herald's tabard stiff with gold embroidered figures. "Back, farther back . . ." Togas and tunics and homespun cloaks fastened with enameled brooches; figures shrinking in size, darker and bowed. At dizzying speed I skimmed the surface, and the shapes were no longer human. They had dropped down onto four feet, or hooves, or pads. I was moving so fast they seemed to move too, backward; crawling and slithering and swimming, shrinking still, while the voice continued to intone its litany: "Farther, farther back . . ." Back to the very beginning, to the shapeless blobs of matter from which we came, back to the primeval ooze and the organic chemicals. I could no longer bear to look at the shapes that squirmed and pulsed along the road. I was moving too fast. When I reached the end I must crash or fall; I could not stop. . . .

The crash jarred every muscle in my body. I lay shaking for a minute before I realized that there was light—the light of my bedside lamp, which I had not turned off—and that the only squirming, pulsing object visible was Tabitha, sprawled across my legs. She suddenly sat up, her head cocked. So the sounds that echoed in my ears were not the remnants of my nightmare. The cat had heard them too.

I got out of bed. Bea's door opened as I ran into the hall.

"What on earth—" she began.

"Roger must have attacked the ghost," I said.

When I turned into the corridor that served the west wing, it seemed unusually dark. The light nearest Kevin's door had gone out, leaving a long stretch of shadow. That was where the disturbance was taking place. At first I saw only a shapeless mass, squirming and twitching like the things in my dream, but considerably larger. I came to an abrupt halt, enabling Bea to catch up with me. She had had enough presence of mind to bring a flashlight. Its beam framed the tableau on the floor: Kevin, kneeling, his hands wrapped around the throat of Roger O'Neill, who lay supine, with Kevin's full weight on his chest. Roger's face was turning blue.

Bea let out a shriek. "Kevin! Stop it at once!"

Kevin reacted instantly. I suppose he had heard that tone, if not those very words, several thousand times in his youth. He let go of Roger and climbed off him. Roger took in air in a long, rasping gasp. Shoving her nephew out of the way, Bea fell on her knees beside Roger.

"Darling, are you hurt?"

"I may never speak again," Roger croaked. His hand went to his throat. "That was a very stupid question, sweetheart."

Kevin invoked a list of sacred names in tones Father Stephen would not have approved. "God Almighty," he finished. "I'm sorry, I didn't know—hey, Roger—"

A carved wooden chest, black with age, stood near me. I dropped down onto it.

"I was going to the bathroom," Kevin explained. "I saw somebody duck out of sight, as if he were hiding; naturally I thought—Roger, are you okay? Let me help you up."

Roger slapped his hand away. He seemed more insulted by Kevin's sympathy than by his attempt to strangle him. "I'm not helpless yet, boy. You caught me unawares, or . . . All right, Bea, cut it out. I am capable of standing by myself."

He proceeded to do so. Her arm around him protectively, Bea turned a furious gaze on Kevin, who was still squatting on the floor. He looked rather pathetic.

"Kevin, you idiot, didn't you read my note? I told you Roger was spending the night."

"I came straight upstairs," Kevin said plaintively. "I was bushed. Hell's bells, Aunt Bea, I said I was sorry."

"It's okay." Roger straightened up. "An understandable confusion. No harm done."

"I'm really sorry," Kevin repeated.

Bea turned her back on him. "Come with me, Roger, and let me put something on those bruises."

She led him away. I stood up. "Night, Kevin. Sleep tight."

It was a good time to leave. Kevin was beginning to lose his temper at seeing his abject apologies rejected, and in another minute he would have taken it out on me. As I retreated I heard his door slam.

Roger was sitting on the bed in Bea's room, his head tipped back, while Bea examined his throat. "Look at those bruises," she exclaimed angrily. "How could he do such a thing?"

"I don't blame him," Roger answered. "I did what he said—tried to hide. It was a stupid move, but he caught me by surprise and I didn't stop to think."

I sat down beside Roger. In addition to the darkening marks on his throat he sported a lump on the jaw and some miscellaneous scrapes across cheeks and chin. He looked terrible.

"Should we go and minister unto Kevin also?" I inquired.

Roger rolled his eyes in my direction. There was an appreciative gleam in the eye nearest me.

"Thanks," he said dryly. "I landed a couple, I think. But he's a lot younger and tougher than I am; he'll survive. Now, Bea, you've enjoyed yourself long enough. That will do."

"I agree," I said. "Let him talk, Bea. I want to hear what happened before the fight. Did you have any luck, Roger?"

"That depends on what you mean by luck," Roger said maddeningly.

"I may strangle you myself if you don't get to it," I threatened.

"I'll make tea," Bea said.

Roger caught her by the sleeve as she turned away. "No. From now on you are not to wander around this house at night."

"I have a hot plate and kettle in my sitting room," Bea said.

"So something did happen," I said.

"Some thing," Roger said, deliberately separating the words. "I'll give it to you from the beginning."

I didn't want a slow, measured narrative. I wanted to know whether he had seen my melting, slimy-faced apparition, and I suspected it was not so much his logical mind as his love of drama that made him select this method. But there was no use arguing with him, so I nodded and settled myself cross-legged on the bed.

"Kevin came home at twelve fifty-three," Roger began. "I gave him ten minutes to settle down, then went out to arrange my equipment. I then returned to my room and took up a position on the balcony, midway between his room and mine. At precisely one forty-seven I heard a soft creaking that might have been the springs of Kevin's bed. Up till then he hadn't made a sound. He must be a quiet sleeper."

He stopped to accept the cup of tea Bea handed him. I could have kicked him.

"I am able to be precise about the times because my watch has a luminous dial," Roger said pedantically.

"I could have figured that out," I told him.

"It is necessary to be precise. After approximately a minute and a half I began to hear murmurs. That continued for—oh, about ten minutes." His voice cracked and he put his hand to his throat. "Oh, hell," he said. "I'll have to cut it short. My pharynx is beginning to swell up. I didn't hear what you two heard. I could not swear there were two different voices. Nor did I see your apparition, Anne. In my opinion you were imagining that. There is no ghost."

Chapter Seven

I SHOULD HAVE been relieved. Instead I knew how Noah must have felt when his neighbors chuckled and told him to stop worrying—it couldn't go on raining for forty days and forty nights. He knew it could, and would. The denials didn't comfort him, they simply added frustration to his sense of doom.

Bea pulled up a chair and sat down by the bed. Quietly she said, "You can't dismiss it as Anne's imagination, Roger. I didn't see anything, but the voices were . . . I don't think I have been able to express to you how much they disturbed me."

"Hey, now, I'm not dismissing anything. I am simply trying to explain that manifestations of this sort may vary according to the personalities and predilections of the beholders. That's true of even so-called normal occurrences. Witnesses of a crime or an accident seldom agree as to the details; you get the most incredible variants, even from honest and sensible people. In a case like this, the phenomenon itself is paranormal, outside the range of ordinary experience. Naturally witnesses interpret it differently."

"Thank you, Sigmund Freud," I said.

"Jung would be more like it," Roger replied. "I didn't see your apparition or hear your lady vampire, but I saw enough to convince me that there is a psychic force operating in this house, at or through Kevin. Now do you feel better?"

I considered the question. "I don't know," I said.

"There was something abnormal about the acoustical conditions in Kevin's room," Roger went on. "I had the feeling that something was muffling the sounds, as if a heavy curtain had been drawn across the windows. It hadn't; his windows were wide open and I could see his curtains moving in the breeze.

"At five minutes after two I left the balcony and hid in the alcove. Fifteen minutes later Kevin opened his door. I was struck by the openness of his movements; he wasn't making any attempt to be secretive. I saw no one but Kevin. However—here I do agree with you, Anne—I am one hundred percent convinced that Kevin saw something. His expression, the way his eyes moved. . . . The light bulb in the fixture near his room was pretty dim; as you may have noticed, it gave up the ghost (excuse me) not long afterward. Nothing strange about that; light bulbs do burn out. But it made it hard for me to see. Increasingly I had an impression of something there; it grew stronger as the seconds passed. I need not tell you that I was snapping pictures as fast as I could. I had an excellent view, straight down the hall. Just before Kevin went back into his room and closed the door, I caught a glimpse of something. The best way I can describe it is as a column of dim light, about four feet high. It was faintly luminous, and it was moving. It passed around the turn in the corridor and disappeared. There was a faint, very brief afterglow.

"I could hear my heart pounding and I knew my pulse was faster than usual, but I had no sense of horror or fear. I took my last couple of shots and waited for a full quarter of an hour before I collected my gear. I didn't stop to examine any of it, just shoved it into the bag. I got back to my room without any trouble and stowed the bag away; then I went to the bathroom. I was on my way back when Kevin came out. Having concluded that he had long since dropped into a deep sleep, I was so startled that I acted without thinking—and he jumped me. The kid has reflexes like a cat's. There's nothing wrong with him physically."

None of us spoke for a few moments, as we pondered the implications of this remarkable story. Roger kept massaging his throat. Finally I said, "You think something is wrong with Kevin mentally?"

"Something is wrong, but it isn't mental in the sense you mean," Roger said hoarsely. "Now I understand why you two were so opposed to discussing this with him. He's probably incapable of discussing it or even admitting it. Do you know the real definition of the word 'glamour'—not the corruption Hollywood has foisted on us?"

I murmured,

"'Oh, what can ail thee, knight at arms,
Alone and palely loitering. . . .'"

Bea nodded. "La Belle Dame sans Merci," she said. "The theme is an old one—the human, male or female, who falls under the spell of a supernatural lover. Gods and goddesses, mermen, succubi . . ."

"Mind you," Roger said, "I'm not saying that Kevin is bewitched by some soulless immortal creature. The thing that is operating here takes that form for him.

Why it has picked on him and what it wants I can't even begin to imagine at this stage. But he needs help; he can't help us. And I am of the opinion that it would be worse than useless, perhaps even dangerous, to tell him what is happening."

"I agree with that, if not with your main premise," Bea said. She was sitting primly upright, her back straight, her hands folded in her lap. The sash of her robe, a soft, flowing garment printed with lilacs and sprays of ivy, was tied in a neat bow.

"You're still hooked on a beautiful fair-haired ghost?" Roger demanded. "Her lover was killed in the Crusades, so she pined away. . . . Or she was ravished by a wicked lord of the manor and threw herself off the battlements. . . . Or her cruel father starved her to death because she wouldn't marry the man he selected for her. . . ."

"I don't intend to discuss the subject any further," Bea said. "You pursue your theory; I'll pursue mine."

Her nose was lifted as if she smelled something nasty. Roger let out a shout of laughter, then clutched his throat. "You're adorable," he croaked.

"Hmph," said Bea. "I'm going to get some ice for your throat."

"No, don't bother. I've got to go. I want to get to work on that film. I'll bring the prints over tomorrow."

"You're going home now?" I asked.

"Why not? I can't wait to see what I got on film."

"No reason, except that Kevin may get suspicious of your sudden retreat."

"Kevin wouldn't notice a bishop in full regalia conducting an exorcism," Roger said. "However, you may have a point. I'll stay."

"You can't go back to that room," Bea said.

"Is that a proposition?"

"Certainly not! I just don't think it's safe—"

"I agree." Roger took her hand. "I'm scared to go back there. I need somebody to stay with me and hold my hand. A nice, warm friendly person."

They didn't notice when I left. I don't know where Roger slept that night, but I hoped for the best. Bea's protests had lacked sincerity.

II

As I drifted off to sleep I thought that if Kevin came bursting in next morning and woke me, wanting to play tennis, I would break the racket over his head. He didn't come, and neither did anyone else. I snored until the sun crept across the room and shone in my eyes.

As usual, morning brought reassurance and the familiar sense of comfort, dulling the alarms of the night. Yet I was conscious of a morbid curiosity, which was to stay with me for some time—a need to know where Kevin was and what he was doing. After I finished breakfast I went looking for him.

Following a not-too-subtle hunch I went first to the tennis court. Sure enough, he was there, and I saw why he had not bothered to wake me up. Debbie was as cute as a button in one of those adorable little tennis dresses dripping with eyelet and short enough to show darling little ruffled panties underneath. Her hair was tied back in a ponytail that kept swinging from side to side in an inconvenient manner. It didn't signify; she had no intention of winning that match anyway. Once or twice she forgot herself and returned a shot with an effortless skill that showed how good a player she really was, but for the most part she managed to play badly enough to accomplish her end. When the victory was official, Kevin bounded over the net— Mercury in white shorts and alligator T-shirt—and threw his arm around her, laughing. She cuddled into his embrace, but when his hand cupped her breast she giggled and pushed it away. This confirmed what I had suspected. She wasn't one of the kind that "does it on a first date." No wonder poor old Kevin had been tired when he came home last night. He was due for some more heartache and hard breathing now, if I was any judge; the two of them wandered off toward the garden, entwined like Laocoön and the snakes. I went back to the house.

Bea had sent the cleaning team to the library; the mahogany surfaces shone, and the traces of our informal meeting the night before had been swept away. I inspected my desk. There wasn't a speck of dust to be seen, but the books had an abandoned look, like babies left on the doorstep of an orphanage. My notes looked yellow around the edges. Pure imagination, of course. They weren't more than eight months old, and paper doesn't turn color that soon.

I started looking through those antique notes. Some of our ideas had been good ones. It would have been a first-rate book. The poetry section, for instance. I sat down at the desk and reached for a pen.

I had been working for about an hour when Kevin appeared. I was about to ask him where Debbie was when I realized, in the nick of time, that I wasn't supposed to know she had been here. So I just said, "Hi," and Kevin sat down beside the desk.

"Working?"

"Trying to."

Kevin slid down onto his spine and stuck his legs out. Moodily he contemplated his knees.

"I've been a lazy rat, haven't I?"

"I haven't been exactly energetic myself."

"No, but you'd have put in some work if I hadn't dragged my feet. It's your own fault, Anne, you're too damned polite. Why didn't you tell me off?"

This was the old Kevin—charming, apologetic, considerate. "Oh, well," I said deprecatingly.

"I'll do better from now on," Kevin said.

"Why should you? One of the things we had in mind when we began was making a few bucks. You don't have to worry about that now."

"Yeah, well, I suppose that's one of the reasons why I haven't felt any sense of urgency; but it's no excuse. Money was only one of our motives. It could be a good book. Besides . . ."

"You don't owe me anything," I said, anticipating him. "Except honesty. If you want out, just let me know. I can get another collaborator, or do it myself."

"That's damned nice of you." Kevin gave me one of his sweetest, most disarming smiles. "Let's see what we can accomplish this summer, okay? If I cop out it's all yours, including what we've done jointly."

He held out his hand.

What could I say? It sounded fair enough. Only . . . three months of intensive work would have given us a book, or most of one. I didn't have a prayer of finishing it now. Yet to reject Kevin's offer would have been ungracious. So I gave him my hand and we shook.

He then proceeded to make me feel even more of a

jerk by putting in two solid hours of productive activity. We had just about finished a rough outline of the first section when Bea came looking for us to tell us lunch was ready.

Fortunately for my conscience, which is all too prone to indulge in masochistic self-recrimination, Kevin went up to his room after lunch instead of returning to work. So I felt free to resent him all over again.

I started helping Bea clear away the dishes.

"Don't bother," she said. "The cleaning team hasn't tackled the kitchen yet. They can deal with this."

"I sort of expected Roger to show up by now," I said.

"I haven't heard from him," she said shortly.

So I went back to the library.

I worked for a couple of hours, stoically ignoring the soft breeze that wafted in from the garden, and the cute gambols of Pettibone, who wanted me to play with her. Kevin never came back. At three o'clock I decided he must have gone for a swim. I could have used one myself. It was another hot day. But I figured Debbie might be there, so I made a martyr of myself, working doggedly on and dripping perspiration onto my papers.

Shortly before four o'clock the doorbell rang. I pried myself off my chair and went to answer it. I hoped it was Roger. For even though I had been genuinely absorbed in my work, part of my mind had been speculating about what he had found on his photographs.

It wasn't Roger. It was Father Stephen.

Bea reached the door before I did. From the draw-

ing room, unseen by either, I saw her greet him and
lead him upstairs.

So Bea had taken the bit in her teeth and proceeded
with her own plan, despite Roger's objections. She
hadn't actually broken her promise; she had waited to
consult the pastor until Roger had had a chance to do
his own thing. I doubted that Roger would look at it
that way, however.

I showered and changed, and then I knocked on the
door of Bea's sitting room. Father Stephen rose when I
came in. One look at his beaming face told me that
Bea had not yet confided in him. No doubt she
planned to stuff him full of cakes (freshly baked) and
tea (China) before she hit him with her news.

"Oh, Anne, I was just about to ask you to join us,"
she said coolly.

"And where is Kevin?" Father Stephen asked. "Still
at work? Such dedication."

"He's probably at the pool," I said. "He spends
every afternoon there and every morning on the
tennis court."

Father Stephen's eyebrows rose a fraction. I had
intended my comment to be one of humorous tolerance, but it had come out sounding bitchy.

"What's wrong, Anne?" Bea asked.

"Sorry, I'm just not in the mood for polite chitchat.
Go ahead and tell him. That's what you intended to
do, wasn't it?"

Bea had every right to resent my manner and my
grouchy voice. Instead she gave me a sympathetic
look. "Is Debbie still here?"

"I didn't know she had arrived," I said mendaciously.

"She came to the kitchen door awhile ago. Kevin

was still in his room. She introduced herself very prettily and said he had asked her over to swim."

"I don't know why you brought her up," I said.

Father Stephen had followed this exchange with a faint smile and a furrowed brow. Another sort of man might have attempted to cast oil upon the troubled waters. He went right to the point.

"Tell me what?"

Bea's eyes shifted. She nibbled on her lower lip; and after a moment Father Stephen glanced at me. "Perhaps . . ."

"No, that's all right," Bea said. "Anne is very much involved; her presence isn't what is inhibiting me. I can't think how to tell you without your suspecting my sanity."

"I can't imagine that I would ever do that," Father Stephen said, smiling.

"Start at the beginning," was my brilliant suggestion.

Bea took a deep breath.

Before she could utter the first word, there was a thud of rapidly approaching footsteps and the door burst open. Roger stood on the threshold. He surveyed the three of us—Father Stephen with a smile of welcome curving his lips, Bea with her mouth open, ready to speak, me—I don't know why I should have felt guilty, but I realized I was trying to squeeze myself into a smaller space. Never have I seen such a malignant look on a man's face.

"Frailty, thy name is woman," he said, glowering at Bea.

"That," I said, recovering myself, "is a misquotation if I ever heard one. She didn't promise—"

"She did too."

Bea started to speak. I think she was about to say, "I did not"; but, realizing where this would lead, she changed her mind.

"Sit down, Roger."

"You promised—"

"That is irrelevant."

Roger threw himself into a chair with such force that the springs wheezed protestingly. "Have you told him?"

"Not yet."

"But you intend to. I can't talk you out of it?"

"I certainly hope not," said Father Stephen. "Between the three of you you have now worked me up to a pitch of unbearable apprehension. Is this to be a confession, or an accusation, or what? For heaven's sake enlighten me before I burst with curiosity and alarm."

"Certainly," said Bea. She faced him squarely, turning her back on Roger. "It began a few days ago, when . . ."

I don't know what Father Stephen expected, but I can assert with some confidence that he had never in his wildest dreams anticipated a story like the one Bea told. Years of experience had taught him to control his countenance, but the look of amiable, imperturbable calm with which he began soon changed to frowning consternation.

As for me, I felt an illogical relief, as well as a childish hope that here, at last, we would find help. This was Father Stephen's specialty. It was rather like telling God. Moreover, at one point in my own narrative I saw the most extraordinary expression pass over his face, a look of reminiscence, as if he were not hearing the story for the first time. But I was doomed to disappointment. His first comment when the story had been told, was one of horror.

"How ghastly!"

There was a pause. I waited for a further comment, but he just sat there, shaking his head dumbly. Roger, who had been consuming tea cakes with absent-minded greed, gave a nasty chuckle.

"Want to hear my chapter before you commit yourself, Steve? I warn you, it will knock all your theories into a cocked hat."

The challenge restored the pastor's powers of speech, if not his composure. "Roger, that cynical manner of yours is an unmitigated pain in the neck. How do you know what theory I may have formulated?"

"You have no choice," Roger said. "You're condemned by your profession to spend your life trying to come to terms with the contradiction between your benevolent God and a vicious universe. I'm going to spare you the humiliation of being proved wrong in this case. I'll tell you what I discovered last night."

Father Stephen listened with wary suspicion as Roger went on with his narrative. Skilled rhetorician that he was, Roger saved the best for last. "I developed the film this afternoon," he said. "Here it is."

From his jacket pocket he withdrew a fat sheaf of prints. Bea held out an eager hand, but Roger shook his head, a maddening smile on his face.

"One at a time, in order, and with commentary," he said.

Pushing teacups out of the way, he cleared a space on the table. We crowded around, Father Stephen as openly curious as Bea and I.

"First," said Roger, "the two cameras I had

mounted on the wall, with threads attached to trip the switches."

His voice had a peculiar note that made me look at him suspiciously. He dealt the picture down onto the table.

It was an excellent snapshot of Annabelle proceeding along the hall. Her tail was lifted and her face had a look of profound contemplation.

Before anyone could comment, Roger added a second photograph to the first. This time Annabelle had apparently heard the click of the shutter or seen the faint red glow of the flash. Her head was turned toward the camera. She appeared to be mildly curious, but not put out.

Nobody but me seemed to think this was funny. I stopped laughing after a minute and Roger said, "I should have anticipated something of the sort. Those damned animals are all over the house. Next time I'll raise the threads a few feet."

"All right, Roger, you've had your fun," Bea said coldly. "You wouldn't have shown us these if you had not caught something important with the other camera. Stop playing games."

Roger looked sheepish. Again I sensed that this was primarily an exciting game to him. Even the bruises on his throat, now concealed by a scarf, had not convinced him that the problem was not academic.

"Okay," he said. "Here we go."

He dealt the pictures out like cards, talking as he did so. "The first three show the hall before Kevin opened his door. Nothing unusual there. Now, here's Kevin. And here, and here . . ."

Father Stephen's breath caught sharply. Neither my description, nor Roger's, had conveyed the appalling significance of Kevin's actions. His movements and his expressions, caught in shots only seconds apart, were as graphic as a motion picture. They left no doubt of what he thought he was doing.

"No sign of any other—uh—object, you see," Roger said, continuing to deal out prints. "Now Kevin's arms fall to his sides. He turns. And now, in this—"

The photo he indicated showed Kevin fully turned, his back to the camera. Beyond him, between a small Chippendale table and a mirror, was the faintest streak of light.

"It could be a flaw in the film," I said.

"Look at these," Roger replied.

There were twenty-four more photographs. The last two showed an empty hall and a closed door to Kevin's room. But the three before these . . .

I grabbed one. Father Stephen and Bea did the same. They were almost identical.

The thing that had begun as a dim streak of light was a luminous column in the last three prints. There was some resemblance to the object I had seen on the first night of my vigil, before the apparition began to shape itself. A narrowing at the "waist" and a blob above the wider shoulder portion that might have been a head were suggestive of a human form, but no details were visible.

"I blew the last one up," Roger said, producing an eight-by-ten glossy. "Unfortunately, enlargement only blurs it."

We passed this print around. The figure was even less distinct, but there were a couple of interesting aspects now to be observed. In the center of the figure was a core of virtually opaque material; one could not see objects through it, as one could through the edges. Also, there was something about the lower part of the form . . .

"Folds." Roger pointed. "See them? Like a long skirt, or robe—or toga."

III

"Toga?" Father Stephen's voice had lost its mellow smoothness. "Roger, there are times when you try my temper. What madness are you hinting at? Roman ghosts that 'shriek and squeal about the streets'? You must be out of your mind to approach this subject so frivolously."

"Who says I'm frivolous?" Roger exclaimed indignantly. "I'm approaching it as I would any other problem, rationally, logically—"

"The problem of good and evil is not susceptible to logic."

"Ha! There you go; I knew you would. Next you'll start mumbling about the devil and evil spirits and the souls of the damned—"

"Roger, you are incredibly rude," Bea cried. "What else can it be but—"

"That's all right, Bea; Roger and I are used to one another." Father Stephen recovered himself. He smiled faintly. "Actually, there are a number of things 'it' could be."

"Including hallucination?" I suggested hopefully.

"There speaks modern, skeptical youth," said Father Stephen. "No, Anne, forget that. It seems to me quite impossible that three sensible adults could suffer from the same delusion."

"Four," I said.

Father Stephen's smile vanished. "Four, yes. That unfortunate young man . . . Something must be done. He is in grave danger."

I said in a rush, "I'm so grateful, so surprised and glad—you believe us, don't you?"

"Roger would say that I am credulous by nature and by training. Certainly I find it harder to believe in the superstitions of modern psychiatry than in—well, even in Roger's theory of an unknown psychic energy field."

"Humph," said Roger. "All the same, Steve, that's what we have. The thing takes different forms to different people. It must; it has no physical shape of its own. It is an impersonal, psychic phenomenon, seemingly unnatural only because science has not yet—"

"Nonsense," Bea said crisply.

The pastor glanced at her. "Quite right," he said, and raised a warning hand as Roger started to protest. "Wait a minute, Roger. You have each told me one chapter of a most interesting story. Now it's my turn. Bea, would you mind terribly if I smoked? It's a filthy habit, but I need something to help me compose my thoughts."

Bea brought him an ashtray while he filled his pipe with the loving, tedious slowness pipe smokers seem to consider ritually important. When the pipe was going, he sat back in his chair, his eyes fixed on the ceiling, and began.

"A few days ago we spoke of Miss Marion Karnovsky, the former owner of this house. My manner must have struck you as somewhat strange— no, Bea, don't be polite, I know I was abrupt and ill at ease. Ordinarily I wouldn't dream of discussing the private affairs of a former friend and parishioner. However, your situation is extraordinary, and what I am about to tell you may shed some light on the case. Besides, in a sense the story is already a matter of public record.

"When I came here, twenty years ago, Miss Marion was already elderly. She was punctilious about her religious obligations, never missing a service, and she treated me with a respect and regard that was, I'm sure, due to my office rather than my personal gifts. I was a rather callow, pompous young man, as I recall.

"At any rate, the years passed, and Miss Marion stopped coming to church. I didn't think too much of it; I assumed her infirmities prevented her from going out. Her elderly chauffeur had died, and she had few friends in the neighborhood—by her own choice, I might add. I was the only person she saw regularly, and when she no longer attended services, I tried to increase the frequency of my visits. But I didn't go as often as I should have done. I usually telephoned before I called on her. That was a mistake, too, though I didn't realize it; it gave her time to prepare a gracious welcome, tea ready in the drawing room, the silver polished till it shone. Oh, she did her best to keep me in ignorance, but I ought to have been more observant. A woman would have noticed that her clothing was shabby and out of fashion; a psychiatrist might have seen other signs. I did remonstrate with her, after the last of her servants left, about the inadvisability of living alone in such a big, empty house. She replied, with a toss of her head—she must have been a handsome girl, high-spirited, as they used to say—that she was quite capable of managing, and that the kindest thing anyone could do for her was to allow her to die as she had lived, in her own home. When she spoke of the ignominy of nursing homes and hospitals, her face showed the first sign of distress I had ever seen her display."

Father Stephen's pipe had gone out. He sat cradling it in his hands, his face drawn.

"I have never ceased to blame myself," he said quietly. "If I had acted sooner, I might have been able to forestall what happened. But"—he gestured with his pipe—"I'm not going to wallow in self-contempt. Believe me, I've done enough of that already.

"I will never forget the day I learned the truth. It was a bleak winter afternoon; the temperature had been below freezing for weeks, and the snow lay icy on the ground. I had an errand in this neighborhood and decided I would stop and call on Miss Marion. I had not seen her for some time.

"When she opened the door she had a shawl wrapped around her shoulders—a gray wool shawl. I can still see it, with its carefully mended rents and tears. She didn't appear pleased to see me, but she led me into the small parlor downstairs—the one that, I believe, Mr. and Mrs. Blacklock have converted into a breakfast room. By comparison to the bleak chill of the rest of the house, it was warm; in fact, the air was unbearably close. The cracks in the windows had been stuffed with rags. Blankets, piled neatly on a sofa, told me where Miss Marion had been sleeping. She was living in this room to conserve heat. A fire smoldered on the hearth. Beside it was a basketful of twigs and small branches—the gleanings of the woods. I had a vision of her hobbling along, stooping painfully to pick up fallen branches. I was sick at heart when I took the chair she offered me.

"But the worst was yet to come. She was troubled. She talked at random for a time, in a hurried and incoherent manner. My own distress was so great I hardly noticed hers. It was as if scales had fallen from my eyes; every object I saw in that room, including its mistress, was further evidence of poverty and discomfort.

"Finally she said suddenly, 'There is something on my conscience, Father. I am trying to gain courage enough to tell you about it.' I asked her if she wished to make a confession, but she shook her head vigorously. 'I don't want absolution, Father. In order to gain that, I would have to promise to refrain from sinning again, wouldn't I? Well, I don't intend to refrain.'

"Paradoxical as it may sound, this speech heartened me. Physically she was in remarkable condition for her age; and the grim humor that twisted her mouth when she spoke reassured me as to her mental state.

"How wrong I was! I did not know how wrong till she began her story. You can imagine my consternation when, in the coolest manner imaginable, she informed me that for ten years she had been sharing the house with a . . . she called it 'my spirit friend.' This companion was the consolation of her old age, affectionate, amusing, helpful. My blood ran cold as she described how they made music together, played card games, talked, told stories. The culmination came when she told me of the source of her guilt. In her need, was she keeping her companion from the heavenly bliss it surely deserved? Or might she consider it a guardian angel taken visible form, a kindness of God?

"I have not the faintest recollection of how I got out of the house. I came to my senses when I got into the car, and I sat there for a long time, unaware of the freezing cold, while I wrestled with my duty. Suffice it to say that the necessary arrangements took far too long. She was the last of her family; it was necessary to go through painful and prolonged legal struggles before I could be appointed guardian. The most terrible memories of my life are the final interviews I had with her, before and after she was admitted to the excellent nursing home I and the court-appointed lawyer selected. She . . . she cursed me. I had no idea she knew such words; though, I admit, most of them came from the Bible. The Old Testament, of course."

He took a handkerchief from his pocket and passed it over his face. "She lived only a few weeks," he said. "I felt a cowardly relief when they called to tell me she had died in her sleep."

"You couldn't have done anything else," Bea said, reaching out to touch his hand.

"Oh, yes, he could," said Roger. "Don't get me wrong, Steve; I know you did more than most people would have done, and with the best of intentions. If she was so poor, who paid for the expensive nursing home? But now—our experience sheds a rather different light on Miss Marion's delusions, doesn't it?"

"It proves I was right," Bea said triumphantly. "Another independent witness saw the ghost; none of us had heard of Miss Marion's experience, so we can't be accused of being affected by it. I'm convinced that the spirit is a kindly one—a sweet young girl, who died an untimely death."

Father Stephen cleared his throat. "Oh, dear," he said. "Did I never say? . . . Now that certainly is an example of my subconscious suppressing the facts. Miss Marion's 'companion' was not female, Bea. It was a young—er—a handsome young man."

Chapter Eight

I THOUGHT BEA was going to hit Roger with the cookie plate. "Ribald" is the only word for the tone of his laughter.

Once he had gotten his amusement out of his system, he apologized profusely. "It's a very pathetic and tragic story," he said. "Steve, stop flagellating yourself, you did the only thing you could have done—being the man you are—and you did it handsomely. And the old lady had many years of . . ." The corners of his mouth twitched violently, but he got himself under control and went on, ". . . of comfort. She was long overdue. Don't you see that your story confirms my theory, not Bea's? Kevin sees a pretty girl, Miss Marion saw a man."

"Not necessarily." Father Stephen's face was still grave, but he seemed to have found relief in telling the story. "A house this old may have known many tragedies, Roger. We know so little; perhaps there is an atmosphere here peculiarly conducive to—"

He groped for words. Bea nodded. "I know what you mean, Father. There is an atmosphere of peace here. We have all felt it; that may be why we are able to live with what is happening instead of running away. Why shouldn't some of the former inhabitants feel the same way?"

Father Stephen looked distressed. That was not how he would have expressed it. He might have expostulated against a viewpoint that was, to say the least, unorthodox, if Roger had not put it less tactfully.

"Honest to God, Bea, I don't know how an otherwise intelligent woman can believe such junk."

Bea flushed. The pastor's presence restrained her from retorting as she would like to have done, so I did it for her.

"Junk yourself. There are several points that support Bea's theory."

"What?"

I counted them on my fingers. "One: Kevin's companion is female, at least to him. Two: I saw the form of a girl with golden hair. Three: Bea and I both heard a woman's voice. Four—and this is what I find most convincing—the portrait in Kevin's room is that of a girl with golden hair. Wait a minute, I know the painting is late in date. That's my point. What if it was painted by someone a century ago, who saw the same thing Kevin sees?"

The reaction was gratifying. Bea clapped her hands in applause; Father Stephen nodded thoughtfully; even Roger looked taken aback.

"Touché," he said. "I hadn't considered that. All the same—"

"Quiet." Bea held up a warning hand. "Someone is coming."

It was Kevin. "So there you are," he said, after Bea had replied to his knock. "I've been looking all over for you. Didn't know we had company."

As always, my mind went through one of those sickening roller-coaster swoops of disbelief to see him behaving and looking so normal.

"I call this selfish," he went on cheerfully. "Hiding up here, eating all the food. I bet it was Roger who finished the cookies. I'm starved."

"There are more in the kitchen," Bea said. "Why don't you bring them up? I'll make fresh tea."

"Okay." Kevin vanished, leaving the door open.

"It is hard to believe," Roger murmured, staring after him. "He looks so . . ."

"So did Miss Marion," Father Stephen said. "Unlike her, he seems to have no conscious memory of what he has experienced."

"Maybe it was like that for her when it began," I said, shivering.

"I'm going to tell him," Bea said abruptly.

"Are you crazy?" Roger shouted. She stilled him with an imperious gesture.

"Not about his—er—dreams, that would be bad, I agree. I'll put it tactfully, don't worry; but I feel we ought to find out whether he has had any conscious experiences. It might be useful."

There was no time to argue the point, if anyone had wanted to—and from Roger's mutinous expression I gathered he did want to. Bea's mouth was set just as stubbornly as his. There was an iron core under her seeming softness, as I had already observed.

Kevin was back in a few minutes. "We ought to do this more often," he said, putting the plate of cookies on the table. "Roger, you look sort of peculiar. Did I interrupt something? What were you talking about?"

"Ghosts," said Bea.

Roger choked on the cookie he had bitten into. I

thought that if this was Bea's idea of tact . . . But Kevin only looked amused and interested.

"In general or in particular?" he asked.

"I was speculating," said Bea, "as to whether this house might be haunted."

"Oh, I'm sure it is," Kevin said lightly. "What would a place like this be without a ghost? You haven't seen anything, have you, Aunt Bea?"

There was not an actor alive, on stage, screen, or television, who could have asked that question as guilelessly. By contrast, Bea's response was obviously false.

"I wondered," she said. "Once or twice—but I assumed I was dreaming. It happened just as I was dropping off to sleep."

"What did you see?" Kevin asked.

"Not see. I thought I heard a voice—a girl's voice."

"Really? That's fascinating." Kevin put his cup on the table and beamed at his aunt. "It must be Ethelfleda."

II

I tripped twice on the narrow cellar stairs. If Roger hadn't been holding my elbow I would have fallen.

Kevin was taking us to see Ethelfleda's tombstone. If that statement doesn't excuse my uncoordinated condition, I don't know what would.

Kevin had explained that Ethelfleda was the woman in the portrait in his room. When Roger asked how he knew the lady's identity, he said simply, "Her name is written on the canvas." Roger's chagrin was almost funny. None of us had noticed, or thought of looking for, an inscription. Kevin went on to explain that he had become curious about the woman after noting the discrepancy between her costume and the date when the picture must have been painted.

"The name made it probable that she was a real person, not just some imaginary medieval damsel. So I figured she might be one of the former inhabitants. I started to look through the records."

"You never said anything about it," I stuttered.

"To you?" Kevin shrugged. "I was already feeling guilty about abandoning the book; should I admit I was wasting time on idle antiquarian research? But I have a minor in medieval history; the period has always interested me. So after a while it occurred to me that one of those tombstones in the crypt might be hers. I looked—and there it was. Come on, I'll show you."

He was right. There it was.

Stiff and elegant in her high headdress and graceful robes, she lay with hands folded at her breast. The face was an idealized version of youthful beauty, without individuality. It glowed softly golden in the light, as did the whole figure; the tablet was not stone but metal, an ornamental brass beautifully engraved. The plate was about four feet long and two feet wide, set into a low rim of stone. At first I couldn't imagine how I had missed seeing it on our first trip to the cellar. Then I realized we had not visited this room; it must adjoin the other chamber where I had first noticed that the paving stones were inscribed. Long ago the two rooms must have been one. The rounded arches, supported by stubby columns, to the left of the door, might have run down the center of the original room. The spaces between the columns had been filled in with brick and mortar.

Bea dropped to her knees, cooing with delight.

"One of my friends used to do brass rubbing. I always wanted to try it. This is a beauty. Look at the locks of hair, and the hook-shapes that indicate folds of drapery. I've never seen one like this; usually the figure alone is of brass, set into stone."

"The brass tablets are less common than the isolated figures, but they do occur." I might have expected that Roger would know all there was to know about the subject. He lowered himself to the ground, grunting with effort. "What's this around the edge of the tablet?"

"Her name," Kevin said. "I couldn't make out the rest of the inscription. I suppose it's the usual thing."

His nose only inches from the monument, Roger crawled along, following the inscription that bordered the sides of the brass. "Damned Gothic script," he muttered. "I guess you're right, Kevin. It's Ethelfleda, no question about it. The rest is part Latin, part English. 'Queen of Heaven be thou propitious unto me.' I don't see any dates, of birth or death, or any biographical details."

"Maybe this one was originally set in a larger stone, which carried that information," Bea suggested.

Roger went on crawling and mumbling. "*'Dormio sed resurgam.'* I sleep but I will arise. Nice pious sentiment."

"I guess that knocks out our ghost, Aunt Bea," Kevin said. "Ethelfleda can't be walking; she died in the odor of sanctity."

His frivolous tone was jarring. Bea frowned at him, and Father Stephen said coolly, "She was laid to rest with the prayers of her faith. That is a crucifix she holds in her hands."

Roger looked up, like a dog begging for a bone.

"I wonder," he said, echoing a remark I had once made, "how far down your millionaire dug when he moved the house."

"Oh, no, you don't, you ghoul," Kevin said, grinning. "You aren't going to disturb Ethelfleda's ashes."

"God forbid," Father Stephen murmured.

When Kevin suggested we adjourn to the courtyard for a drink, Father Stephen said he had better be getting home. We accompanied him to the door, where he took Bea's hand and looked at her intently.

"Come and see me tomorrow," he said. "We can continue the discussion."

Kevin smiled patronizingly. "You don't have to stop talking religion on my account," he assured them.

"No, no, I—er—must be getting back."

"It was good to see you," said the young lord of the manor. "Come again anytime. Roger, I can talk you into a drink, can't I?"

They went off together. I lingered to hear Father Stephen say softly, "It is imperative that we talk about this, Bea. I'm very concerned. Promise you won't do anything rash until we have had a chance to discuss the matter further."

"Very well," Bea said.

When he had gone she turned to me. "That was a surprise, wasn't it? I knew I was doing the right thing, but I had no idea it would be so successful."

"I don't know, Bea," I said uneasily. "Do you think—"

"I know I am on the right track." Her face was aglow. "Now that we know her name, we can find out more about her, and then . . ."

"Lay the troubled spirit," I said.

"You have doubts. Why?"

"I don't know," I said again. "It doesn't seem . . ."

"I'm sorry you feel that way." Bea laid a friendly hand on my arm. "I couldn't be more pleased, Anne; not only have we a definite clue to follow, but we can be certain that this spirit has no evil intentions. I've never been afraid of it; now I feel only the liveliest pity. If only you could share my faith."

"I wish I could," I said honestly. But I wondered: was Bea's faith a light in darkness, or a veil that dulled her senses to reality?

III

Roger offered to take us out to dinner. To my surprise Kevin accepted with alacrity. He seemed to enjoy himself. Among other matters, and with equal casualness, he talked about Ethelfleda. He had not yet succeeded in locating any material that mentioned her name.

"We ought to get a professional librarian in to catalog the books," he said. "I don't think it has ever been done."

"You won't find printed books from Ethelfleda's time," Roger said.

Kevin gave him a look of weary tolerance. "I know, Roger, I know. But there may be manuscripts—deeds, wills, and the like. If they exist, I haven't found them."

"Maybe I could give you a hand," Roger offered.

Kevin's reaction was exactly what it ought to have been—a becoming blend of surprise and appreciation. "If you have time, that would be great."

"I have an ulterior motive," Roger said.

"You told us before you have designs on my house," Kevin said with a smile.

"It's not that exactly. I'm having problems with my—er—plumbing. Wondered if I could ask you to put me up for a few days till it's fixed."

"Sure, no problem. That is, if Aunt Bea doesn't mind."

"Not at all," Bea said.

"It'll be nice for you to have someone to keep you company," Kevin said.

After dinner Roger dropped us at the house and drove off "to get my things." I assumed the "things" would include additional apparatus for ghost-hunting, and wondered if he planned to spend his nights in the alcove taking pictures. I would not have cared for the job myself, even if Kevin was now aware of his residence in the house. The more I thought about his attack on the presumed burglar, the more it bothered me. Kevin was no coward; it was perfectly in character for him to tackle an intruder single-handed. What was out of character was the ferocity that had made him go on throttling a man who was already subdued. That sort of hand-to-hand violence didn't suit an ex-pacifist, a man who consistently eschewed contact sports. He had told me once that he hadn't even played basketball, though his high school coach had tried to persuade him to try out for the team. Kevin's personality had changed in other, subtler ways; might the change include a new propensity for violence?

He didn't come to the library with us. After a few minutes he popped in long enough to announce that he was going out for a while—not to wait up. So I cleverly deduced he had called Debbie.

Bea fussed around, straightening books and papers,

shifting vases of flowers, and otherwise killing time. Tabitha tried to get on my lap but was challenged by Pettibone, and after an exchange of growls and swipes Tabitha gave up the contest and stalked off, her tail waving indignantly. I scratched the kitten under the chin.

"Can I get you anything?" Bea asked.

"You could hand me that book from my desk—the one on the blotter. Sorry to be so lazy; in my house we say, 'I can't get up, there's a cat on my lap' when we don't want to move."

"A reasonable excuse," Bea said, giving me the book. "Are you getting any work done? I feel bad about the way your summer has been wasted."

"You can't blame yourself for this situation," I said. "And I surely couldn't have anticipated it."

Bea sat down next to me. Her hands were twisting nervously.

"I must say this, at the risk of being misunderstood," she said. "I've grown very fond of you, Anne. I would like to think we will always be friends."

"But you wish I'd get the hell out."

"No, I don't want you to leave! That's just the trouble. Not only do I enjoy your company, I depend on you. I would be lost without your stability, your sense of humor. But I have no right to ask you to stay. At best, this is a waste of time for you. At worst . . ."

"Do you think there is danger?"

"No, I honestly don't. But I have no right to ask you to risk a nervous breakdown or a terrible fright on the basis of my hunch. Unless you feel something for Kevin that gives you a personal interest in his welfare."

"I've always had a great affection for Kevin," I said.

"Lately my feelings have swung back and forth like a pendulum. The only thing that makes me wonder whether I may not care more for him than I had realized is the way I'm reacting to Debbie."

"I noticed that."

"You did?" I laughed wryly. "You would think I could make up my mind about something as basic as whether I'm in love with Kevin or scared to death of him."

"He may be using the girl to make you jealous," Bea said.

"Not likely. Bea, let's leave it this way. If I decide to cop out, I'll give you fair warning. I'm so confused I don't know what to do."

"Whatever you decide," she said.

I was trying to concentrate on *Currents in Modern American Poetry* and Bea was furrowing her brow over a massive tome on medieval architecture when Roger came in, draped with cameras and wires.

"I passed Kevin on the way back," he said, unloading his equipment. "Where's he off to?"

"Late date, I presume," I said.

"Well, thank God for that girl, whoever she is. She may keep Kevin out of our hair for a while." Roger dropped into a chair. Tabitha climbed onto his lap, giving me a snooty look. Absently Roger stroked her.

"It is the oddest sensation," he muttered. "Seeing that kid, so open and healthy-looking, and remembering how he looked last night, his eyes out of focus and his hands moving over something I couldn't see. Like Jekyll and Hyde, or—"

"Or Elizabeth-Betty-Beth," I said. The others looked at me inquiringly. "Have you ever read *The*

Bird's Nest by Shirley Jackson?" I asked, "or *The Three Faces of Eve?*"

"Oh." Roger nodded. "Multiple personality. I can see why you keep returning to that, Anne, but it won't work. That particular illness isn't infectious."

He began examining his cameras. There were a dozen or more of them. "What did you do, go out and buy those?" I asked.

"No, I borrowed them. That's why I was so late getting here this afternoon; my friend lives in Haverford."

Bea dropped her book. "You didn't tell him why you wanted them, I hope. If word of this gets out, Roger, I'll never speak to you again. I won't have this house besieged by your odd friends and by reporters."

"You ought to know me better than that. I told him *my* house was haunted." Roger grinned. "I had to promise him he could come for a visit later. I'll have to think of an excuse. Tell him I exorcised it, or something."

"What are you going to do with so many cameras?" I asked.

"Set them up, of course. I think I'll start with the Great Hall. Wish I had a hundred of the little critters; it's going to take a long time to cover the entire house."

"Why the Hall? The only place we've seen anything—"

"Was where we happened to be. For all we know, there may be a nightly jamboree elsewhere, especially in the areas you don't normally enter—which happen to be, in most cases, the oldest parts of the house." Roger was squinting into the camera lens; I don't know what he was looking for, or at. Now he put it down. "We have to go at this methodically," he said seriously. "In cases such as this there is usually a focus, or center of derivation. I am not convinced that Kevin's room is that center. The thing we saw was moving away, remember? I'd like to know where it was going."

"How about the cellar?" I said in a low voice.

Roger was on the verge of laughing. He took a closer look at me and thought better of it.

"Hey, Annie," he said affectionately. "Stop that. You're giving yourself an unnecessary case of the horrors. Didn't Steve say your medieval maiden was at rest?"

"They may have *put* her there," I muttered. "That doesn't guarantee she *stays* there."

"I'll set up the cameras in the cellar tonight, instead of the Hall," Roger promised. "I doubt that I'll get anything, but maybe it will set your mind at ease."

"Fine with me," I said. "But don't expect me to help you set things up. I wouldn't go down into that place at night for the Nobel Prize in literature."

"He's teasing you, Anne," Bea said. "He doesn't believe in Ethelfleda."

"I'm not teasing her, I'm trying to reassure her," Roger said indignantly.

"You aren't succeeding," I told him.

Roger patted me—the same friendly, casual touch he had bestowed on the cat. "What are you reading, love?" he asked Bea.

"One of the books Kevin found," Bea replied. *"English Manor Houses.* It has a chapter about this house."

"Really?" Roger sat up straight. Tabitha, who had

been writhing lithesomely under his caressing hand, was caught off balance and rolled ignominiously onto the floor. Roger apologized and picked her up. "Give us a synopsis, Bea. Any new information?"

"It's all new to me. The book was written before World War One. According to the author, this is one of the few surviving examples of a fortified manor house. Once it was walled, with a moat and portcullis and all the rest; but those portions were torn down or allowed to fall into ruin during the eighteenth and nineteenth centuries."

"No need for them," I said.

"What?" Roger stared at me.

"I meant . . ." I had spoken without thinking, but it did make sense. "No more civil wars or threats of invasion by that time."

"There was Napoleon," Roger said. "And Hitler."

"But they didn't make it."

"What the hell are we talking about?" Roger demanded. "You're distracting me. Go on, Bea."

"The wing containing the Great Hall and the chapel, with certain chambers over them, dates to the fifteenth century," Bea continued. "The other wings were extensively remodeled, some in Elizabethan times, others—"

"Never mind the later stuff," Roger interrupted. "Is there anything earlier than the fifteenth century?"

His voice was oddly urgent. Bea looked at him in surprise.

"What do you want for your nickel? That's pretty old."

"I just wondered."

"Clever man. You are right." She read from the book. "'The most remarkable feature of Grayhaven

Manor is the remainder of certain sections of stone-work that seem to date from an earlier structure on the site. One portion of the crypt, with its typically massive stone columns and flat Romanesque arches, is suggestive of Norman architecture. The curious carvings on the pillars . . .'" Here she interrupted herself to comment, "I didn't see any carvings, did you?"

"I didn't look," Roger muttered. "Go on, go on."

"'. . . are reminiscent of the doorway jambs of the church porch at Kilpeck, Herefordshire, which date from the year 1134. Even more remarkable is one stretch of stone foundation, exposed by reconstruction then in progress, which suggests Saxon masonry. Unfortunately it was impossible to trace these foundations, since such an effort would have necessitated removing the upper courses, at considerable risk to the stability of the structure—an effort which the present owners quite understandably refuse to consider. One is driven to suspect, however, that the present manor house is the latest of several dwellings that once occupied this spot, the earliest of which may precede the Conquest.'"

"Wow," I said, impressed in spite of myself. "No wonder Karnovsky fell for this place. It is really old."

"It's a good thing he moved it when he did," Roger said.

"What do you mean?" Bea asked.

"Didn't you tell me that the original site was in Warwickshire, near Coventry? Remember what happened to that area in World War Two?"

I have never been able to understand the morbid interest some people have in that war, but even I had heard of Coventry. Something stirred, deep down in the dim recesses of my brain; but before I could encourage it to show its strange little head Roger stood up and transferred Tabitha to his vacated chair.

"I'm going to work," he announced. "Don't want Kevin to catch me in the basement; I'd have a hard time inventing an explanation for being down there this time of night."

Gathering up his cameras, he went out. After a moment Bea gave me a half-smile and a little shrug, and followed. I had no inclination to join them, and I wondered why the place affected me so much more unpleasantly than it did the others. Maybe I was more susceptible to conventional horror stuff—crypts and bones and tombs. Though there wouldn't be bones left by now, not after four hundred years. Unless . . .

Once—I forget when and where—I had run across some articles describing the disinterment of various ancient British kings, when repairs were being made on the tombs at Westminster Abbey. I don't know why I read the damned things, unless it was morbid fascination. Some of the details kept turning up in my nightmares for years afterward. And wasn't it Pepys, that seventeenth-century bon vivant and diarist, who had boasted of having kissed a queen, and held the upper part of her body in his hands? The queen was Catherine, wife of Henry the Fifth, who died in 1437, two and a half centuries before Pepys had pressed his lips to her dried, mummified face. He had described the body as still covered with flesh, like tanned leather. Ghoulish, perverse—but they were more practical about death in Pepys' time. They saw so much of it. The moldering heads of executed traitors grinned down on them as they passed under Temple Bar, and public executions provided outings for the whole family. Peddlers sold snacks to be nibbled while the condemned man dangled, twitching, and spectators fought to buy pieces of the hangman's rope.

In 1744 they had opened the tomb of Edward the First, who died in 1307. The king's body wore royal robes, a crimson-and-gold tunic, and a mantle of red velvet. He had been six feet two inches tall, and all of those inches were intact four hundred years after he died.

And in the late sixteen hundreds a workman found a hole in the tomb of Edward the Confessor, king and saint, who passed on to his presumed reward in 1066. Through the aperture the workman saw the saint's head, solid and entire, the upper and lower jaws full of teeth.

Six hundred years, and still all those teeth.

I wrenched my mind from the subject. Roger was right; I was scaring myself. The room seemed very quiet. I wished I had asked him to close the windows. They stood open to the night, tall rectangles of darkness. Something close at hand let out a sharp rasping breath. I missed a couple of inhalations until I realized it was only Belle, snorting in her sleep. I had a crazy, cowardly fear of getting out of my chair, with its protective high back and arms.

What was taking them so long? All they had to do was set up a few cameras. Roger's notion of threads strung around the room, to trip a ghost, was perfectly ludicrous. Everybody knows ghosts are immaterial. If they can pass through doors and walls, they are not likely to disturb a thread.

Suddenly I knew I had to find out whether Ethelfleda was really there, under the brass slab. Maybe it didn't really matter. Many of the ghost stories I had read implied that spirits tend to hang around the place where the body is buried. That gentle scholar, M. R. James, who wrote some of the most gruesome ghost stories in the English language, had one about a couple of children who had been murdered by a nasty old man for purposes of black magic. He had hidden their bodies in a disused wine cellar, but their vengeful spirits murdered him by the same method he had used on them—tearing the heart out of his living body.

If the lights had gone out just then, I would have had a stroke. Once again I got a grip on my unwholesome imagination. The point about such stories was that they suggested that where there was a ghost, there must be a body. However, that was fiction. I was not familiar with the body of "true" supernatural literature, if there is such a thing. All the same, I thought I would feel better if I was sure Ethelfleda's remains, whatever their condition (better not think about that) had not been shoved into a packing crate and moved to Pennsylvania. I had an insane image of myself in the cellar, laboring with pickax and chisel to lift the tombstone. Which was ridiculous. Even if I had the strength and the inclination for such a ghastly job, I couldn't attempt it without Kevin's knowledge.

All at once I sprang out of the chair, forgetting morbid fancies. There was an easier way of learning what I wanted to know. It had been less than sixty years since the house had been moved from England to America. The job couldn't have been done without satisfying a complex web of legal requirements. There must have been a mass of papers pertaining to the transaction—packing and shipping bills, lists of contents—"one coffin, containing miscellaneous bones and teeth, scratched, broken, stained. . . ." How much to ship Ethelfleda's ashes across the Atlantic? If she wasn't on the list, I could safely assume she had not made the trip. Rudolf Karnovsky might have been an eccentric, but he was also a businessman, and businessmen love lists, receipts, and permits.

Where would such papers be? There was a chance they might be somewhere in the house, in the library or one of the attics. I decided I would look—tomorrow. In daylight.

I didn't mention my idea to Bea and Roger. Maybe I was becoming overly sensitive to Roger's poorly concealed amusement. I concluded I would try it out on Bea the next day, or on Father Stephen. He might think I was weird or heretical, but he wouldn't laugh at me.

I was getting ready for bed when I realized there was another possibility of locating the papers I wanted. Miss Marion had been the last descendant and heir of old Rupert. Personal papers, which would surely include those dealing with the house, would have gone to her. And her conservator and guardian had been Father Stephen.

Chapter Nine

BEA ALMOST GOT out of the house without me next morning. I happened to catch her in the hall, when I came yawning down in search of coffee, and when I saw her neat pink suit and white gloves I knew she was on her way to pay the promised visit to Father Stephen. So I said, "Hey, wait for me," and it was not until she gave me a queer, considering look that I remembered I had not been invited.

"Oh," I said. "Sorry. I assumed . . . Stupid of me."

"You're welcome to come, of course. I thought you weren't interested."

"Not interested?"

"In my ideas. They sound foolish, I suppose, to someone who doesn't . . . well . . ."

There was a brief embarrassed silence. Maybe it was her formal clothes; I don't know. For the first time I felt ill at ease with her, the way I did when my Aunt Betty came for a visit, the one who's the social queen of Hagerstown, Maryland, and who looks at me as if I had just crawled out of a hole in the ground.

Then Bea laughed. "It's all Roger's fault. He's got me on the defensive. Please come. I'd appreciate your company."

I went to the driver's side of the car. Even after those short weeks I knew many of Bea's habits and foibles. She really didn't enjoy driving and was happy to let someone else do it. I'm no hot-rod type, but it was a pleasure to drive that car. I had never handled a Mercedes before, and I didn't expect to again.

As we glided smoothly down the drive, I caught her looking at me out of the corner of her eye with that same speculative gaze. Self-consciously I tried to mash down my frizzled locks.

"I'd have made myself more beautiful if I had known you wanted to leave so early," I said.

"You *are* beautiful," Bea said. "But—I hope you don't mind—there I go, apologizing again."

"Spit it out," I said. "I look like a slob, don't I?"

"I wouldn't use that word; but you don't look as pretty as you could. I suppose it matters more to my generation than it does to yours, and I'd be the last to claim that appearance matters a hoot."

"It does matter, some. I really don't enjoy looking like Little Orphan Annie." I laughed, to show how little the matter concerned me. Bea did not echo my laughter.

"You have beautiful hair," she said seriously. "That copper-gold shade is very rare, and unlike many redheads, you don't freckle or turn a nasty shade of rare roast beef in the sun. All you need is to have your hair styled properly, instead of whacking it off when it gets in your eyes."

If my Aunt Betty had made that suggestion, I would have shot back a flippant reply and gotten my revenge by driving too fast. But Aunt Betty wouldn't have larded the suggestion with big gobs of flattery, or spoken as if she really cared about my feelings, instead of what her friends would think of me.

"I don't have the time to fool with it," I said.

"Would you let me see what I can do? I'm no professional, but—"

"But you couldn't make it look any worse."

"I've been dying to get my hands on you since I first met you," Bea confessed. "You'd be a really striking-looking woman with a proper haircut and glasses that suit the shape of your face and—er—"

"Some halfway decent clothes." I glanced down at my faded jeans—there was a hole in the right knee—and my clean but worn T-shirt, with its emphatic slogan: "Women belong in the House—and in the Senate."

"I guess it wouldn't be a betrayal of the feminist movement to wear a skirt occasionally," I said.

Actually, the idea fascinated me. I was so absorbed in visualizing the new, beautiful me, that I almost drove through the village. Bea nudged me in time. I made a swooping turn into the driveway of the parsonage.

I don't know whether Father Stephen expected me. He greeted me with the same warmth he showed Bea and ushered us into his study. It was a strictly masculine room, with deep leather chairs and animal prints on the walls, but it was painfully neat. We had scarcely taken our seats when an elderly woman wearing a starched white apron entered, carrying a tray with coffee and hot rolls. I gathered from the way she looked at me that she had seen my type before and was resigned, but not enthusiastic.

"I don't know what I would do without Frances," Father Stephen said, after she had gone. "But there are times when her notions of what constitutes proper behavior for a man of the cloth makes me as restless as a teenager. She leaves my desk alone, thank heaven, but sometimes I have a reprehensible urge to dance wildly around the room, or scatter crumbs."

As he had probably planned, this seemingly ingenuous confession made me more relaxed. But I was careful to cross my legs left over right, in an attempt to hide the hole in my jeans.

"Where is Roger?" Father Stephen asked. "I'm surprised he would pass up a chance to play devil's advocate."

"He went rushing off to develop his latest photographs," Bea said. "Leaped out of bed at the crack of dawn. . . ." She turned a pretty shade of tomato red. Father Stephen tactfully pretended not to notice, and after a moment Bea went on, "To be frank, Father, that's why I called to ask if I might come early. I wanted to talk to you without Roger being here, jeering at everything I say."

"I see. Has anything new occurred?"

Bea shook her head. Father Stephen turned to me. "What about you, Anne?"

"I've been sleeping like a baby since I changed rooms," I said, somewhat inaccurately. I went on to tell Father Stephen about Roger's cameras, and his decision to plant them in the cellar. Father Stephen smiled and shook his head.

"Roger and his playthings. He seems not to recognize his own inconsistency. I thought he denied that your disturbances had anything to do with the brass."

"The cellar was a concession to me," I admitted. "Last night I started getting weird ideas."

"You began to wonder whether Ethelfleda's earthly remains are in the crypt," Father Stephen said. My surprise showed on my face. He laughed outright, his eyes twinkling. "I ought to claim that I read your mind; wouldn't you be impressed? Conditioned as we are by long centuries of traditional beliefs, it is not surprising that such a thought should occur to both of us. But I'm sure you decided, as I did, that the question is irrelevant. In any case, we would never be able to determine the facts. Even if Kevin would permit—"

In my excitement I interrupted him. "We wouldn't have to dig her up. There must be records, lists, made when the house was moved."

"Hmm. That's clever, Anne."

"And I thought you might have those records, if they were part of Miss Marion's estate. You were her legal guardian—"

"No, no; the legal aspects were handled by a young lawyer appointed by the court—a member of the firm that had represented the Karnovsky family locally. She gave them very little to do, in fact, having only a small income, and, of course, title to the house."

"But these would be papers dealing with the house," I said. "Wouldn't they have to be available to a prospective purchaser? To prove the title was clear?"

"Very possibly. The point I was endeavoring to make was that I have no papers of any kind. I suppose I might ask Jack—John Burckhardt, that is—the lawyer in the case. I don't know what excuse I could give for my curiosity after so long a time."

"Kevin would have a logical excuse," Bea said. "He is the only one who could legitimately inquire."

"I don't think we ought to involve him," I said.

"But he is already interested in Ethelfleda," Bea argued. "He didn't appear to be upset by my questions yesterday, or—"

Father Stephen brought his hand down sharply on

the table. The gesture was so violent and the distress on his face so pronounced that Bea stopped talking and we both looked at him in surprise.

"That is the difficulty, don't you see?" he exclaimed. "Kevin's unconcern is, in my opinion, a most alarming symptom. I have the feeling that we are dealing with something extremely unstable, like a heavy stone balanced on edge. The stone may appear solid, but the slightest touch could send it toppling over."

After a moment I said hesitantly, "Have you seen something in Kevin that we've missed?"

"I can't produce evidence you would find convincing, Anne. I can only cite my own feelings. But I've had a good many years of experience in such matters. Admittedly, I have never run into a genuine example of possession—"

"Possession!" Bea cried. "You can't be serious."

The pastor sighed. "Confound it, I didn't mean to say that. My tongue ran away with me. Let me put it this way. We must consider the possibility."

"I can't," I said. "I've already stretched my imagination till it hurts. That's too much."

"He has changed," Father Stephen said. "Hasn't he?"

I didn't answer; but after a moment he nodded, as if acknowledging a reply. "I won't press the point. I am far from convinced myself. We haven't enough information as yet to defend any interpretation."

"Exactly," I said. "What about Ethelfleda? That's information we might be able to get."

Father Stephen shrugged. "There is no reason why I shouldn't ask. I could tell Jack that the present owners of the house are interested in its history."

"Father, we can't let you lie for us," Bea said.

"That's not a lie, it's the truth. Perhaps not the whole truth—but that's my problem. It may prove to be a vain quest. For all we know, the relevant papers may have been handed over to Mr. and Mrs. Blacklock at the time of purchase. I'm afraid I'm not familiar with the procedure."

"It would be nice if you would try," I said firmly. Let Bea and Father Stephen worry about his conscience. I myself approve of lying in a good cause. What kind of world would this be if everyone told the truth all the time?

"I'll be happy to do so. But I must make it clear to both of you that I think you are on the wrong track. You especially, Bea. You mustn't fall into the error of materialism. I need not cite Scripture to you—"

" 'Then shall the dust return to the earth as it was: and the spirit shall return to God, who gave it,' " Bea murmured. "I agree, Father, that the whereabouts of Ethelfleda's remains are unimportant. All these theories—Roger's foolish toys—none of them can help me decide what I ought to do."

"There is a ceremony—"

"No, Father. Not exorcism."

Father Stephen grimaced. "I dislike the word too. To conduct such a service would make me feel like that ineffectual idiot in the book that was so popular a few years back. A vile canard, not only on the cloth, but on every aspect of the Christian faith! However, it is an accepted and recognized rite of the Church. Why are you so opposed to it?"

Her eyes downcast, her hands nervously pleating the soft cotton of her skirt, Bea spoke rapidly. "I couldn't give permission for something like that without consulting my sister and brother-in-law. I'm only a guest in their house, after all. And even if I wanted to worry them, and perhaps interrupt their trip, they would never consent."

"It undoubtedly would worry them," Father Stephen agreed with a wry smile. "But what makes you suppose they would not consent?"

"You've met my brother-in-law," Bea said.

I hadn't met the gentleman, but I saw her point. I had a feeling that if I ever did meet Mr. Blacklock, I would find an older version of Kevin—charming, gentle, stubborn, skeptical. No, a man like that wouldn't cable back, "Proceed with the exorcism." He would cancel his trip, fly home—and gently but forcibly evict the crazies who were trying to tell him his son was haunted.

"It's difficult," Father Stephen said thoughtfully. "But I have the feeling you aren't being honest with me. What is your real reason for rejecting my suggestion?"

Bea sat in silence for a time, her head bowed. When she spoke, her voice was so low I had to strain to hear it.

"It means—casting it out—into darkness, annihilation."

"Ah." Father Stephen nodded. "I feared as much."

"No, listen to me—please. Is there any limit to the mercy and loving kindness of God?" Even I knew the answer to that one. Bea didn't wait for Father Stephen's reply. Passionately she went on, "Then how can we be other than merciful to a soul He would save? If we—"

"Stop." Father Stephen's voice was not loud, but its stern tone made it as peremptory as a shout. "Be careful, Bea. You are starting down a perilous road. Oh, I understand, and I admire your compassionate heart. But you are making an unwarranted assumption."

"You think it's evil," Bea said.

"Evil exists."

Bea's tightly clasped hands and tormented eyes showed how much she disliked being at odds with her friend, but the strength of her convictions overcame lesser scruples. How long they would have argued, and what the outcome might have been, I will never know. They were interrupted by a vehement bang on the door.

"Roger," Father Stephen said. "I know that knock of his. Bea, we aren't really in disagreement; I beg of you, don't do anything rash. These matters—"

Roger, tired of waiting for a response, shoved the door open. "So there you are," he said, glowering at Bea.

"Come in, Roger," said Father Stephen.

"I am in. What have you been saying about me?"

"The usual slurs, insults, and sneers," said Father Stephen.

"No, seriously," Roger said.

"We haven't agreed on any course of action, if that's what you mean," Bea said.

"No exorcism?" He returned her startled look with a grim smile. "Given the current state of the so-called literature on the subject, and Steve's anachronistic views about good and evil, that was a logical guess. Why not try it? It's stupid but harmless."

"What makes you so sure of that?" Father Stephen demanded.

"You'd like to believe in demons of darkness,

wouldn't you? It would get you off the old uncomfortable hook—if God is all-powerful and utterly good, why does He inflict so much pain on the world? Grow up, Steve. There is no such thing as an evil spirit—none, at least, that would be moved by the sight of a meaningless symbol."

"What about Borley Rectory? Helene Poirier? The Illfurt case?"

The names were Greek to me, but Roger settled back with a smile, as if he felt on familiar ground. "Classic cases of hysteria—the last two, certainly. As for the poltergeist at Borley—"

Bea rose. "If this is going to degenerate into idle gossip about ghosts, I'm leaving."

"Don't you want to see my photos?" Roger asked.

"Well . . ."

"I do," I said.

Roger waited until Bea had resumed her seat before he said cheerfully, "They really aren't worth looking at. I got what I expected—nothing."

What he had was a series of rather blurry shots of the small cellar room where Ethelfleda's brass constituted the pièce de résistance. These had been taken by a new gadget—a camera that swung on a limited curve, automatically taking shots at set intervals. The other cameras, which only operated when the switch was tripped, had not produced anything.

I studied one of the photos. It had been taken at an angle, showing Ethelfleda's brass and another stone beyond.

"This is odd," I said. "I thought the brass was flat against the floor. This line here, between the brass and the stone—it looks like a gap, a space almost an inch wide."

Roger glanced carelessly at the picture. "It's just a

shadow. I told you the crypt was not the center of the disturbance."

"Then what is?"

"Aha. Time will tell, my dear. Wait till I finish my investigation."

I think he was hoping someone would press him for further details. Nobody did. We broke up soon after that, Father Stephen saying only, "Please keep me informed, Bea. I am ready to act whenever you say the word."

The sun was high in the sky when we emerged from the house. Roger refused a ride, saying he preferred to take his own car. He would follow us shortly.

"I wish he wouldn't do that," Bea said, as we got into the Mercedes.

"What? Drive himself?"

"No, no; I'm talking about his attitude. This is only an intellectual game to him; he isn't taking it seriously."

"I feel the same at times," I admitted. "My emotions seem to swing from extreme concern to utter skepticism. Makes me wonder about my stability."

Bea didn't give me the reassurance I wanted. From her abstracted frown I realized she was thinking about something else.

Like Father Stephen, I was uneasy about her. Not only had she personalized the bizarre phenomenon that troubled the house, but she had developed a passionate sympathy for it. She had no children of her own. That line of reasoning might or might not explain Bea's reaction, but it didn't give me a clue as to how to deal with it. She wouldn't confide in me. She had written me off because of my lack of faith.

When we got back to the house Bea went upstairs to change, and I—this is hard to believe, but it's true—I stood in front of the big mirror in the hall and started pulling my hair into different positions to see how it would look. Bea caught me at it when she came down. So we went to her room and she bustled around collecting scissors and combs and towels, and she gave me a haircut.

By the time she had whacked off nine-tenths of my hair, I hardly recognized myself. My face looked enormous and felt indecently exposed. Bea didn't bother to ask me whether I had any makeup; it was obvious that I didn't. She had quite a collection of little bottles and boxes and brushes, which she dumped out onto the top of the dressing table.

"They give these away as sales gimmicks," she explained, rummaging through the miscellany. "I can never resist freebies, even when they are the wrong shade for me. There's sure to be something here."

I felt like the Sistine Chapel ceiling—if it was bare plaster before Michelangelo started work—and about the same size, when she began. I must say the results were artistic, in both cases. When I put my glasses back on, the face didn't look like anybody I knew, but it looked good.

I admired myself, and thanked her; then I went to my room and admired myself some more, and changed into the only outfit I owned that could live up to that unrecognizable face—a print skirt and a low-necked white blouse. Posturing in front of my mirror, I wondered what Kevin would think of the new me. Would he notice? Would he laugh? In a sudden fit of shyness I changed back into my jeans. I wanted to wipe off the makeup, but was restrained by the knowledge that it would hurt Bea's feelings. I felt ridiculous.

Kevin didn't show up for lunch, which made me feel even more ridiculous. Roger was there; the conversation was banal to the point of boredom. No one raised the subject that should have been uppermost in our minds. After we finished, Bea shooed me out of the kitchen, saying she preferred to clean up alone, and Roger, with a conspiratorial wink and jerk of his head, took me aside.

"What is she up to now?" he demanded, as soon as we were out of the room. "She won't talk to me. What's she mad about?"

"She thinks you are taking this too lightly," I said.

"Lightly! My God, I'm spending all my time on it. Listen, Annie, you don't seem to be susceptible to this superstitious nonsense that affects her and Steve. Can I talk to you? I need a sounding board."

What he really wanted was a Ms. Watson, to follow him around and make admiring noises. "Amazing, my dear Roger." Well, I had been offered that job before. Maybe I had been wrong to turn it down.

"I'll give it a shot," I said. "But no commitments."

"Good Lord, girl, I'm not asking you to marry me," Roger said impatiently. "Come along."

"Where?"

"The cellar." He gave me a measuring look. "Unless you're chicken."

"Ha, ha," I said merrily. "I was just kidding last night. There is nothing down there to be afraid of."

"That's what I said."

I had convinced myself that my mood of the previous evening had been only a passing streak of morbidity, now conquered; and sure enough, as we made our way through the gloomy underground ways I felt nothing more than a mild touch of claustrophobia. Roger had brought a strong electric torch, larger than the usual flashlight, to augment the basement lights. I had expected he would go to the room that held Ethelfleda's brass. Instead he opened the door of the neighboring room.

"You notice that this partition is relatively modern," he began, flashing his light at the right-hand wall with its blocked arches. "Originally this room and the next were one. Agreed? We also agree, I trust, that it served as a crypt under the chapel in the fifteenth-century manor house. Actually, this part of the house is even older. The masonry is Norman, which makes it—"

I was getting tired of listening to a lecture. "Ten sixty-six," I said. "William the Conqueror."

"Don't show off. Say 1100 for these walls. I looked for the Saxon stones that book mentioned; can't find them. I suppose that part of the foundations was repaired. But they are surely here. That proves there was a building, possibly a house, possibly a church, on the site in 1000 A.D., maybe earlier."

"So what?"

Roger gave me a disapproving look. Watson never said "So what?" I'm sure it was my flippant attitude that moved him to prolong his speech.

"Did you know that Warwickshire, where the house used to be, was one of the last parts of England to be brought under Roman control? It was thickly forested and thinly settled; the terrain was too tough for primitive farmers. Two of the famous Roman roads cut across the northern and southern corners, but there weren't many settlements. After the Romans pulled out the Saxons invaded, somewhere around five hundred A.D."

"Then came the Danes, and then came the Normans," I said impatiently. "What the hell are you driving at, Roger?"

"I am suggesting that the Saxon building was a church, not a house," Roger snapped. "To use stone instead of wood, or wattle and daub, at that period, when fortifications were still mainly of beaten earth—"

"You mean your hypothetical Norman lord tore down a church and built his manor on the foundations? I doubt it, Roger. Like all the other bloody-minded killers of the Middle Ages, the Normans were good Christians."

"That's part of my argument. Are you going to shut up and listen without interrupting me every five seconds?"

"If you'll get on with it."

"I'm through talking for the moment. I want to show you something."

He went to the far corner of the room and shone his lamp on the floor. When I hesitated, he gestured impatiently.

That whole room was paved with old tombstones. The one Roger's light indicated was so worn that only the faintest shadowy traces of the original carving still remained. Stooping, Roger traced one of the designs with his finger. "Do you see it?"

I shrugged. I think it was a shrug, not a shiver. "A stick with two branches? A caduceus? A butterfly with a long tail?"

"Don't be ridiculous. It's an ax, can't you see? A double ax. See here. And here."

He moved from one stone to another, pointing. "This stone has the doves as well," he said obscurely. "And the horns. Here—doves, ax, horns."

"I suppose they could be."

"Oh, damn, you aren't looking. Here—this way."

Taking my hand, he dragged me out of the room and into the one next door. Ethelfleda's brass shone bright in the lantern light. Roger pulled me down to my knees and pushed my head close to the surface of the brass. He stabbed at it with his forefinger.

"Steve assumed it was a cross. The shape isn't unlike, I admit."

The object he indicated was half concealed by the slender, flexed fingers. A long stem or shaft protruded below. Above the clasped hand were two branches, at right angles to the shaft. They did seem thicker and more angled than the arms of a cross, and the stem did not extend far above them.

I pulled away from Roger and struggled to my feet.

"You're seeing things," I said rudely. "What would she be doing with an ax?"

"Your generation is hopelessly illiterate," Roger snarled. "Doesn't the term 'double ax' mean anything to you?"

"Why don't you just tell me?"

"Because," said Roger, with deadly patience, "I want to see if the evidence I have collected conveys the same meaning to you that it does to me. That's probably a vain hope; you are too ignorant. However. Next exhibit."

He shone the light up, moving it slowly over the arches and capitals of the pillars forming part of the east wall. At one time the tops of the pillars and part of the adjoining arch had been carved, but it was no wonder we hadn't noticed this before. Almost all the carvings were on the sides of the columns, within the shallow niches formed by the brick and mortar that closed the arches. They had a naive charm, like that of primitive art, and seemed to consist mainly of repre-

sentations of animals—deer, and funny, unana-
tomical lions, rabbits, foxes, and birds.

"Somewhat unorthodox for a Christian chapel,
wouldn't you say?" Roger inquired.

"Why? There shall be a 'melodious noise of birds
among the branches, a running of skipping beasts' . . .
'and the voice of the turtle is heard in our land.'"

"So you do know your Bible."

"The Bible as Literature, English 322, Monday,
Wednesday, Friday," I said.

"Hmph. All right, we're almost finished down here.
Just a quick look at the other tombstones."

Two of them, carved in stone, which had not
survived the centuries as well as the brass, bore effigies
of women wearing long archaic gowns. Silently Roger
indicated the worn traces of objects held by both
women. It was impossible for me to identify them.

Relieved to be on my way out, I relapsed into
sarcasm.

"Maybe one of them is haunting Kevin," I said.
"It's no fair for us to accuse Ethelfleda just because
her monument is easier to read."

To this ill-timed jest Roger replied with a grunt.

I was not as stupid as Roger thought. I could follow
his general argument; it had something to do with the
religious beliefs of the former inhabitants of the
house. I was not convinced of the reality of his double
ax, whatever it might signify, but if the ladies in the
crypt were clutching that ominous symbol instead of a
Christian cross, he might be excused for wondering
about the nature of their beliefs. Therefore I was not
surprised when the next stop proved to be the chapel.

It was so still. Even Roger was quiet for a moment,
as if he felt the hush and tranquillity. Then, with an
air of deliberate violation, he said loudly, "Damn.

The lighting is terrible. Did you have a chance the other day to examine the reliefs here?"

"I didn't. But I have a strange feeling I'm about to. Roger, why don't you just *tell* me?"

I knew I wouldn't get off so easily. Roger made me look at every carving. There weren't many. The ribbed columns were plain, spreading up without a break into the ceiling ribs. Only the inside arch of the door and the window traces were carved, with garlands of flowers and hanging fruit and with the same motif of running animals.

Above the altar, under the high window, was a single bas-relief, on a separate block of stone that was not part of the wall.

"Mary, Queen of Heaven, mourning over the dead Christ," I recited. "It may be a pietà, Roger, but it's no Michelangelo."

"Look closer. Have you ever seen a pietà like that? Look at Mary's crown and robes. Usually she is shown in the wimple and gown worn by women in the Middle Ages. Look at her . . . son. Beardless. Naked. And where's the Cross?"

"I haven't seen many pietàs," I said crossly. "I suppose they vary. Like the pictures of Jesus painted by various ethnic groups—he's black in Africa and has slanted eyes in Japan. Which makes good sense psychologically and theologically."

"Oh, bah." Roger threw his hands out. "You're hopeless. Never mind. What I really need from you is muscle, not brain. Give me a hand with this."

He jerked the cloth from the top of the altar. I bit back an exclamation of protest; the violence of his gesture had struck a deeply buried core of emotion. He bent, inspecting the stone under the altar table.

"It's not flat up against the wall," he said. "I caught a glimpse of something on the back surface; but there isn't room to get behind it. We'll have to pull it out."

I didn't say anything. Misinterpreting my silence, Roger said impatiently, "It won't be difficult. We needn't lift it, just push it out from the wall. I need someone to guide it from the other side."

I have to admit Roger did most of the work. All I had to do was nudge my corner when the stone pressed against the wall. Finally Roger let out a grunt of satisfaction. "That's far enough. Come here and have a look."

The back of the stone was carved. The relief work was so deep that parts of it stood almost clear of the background, like sculpture in the round. A narrow rim of stone as deep as the deepest part of the carving framed it, as if it were set down into an open box. After a moment I realized why the perspective looked so queer. I was looking at what was meant to be the top of the stone. It had been tipped over onto its side.

I realized something else, and that was how amateurish the other carvings were. This wasn't the work of a Lysippus or a Phidias, but it was professional, produced by a trained craftsman. It was also older, by half a millennium, than the earliest of the other reliefs.

The central figure was a bull, carved with such realism that its bellowing was almost audible. It had reason to complain; ropes bound it to a flat altar, and a man in long robes, wearing a hood, was cutting its throat. Blood gushed down into a footed bowl.

"Greek," I said experimentally.

"Roman copy," said Roger, like an antiphonal chorus.

"It reminds me of something."

Roger said, "It reminds me of something too; but what I'm thinking doesn't make sense. Wait a minute. I remember reading . . ." He made a movement toward the door, then caught himself. "First help me get this back in place." Another dart toward the door. "No, I want to get a photograph first. Wait here."

I was tired of being ordered around, so I followed him. Before he reached the door it opened, and I saw someone standing in the doorway.

I didn't recognize Kevin at first. The room was shadowy, and the hunched pose of the still figure made it look abnormally large and threatening. Even after I had identified him I felt his anger. It fanned out like a blast of hot air.

"What the hell are you doing?" he demanded.

I scuttled forward and stood shoulder to shoulder with Roger. (I have these heroic tendencies now and then, though I try to control them.) Roger was visibly taken aback by the viciousness of Kevin's voice. When he spoke, his tone was conciliatory.

"I looked for you to ask if it would be all right. Couldn't find you. You did say it was okay for me to—uh—do some research."

Kevin didn't speak for a moment. Then, "I guess I did," he said. He sounded confused. "What are you looking for? What are you doing in here?"

"We found something interesting," Roger said—answering neither question. "I was going to show you. Glad you're here. Come and have a look."

By the time Kevin reached the altar and squatted down to inspect the relief, he was his normal self. "Looks Greek," he said interestedly. "One of Rudolf's acquisitions? He's got a Roman sarcophagus in one of the bathrooms."

"I hadn't thought of that," Roger admitted. "It's a funny place to put it, though, under a Christian altar."

"Maybe Rudolf was Jewish and considered all other religions equally heretical. This is Mithraic, isn't it?"

"Could be," Roger said.

I was about to ask for elucidation when my faithful memory dredged up some half-forgotten data from a history course I had once taken. The god-hero Mithra was Persian originally, but his cult became popular in the Roman Empire, especially among the legions. It was a religion for men, for soldiers; women were not welcome. The sacrifice of a bull was one of the rituals.

Having settled this, we prepared to leave. Roger asked Kevin if he could take a photograph of the carving, and Kevin said sure, he would appreciate having a copy. Roger trotted off to get his camera. Kevin looked at me, frowning.

"It was Roger's idea," I said cravenly.

"You look different," Kevin said.

"I do? Oh—Bea cut my hair. It was—er—hot."

"Looks good."

"Thank you."

Kevin continued to study me with a puzzled expression. "I was thinking—this has been a dull summer, we've hardly left the place. Do you want to go somewhere? A movie, maybe?"

It was absurd—like one of those old films, the ones with Doris Day or someone of that sort: the heroine takes off her glasses, buys some pretty clothes, and *voilà!* the hero sees she is A Woman.

"*Is* there a movie?" I asked.

"Must be one somewhere."

"I don't feel any need to be entertained, Kevin." And—God help me—I added, "There's so much going on here."

"I'm glad you feel that way. Most girls would be bored sitting around all day."

I didn't even complain about the word "girls." "Bored?" I said thoughtfully. "No, I haven't been bored."

We started walking. Kevin slipped a casual arm around me. I didn't feel repelled. Not at all.

II

That day was memorable for another reason. I got a letter from Joe.

Not a miserable postcard, a real letter.

We didn't bother much about the mail. The box was at the end of the drive, over a mile away. When one of us happened to be in the neighborhood, he or she collected the contents and dumped it on the hall table. So far I had received the postcards aforementioned, a couple of irritable scrawls from my mother asking why I never wrote, and a few circulars forwarded by the friend who had sublet my apartment.

The letter from Joe caught my eye as I passed through the hall. It was on top of the pile and it was bright with foreign stamps, stuck on every which way. I stood there looking at it for a moment. Perhaps the great news of my transformation into A Woman had crossed the Atlantic by mental telepathy—only it would have to be clairvoyance, instead of mental telepathy, because the letter had taken five days to get here. I took it up to my room.

If I had been inclined to believe in ESP, the letter would have proved to me that Joe would always misinterpret any vibes he got from my direction.

I don't give a damn what you do, Anne, it's your life, but I think you owe it to me to be honest with me. I never liked your crazy idea of living with Kevin this summer, but you went ahead without consulting me. Do you realize you haven't written since that first note? And that wasn't even a letter, just a couple of lines. If your feelings have changed, say so. Mine are the same. I don't have time to do much screwing around. This place is a gold mine. I've been working my tail off, ten hours a day.

And so on. After two pages about his work, most of which was unintelligible to me, he ended abruptly, "Answer this right away. Love, Joe." The "love" had been inserted, with a caret, as an apparent afterthought.

If he had taken a course in how to write letters designed to infuriate the recipient, he couldn't have done better. The arrogant, demanding tone brought back all the old irritations—his bland assumption that the housework was my responsibility, his bored look while I talked about my work, his insistence that I stop whatever I was doing while he talked about his. Incredulously I remembered that once I had thought such things amusing.

III

We went to the movies that night, Kevin and I—and Roger and Bea. Roger invited himself, ignoring Bea's coughs and frowns. He seemed keen on the idea. So we all sat in a row in a little local theater whose aisles were sticky with spilled cola, and ate popcorn, and watched one of those comedies where everybody eventually goes to bed with everybody else. Afterward Roger suggested we go someplace and get a malt—it seemed to be some kind of a ritual—but we couldn't find anyplace that was open, so we went home.

That night I dreamed again, dreamed I was running down an interminable road lined with stiff-faced statues, running with stumbling, desperate speed because something was after me. I didn't dare turn to see whether it was gaining, because I knew it was too horrible to face. Just as I felt its hot breath on the back of my neck I saw Joe, and I put on a last, frantic burst of speed. But when I got to him he stepped aside, and I fell, down, down, down into darkness . . . and woke with my heart thumping and a sick taste in my mouth.

The night was hot and humid. My windows were wide open. The outside lights cast a dim glow into the room. I don't know how long I lay there, increasingly drowsy and relaxed as the nightmare faded back into the place from which it had come. I was still awake when I heard a door open and close.

Night sounds in that house were legitimate causes for alarm. I sat up in bed and listened. Nothing; but now I was tense and alert again. I knew I couldn't go back to sleep until I made sure that what I had heard had been Bea on some harmless errand. The opening door had to be hers; it was the only one close by.

When I tapped lightly on her door I got an immediate response. She was sitting on the cushioned seat that ran around the inside of the bay window.

"Did I wake you?" she asked. "I tried not to make any noise."

"I was awake. Bad dream."

"Sit down and tell me about it." Bea patted the cushion next to her.

"Thanks, but I'm okay. Just my damned subconscious whining at me. It does that all the time." But I sat down. "What are you doing up at this hour? It must be three A.M."

"I've been in the old wing," Bea said calmly. "In the hall near Kevin's room."

"For God's sake, Bea! You promised Roger—"

"I didn't promise. He demanded; I did not agree."

"Where is he?"

"Downstairs. In the chapel, I think; he has some silly theory about the place."

"Why didn't you ask me to come with you, if you were determined to go? You had no right to take such a chance."

Bea studied me thoughtfully. "Was it that bad?" I gesticulated and sputtered. She nodded. "I know it was; you tried to tell me. Odd, how difficult it is to communicate states of emotion. You forget, though, that I am the only one who had never seen anything. I was curious. I also felt we ought to keep watch every night. The manifestation may stop, or become intermittent."

"You're right," I said, after a moment of reflection. "Roger seems to have lost interest in Kevin's lady, but I ought to have kept an eye on Kevin. I'm not as brave as you. I'd rather play ostrich. If I don't see something, I can pretend it isn't there."

"Kevin never opened his door tonight," Bea said.

"Then maybe it's ended."

"Maybe."

I knew that expression—her eyelids drooping, half

hiding her eyes, the tiny muscles at the corners of her mouth taut to hold the words back.

"You did see something."

"You would say I was dreaming. Maybe I was. It was so quiet; I kept nodding off."

"Well?"

Bea shrugged. "The conventional apparition, straight out of a ghost story. Transparent and floating. It was Ethelfleda, the way I have pictured her in my mind, costume and all. But when I blinked and pinched myself, she was gone."

"My God."

"It was not frightening. And, of course," she added calmly, "not conclusive. It proves nothing."

"Promise me you won't do that again without telling me."

"I don't need your skepticism, Anne," Bea said. "I need your support. If I can't have it, wholehearted and without reservations, I don't want it."

Was that all anyone ever wanted? I wondered. Unquestioning cooperation, mindless trust? I fumbled in my weary brain for words. I couldn't give her what she asked, but by sheer instinct I found a substitute. "You have my love," I said. "Won't that do?"

We had a nice emotional session, hugging and kissing and a little crying. My mother is not a hugging woman.

Chapter Ten

As Bea had admitted, her experience didn't prove anything; it could be interpreted (and probably would be, by the parties concerned) as evidence supporting either theory—Bea's wistful, wandering spirit, or Roger's claim that the some *thing* in the house took different forms for each of us, depending on our individual predilections. On the whole, I preferred Bea's interpretation to Roger's. Only a nasty, sick subconscious could call up the ghastly vision I had seen.

Debbie turned up again the following morning. I'd overslept and decided to take a walk in the garden to clear my fuzzy brain. Somehow I happened to stroll toward the tennis court, and there they were. Her dress had even more ruffles than the other one. It was pink, with little red strawberries embroidered on it. I felt like Jane Eyre watching the brilliant and lovely Blanche flirting with Mr. Rochester.

After a while I crept away, unseen. I didn't ask myself why the sight of them together made me ache inside. Maybe I wouldn't have minded so much if she had not been my exact antithesis—rounded and curved where I was flat and angular, ruffly and pink where I was grubby and tattered, feminine and cute and birdbrained where I was . . . but why go on?

I found old Mr. Marsden spraying roses and cursing Japanese beetles. I thought they were rather attractive insects, greenly iridescent in the sunlight, but when he showed me the mangled corpse of a rosebud they had devoured I began to share his feelings. They were vulgar bugs, coupling furiously all over the bushes— no sense of modesty at all. I took up a jar with a little kerosene in it and began capturing them. They were so preoccupied with eating and sex that they were easy to catch, and I discovered a hitherto unsuspected streak of sadism as the writhing collection mounted up.

After we finished the roses, Mr. Marsden let me weed the perennial border. He wouldn't allow me to do anything more complex, though I itched to wield his neat little clippers and tie things to stakes. Even then he stood over me for fifteen minutes to make sure I was pulling up the right shoots.

I was still on my hands and knees when I heard a distant voice bellowing my name. It was a baritone voice, but I was unable to delude myself that Kevin wanted me. Roger's gravelly tones were unique.

I yelled back and went on weeding. This procedure continued for several minutes, with Roger's voice rising impatiently. When he finally located me he gave me a hard whack on the rear.

"What are you doing?" he demanded.

"What does it look like?" I sat back on my heels and deposited a handful of weeds in the basket.

"Well, stop it. Bea's been calling you for ten minutes. Lunch is ready."

"How nice of you to come in search of me."

"Kevin's girl friend is staying for lunch," Roger said, not offering his hand to help me to my feet.

"Great." I tried not to look at my earth-stained knees and the black rims under my nails.

With more tact than I would have expected, Roger ignored my spiteful tone. Or maybe he didn't even notice. "I'm going to Pittsfield after lunch," he said. "Want to come along?"

"What for?"

"I," said Roger, "need to find a library. There's something I want to look up. Bea is going to do some shopping. You may, of course, suit yourself."

"Are you hinting that you want to use my research expertise?"

"No. I would like to talk to you, if you can spare me an hour of your valuable time later this afternoon."

"I'll try to work you in," I said.

I went in to lunch just as I was, except, of course, for washing my hands and beating some of the dust out of my pants. Debbie was sweetly deferential to Bea and Roger. She took one look at me and mentally crossed me off her list; I could almost see her pretty little hand with its shiny pink nails drawing a black line through my name.

I told Roger I would be delighted to go to Pittsfield. We took the Mercedes, and he let me drive. When we got in the car I realized why he had asked me to come. Things between him and Bea were a little tense. They were so polite it was obvious they had had a falling-out about something. I assumed they had run into some snag in their romantic life; it didn't seem possible that two reasonable adults could come to blows about a subject as bizarre as what kind of ghost was haunting Grayhaven.

In this, as I was to learn, I was exceedingly naive. I ought to have known that their respective "theories" were only the tips of two enormous icebergs of habit, conviction, and belief.

Anyhow, by chatting nonstop about one thing or another, I kept a conversation of sorts going. We left the car and went our respective ways, having agreed to meet later at a coffee shop near the parking lot.

I don't remember exactly what Bea and I did. We looked at a lot of clothes, and needlework, and a craft shop. I bought a dress. I had not planned to buy a dress. However, I had gone to my room before we left and had taken fifty dollars from my emergency cash supply.

The dress cost forty-eight dollars. It wasn't the most expensive garment I had ever bought, but I had never spent that amount of money on a plain cotton sundress. It was a luscious shade of green, like lime ice, with spaghetti straps that tied on the shoulders. I won't say that Bea talked me into buying it. She didn't exactly discourage me, though.

We were twenty minutes late meeting Roger. He was sitting at a table, with an empty glass in front of him. I expected some sarcastic remark, but he was meek as a lamb.

"Have a nice time?" he inquired.

"Very nice," I said. "And you?"

The shop was almost empty. It was one of those arty places, with abstract painting on the walls and prices designed to scare away the hoi polloi. Roger put his elbows on the table and his chin in his hands. He heaved a deep sigh.

"I got what I wanted. Can we talk about it, or are you going to go on treating me like an enemy agent?"

"I have no idea what you mean," said Bea.

"I don't know how it happened," Roger said plaintively. "Maybe it's as much my fault as yours. I do tend to think of this as an abstract problem in logic—or nonlogic, if you like. But try to see it my way, Bea; it's hard for me to feel any urgency about the situation when I see that boy looking so damned healthy, and behaving as if he hadn't a care in the world except how to make time with Debbie." He broke off then and gave me a sharp look. "What are you grinning about? Oh—my archaic slang, I suppose. That isn't the term you would have used?"

"No."

"Never mind. Bea—if you take this seriously, so do I. I honestly don't believe Kevin is in imminent danger. I'm not saying the situation is good; I don't know what it is. But I want to work with you, not against you. Can't we discuss our ideas calmly and reasonably, and try to see one another's point of view?"

Bea was obviously moved by the appeal. "I don't know, Roger," she said slowly. "Our viewpoints are so far apart—"

"Then we'll find a way to bridge the gap." He took her hand. "Just talk to me; don't shut me out."

"I'll try."

It wasn't much of a response, but Roger looked relieved. "Wonderful! Can I tell you what I've been working on? In some ways it substantiates your theory," he added, with what he obviously thought was a crafty look.

The corners of Bea's mouth twitched. "Roger, you're incorrigible. All right, go on."

Roger reached under the table and brought out his briefcase. He opened it and began removing papers.

"My first subject," he began, "is the stone under the

altar. Clearly an import; the marble is foreign, probably Italian. It could have been a relic, as one of you suggested; but if that were the case, one would expect an inscription explaining its origin. Nothing of the sort was visible.

"The next clue was Ethelfleda's brass. The inscription there was peculiar, to put it mildly. No dates, no family name or parentage, and a couple of ambiguous epitaphs. I took a closer look at the presumed 'cross' she was holding, and—as I told Anne yesterday—I decided it was not a cross."

Roger paused. Having heard this much of his argument, I knew he was about to embark on the most farfetched part of it, and was trying to organize his material in the most convincing manner.

"The object in Ethelfleda's hands is a double ax. It's a very ancient religious symbol, primarily connected with Crete and the old Minoan Empire, but it is also found in England, carved on one of the monoliths of Stonehenge. The date would be around 1800 B.C.

"The Minoans worshiped a mother goddess, Mistress of Trees and Mountains, Lady of the Wild Animals. One of her symbols was the double ax, which was usually carried by priestesses—women. Some of the other symbols of the cult were the snake, the dove, and the bull.

"A number of ancient civilizations worshiped a mother goddess, who represented the fertility of nature. Often she had a male counterpart, sometimes a consort, sometimes a son, who died and was reborn, just as the new crops were born again after the bleak cold of winter."

I decided it was time to interrupt the lecture. "I see what you're getting at, Roger. The running animals in the friezes in the crypts and chapel could refer to the goddess in her role as mistress of animals. The bas-relief over the altar doesn't represent Mary and Christ, but the Great Mother and her lover, whatever his name was. But you're going too far if you expect me to believe that a prehistoric religion survived for two thousand years in a remote corner of England. And what about the bull? I thought you said that was Mithraic. Mithraism was the original male chauvinist religion; no women allowed, no female gods."

Roger scowled at me. Then he remembered he was supposed to be demonstrating open-mindedness and patience. He produced a pained smile. "I was going to work up to that gradually. Obviously I don't believe the fifteenth-century women of Grayhaven worshiped an ancient Minoan goddess. But I think the belief in a mother goddess spread farther and survived longer than we imagined. The worship of Cybele was popular in Rome years after Crete fell, and she was only another version of the same principle. The Roman legions carried her cult to England; and there, if I am right in my surmises, it met and blended with another, older branch of the same faith—one that had been brought to Britain by the craftsmen who helped build Stonehenge. The old pagan religions were still prac-ticed by the peasants for hundreds of years after Christianity became the official religion—longer, if scholars like Margaret Murray are right. She main-tained that the witch cult of the Middle Ages was a survival of the prehistoric religion, condemned as heresy by Christian priests."

"Are you saying," Bea demanded, "that the chapel is a pagan temple, dedicated to a heathen goddess?"

"No, no!" Roger chose his words carefully, watching Bea's reaction. "Remember that in the early centuries the Christian Church was marked by innumerable schisms and heresies. People had a hard time understanding the new ideas, especially when there was a superficial resemblance between Christian dogma and certain pagan cults. To an unsophisticated person, the worship of the Virgin and her resurrected Son might seem—well, it might seem to have something in common with the ancient faith of the mother goddess and her dying, yet immortal consort. Such a worshiper might see nothing wrong with assimilating the two, just as Cybele had been identified with another, older mother goddess. By recent times the old ideas had been forgotten; I'm sure your chapel has been an orthodox, respectable place of Christian worship for centuries. But—and this is my point— for millennia before that, it had been a focus of genuine, fervent faith in a higher being. There may have been a crude little temple on that spot two thousand years before Christ. I would be the last to deny the power of such faith; in fact, it's the basis of my theory."

He stopped, his eyes fixed on Bea like those of a dog that hopes for a bone, but rather expects a kick.

"About that bull—" I said.

"Shut up," Roger said. "Bea?"

"You're awfully long-winded," she said. "Do you always lecture at such length?"

She was smiling. Roger let out a long, exaggerated sigh. "Then I haven't offended you?"

"We are not all so narrow-minded and ignorant as you suppose."

"I never said—"

"However," Bea went on, "I think you're stretching things. You haven't any proof of the transitions you mentioned."

"It's only a theory," Roger said humbly.

"You haven't explained the bull," I said.

"Oh, damn the bull." From the mass of papers on the table he extracted an eight-by-ten photographic print. It was a copy of the relief on the stone under the altar. He passed it to Bea, who examined it with interest.

"That confused me at first," Roger said modestly. "As you observed, Anne, the sacrifice of a bull was a ritual of Mithraism, and that sure as hell didn't fit my picture of a mother-goddess religion. Then I remembered something. I found the reference today." He picked up another paper and read aloud.

" 'The taurobolium—bathing in the blood of a bull caught in a solemn ritual hunt—at first may have been a rite effective in itself and not attached to a particular deity. By the second century A.D., in the western empire, it was connected with Cybele, among others.' Ha," he added.

"Clever man," I said.

Roger ignored me. "Don't you see, Bea, we're working along the same lines. The centuries of worship in and around that house have permeated the very stones and produced a spiritual energy field that still operates. I don't believe it is evil or dangerous in itself, but such manifestations can be harmful if they are misunderstood. That's why—"

"We are not working along the same lines," Bea said. "How can we? It is Kevin's soul I fear for. How can you help me save it if you don't believe it exists?"

II

Can a woman who believes in the immortality of
the soul find happiness with a heretic? I would have
considered that a ludicrous question before I saw
those two in action. But their discussion did clear the
air in a way; they argued, but at least they talked. They
talked all the way home. I couldn't have gotten a word
in if I had wanted to.

Roger's theory was seductive. I loved the way all the
pieces fit neatly together. Even little things—the
behavior of the pets, for instance. Naturally they
would feel comfortable with the Mistress of the Wild
Animals. And She, patroness of fertility and the
simple, uncomplicated mating of all species, would be
more than willing to accommodate her unconscious
worshiper with a suitable partner.

It might even explain why I was beginning to lust
after Kevin.

Yes, I liked Roger's theory. Not that it was any more
sensible than Bea's belief in ghosts, but it *sounded*
more scientific. We liberal-arts majors are always
impressed by science.

I pondered these things as I drove and paid no
attention to the conversation in the back seat until
Roger nudged me.

"Well, what do you think?"

"About what?"

"About telling Kevin some of our discoveries.
Haven't you been listening?"

"Kevin is a worshiper of the mother goddess," I
said. "Wild, free, healthily lecherous." Catching a
glimpse of Roger's exasperated face in the rear-view
mirror, I said, "Oh, hell, how should I know? My

opinion, for what it is worth, is that we keep him out of this. I don't believe in sticking my hand into a hole when there might be a snake inside."

"All right, we agree," Roger said. "We ought to monitor his room, however, particularly at night. I'll set up a camera and a tape recorder, if I'm not on the spot at the witching hour."

"A tape recorder—of course," I said. "That would be an objective witness. Why the hell didn't you think of that before, Roger?"

"Mine was busted," Roger said.

III

Kevin was in the library, so deeply absorbed in his book that he didn't hear me enter. The animals were with him—Belle in her favorite place at his feet, Amy sprawled on the rug, all long legs and floppy ears, the cats lying around at respectful distances from one another. It was almost time for them to be fed. They were waiting for Kevin to move; then they would converge on him, making suggestive noises about din-din. Yet after Roger's lecture, the scene had an almost heraldic significance: the animals at peace in the sanctuary of the Lady, the young priest lost in meditation, but ready to serve.

I must have made some sound, deep in my throat. Kevin looked up. "Hi, there. Did you have a good—"

"No," I said. "I mean . . . excuse me, I forgot something."

It took me a while to find Roger. I finally ran him to earth in the chapel, where he was looking under the pews, flashlight in hand.

"I've got to talk to you," I gasped.

"Sure." Roger made a courtly gesture toward one of the pews. I shied back.

"Not here. Let's go outside."

We found a bench in the perennial garden. Columbines the color of morning sky danced in the breeze.

"What's up?" Roger asked. "You look worried."

I pressed my hands to my head. "It doesn't seem so inevitable out here . . . I just saw Kevin, with all the animals around him. Roger, that hokey ancient religion you were talking about—you said the goddess had a male counterpart."

I had to listen to a passionate speech about today's ignorant, untaught youth. "Even you must have heard of Osiris," he went on. "One of the dying gods whose resurrection symbolized the new crops. His mating with the Mother—"

"There was a book," I interrupted. *The King Must Die.*

"Yes; well, that was an element of some of the cults. The king represented the dying god; his blood fertilized the land he ruled and brought good fortune to his people. Murray believed that the god of the witches was a survival of this old belief. He had to be sacrificed periodically to ensure—"

"Kevin," I said. "What about Kevin?"

Roger's eyes bulged. "My God—are you suggesting—"

"You were the one who suggested it. Are you trying to tell me you didn't remember that aspect of the good old religion? It follows, inevitably, if your crazy idea is right."

"Wait a minute—calm down. Let me think." Roger brooded, his expression increasingly grim.

"I have now got a theory of my own," I said.

"You have definitely captured my attention," Roger said. "Go on."

"What if the old religion is still being practiced, here in the neighborhood? There are a couple of covens of 'witches' at the university; people are dabbling in black magic and weird cults, mostly for erotic kicks, but in part because modern skepticism has left them groping for something to believe in. Kevin was here alone for a couple of weeks before I arrived. Plenty of time for them to contact and convert him. They may be using drugs." In my mind's eye I saw Kevin's face as he caressed his invisible lover—rapt, luminous. "Drugs and hypnotism," I went on, increasingly convinced. "And—well, things like that. Damn it, Roger, if you were looking for a young male god, you couldn't find a better specimen than Kevin. What if all this has a factual explanation, and the phenomena we've seen were tricks, produced by human agents?"

"Hmmm." Roger scratched his head. "You have shaken me, Annie, I admit it. I won't ask you *how* such phenomena could have been produced; I've read enough about fake spiritualist tricks to know that almost anything is possible. But I do have one question. They? Who, for God's sake? You can't drag in a new character at this point; the villain must be someone we know, someone who has access to the house."

"But there are lots of people we don't know well," I argued. "How about Dr. Garst? A physician could get drugs. His chubby niece could be part of the plot, she's the type who would be turned on by a little black magic. Even Debbie . . . All right, smile! You can't dismiss people as harmless just because they are stupid and look like soap-opera characters."

"I wasn't smiling; I was grimacing. I am well aware of the fact that some of the most accomplished mass murderers of all time have been sweet little old ladies or ineffectual men. But I can't see Garst as the mastermind. Damn it, he's too straight. It wouldn't surprise me to learn that he has his private vices, but I doubt they are as original as the one you suggest."

"There are other possibilities."

"Aha," Roger said softly. "I wondered whether you would come out with it. A man who is an antiquarian by inclination, with a morbid interest in outré cults; someone who pointedly sought your acquaintance and has managed to worm his way into the house."

"Huh?" I stared at him. "You? You make a good case, Roger, but I wasn't thinking of you. I was thinking of Father Stephen."

"Steve?" For an instant his face mirrored my surprise. Then he threw his head back and howled with laughter.

After a while I got up and started to walk away. Roger caught my wrist and dragged me down onto the bench. "Wait," he gasped. "Give me a minute. Sorry, I couldn't help it."

"I don't think it's funny."

"You're right." Roger mastered his amusement. "The situation isn't funny, but to think of Steve in a goatskin and horns, performing a Black Mass . . . You don't know him."

"Maybe you don't either."

"Maybe not. I have lived long enough to realize that we can never be one hundred percent certain about anybody. I would stake my life on Steve's sanity and saintliness; but there are forms of mental illness, brain tumors . . . For the sake of argument I'd have to agree that he must be considered." Roger thought a minute, and added, "Rather him than me, if it comes to that. I'm flattered you didn't consider me."

"Oh, I haven't eliminated you," I assured him. "You think I may be right, then?"

"*May* is the word, Annie. You've made a strong case, but remember that none of my equipment has given us any evidence of trickery. The cameras ought to have caught someone—if there had been someone to catch."

"Maybe they weren't in the right place at the right time."

"A hit, a palpable hit. Hmmm. It's going to be difficult covering all the possible means of entrance to the house—"

"But what about Kevin, in the meantime? He could be in deadly danger—not his soul, whatever that may be, but his life. We've got to do something fast."

"The only theory that puts Kevin in imminent danger is Bea's," Roger said. "Even that isn't really imminent; Kevin is young and healthy, he shouldn't be in danger of damnation for decades to come. As for your idea, and mine—you haven't convinced me completely, Annie, not by a damn sight—take comfort in the thought that the old religion has specific timetables and major festivals, like the Christian Church. One of them has already passed—Midsummer Eve, which is in June. The next big one isn't till fall."

"Hallowe'en?"

"All Hallows Eve. Nothing is going to happen to Kevin before then—if then. So we have plenty of time."

"I wish," I said, "that didn't have such an ominous ring to it—like in the category of famous last words."

IV

Roger went trotting off to rearrange his gadgets. He looked depressed. He might not be convinced, but his hope of getting a story with which to dazzle his friends and rivals in the Society for Psychic Research had been shaken. In his way he was as superstitious as Bea.

So now we had three theories—four, if you considered Father Stephen's hints about diabolic possession as distinct from Bea's—and nothing to prove or disprove any of them. I began to wonder how many scholarly reconstructions were based on equally tenuous proofs.

I returned to the library, but Kevin was gone, and so were the animals. The kitchen was the logical place to look next; they were all there, the pets busily munching, and Kevin perched on a stool eating carrot sticks almost as fast as Bea cut them. I covertly examined his bare brown arms for needlemarks. Their absence didn't prove anything, of course.

"Find it?" Kevin asked.

"What?"

"Whatever it was you forgot."

"Oh. Yeah, I found it."

Kevin offered me a carrot. "Speaking of forgetting, Father Stephen called earlier," he said to Bea. "He sounded urgent."

"You might have told me," Bea exclaimed. She put down the knife and wiped her hands on her apron.

"I forgot," Kevin said placidly.

Bea left the room. Kevin continued to crunch. After a while he said, "You doing anything particular tomorrow?"

"No, nothing in particular."

"We might try to get some work done."

"That would be a change."

"Don't blame it all on me. Seems as if I hardly see you anymore. I hope you're enjoying yourself."

His tone was not sarcastic, only mildly reproachful and a little weary. "I wasn't complaining," he added. "I'm sorry I haven't been a good host."

"That wasn't the deal, Kevin. I'm not complaining either."

"It's been a peculiar summer," Kevin said, half to himself.

"Are you all right?" I asked tentatively. "Feeling all right, I mean?"

"I haven't been sleeping too well lately. Probably the weather; my room doesn't get much ventilation, that damned balcony cuts off the breeze. I guess maybe I'm going through some kind of agonizing reappraisal, that's why I feel so confused. All my ideas and plans are screwed up."

"Do you want to talk about it?"

"I was hoping you'd ask," Kevin said with a grin. "I hate friends who dump on me, but I love to be the one doing the dumping. It's just so damned hard to get any privacy around here. How long is Roger planning to stay?"

I had been wondering myself. "I don't know," I said. "It isn't up to me to ask."

"Nor me; his being here is no skin off my nose, and I guess it's nice for Aunt Bea. You think they have something going?"

"Would you mind if they did?"

"Hell, no. She deserves some fun after old Harry. I wouldn't have thought Roger was her type, but it's none of my business. Tomorrow okay with you, then?"

"Fine. Oh, and Kevin—if your room is too hot at night, why don't you change?"

"I might at that."

I didn't press it. Bea returned, trailed by Roger. They were deep in another argument.

"Why can't I go?" he demanded. "Steve won't mind; he and I—"

"Because I don't want you," Bea said. "Kevin, if you don't stop eating those carrots, I'll have to cut a whole new batch."

"But you hate to drive at night," Roger persisted. "And it looks like rain."

"I can manage. It's only a few miles."

"At least take Annie."

Bea considered the suggestion. Behind her back, Roger winked and gestured at me. I knew what he wanted—a spy in the other camp. Well, I was curious myself.

"I'll be glad to," I said.

"Thank you, dear."

We had drinks and snacks on the patio. Roger couldn't take his eyes off Kevin. His stare was so unblinking that Kevin began to squirm. "What's the matter, am I sprouting horns or something?" he demanded.

"No, in fact you look fine," Roger said. "Better than

you did when I first met you. Tanned, sleek, bulging with muscle—"

"You make me sound like a prize bull," Kevin complained.

"Uh," Roger said, startled. "I only meant you look—er—healthy. Are you doing anything in particular—exercises, yoga, vitamins?"

He was as subtle as a sledgehammer. I wanted to kick him. But Kevin didn't seem to find the question out of line. Men do take their muscles so seriously.

"It must be Aunt Bea's cooking," he said with a smile. "Of course I've been swimming and playing tennis every day. Daily exercise is a good idea; you ought to swim, Roger, it's the best activity for a man your age; no strain on the heart."

Which was one up for Kevin. Roger looked a little annoyed.

When dinner was over we left the men to do the dishes and Bea went upstairs to get her white gloves. It was still light when we drove off; the long, lovely shadows of evening were quiet on the grass, but Roger's prediction of rain looked more likely. Huge thunderheads, bloodstained by the sunset, pressed down on the ridge.

"What is Roger up to?" Bea asked suddenly.

"What do you mean?"

"Those questions about Kevin's health. Roger is as transparent as a child. I know you're on his side, Anne, not on mine, but I thought—"

"Hey!" I turned to her. With a peremptory gesture she indicated that I should keep my eyes on the road. "I'm not on anybody's side," I protested. "I'm trying to keep an open mind."

"Then do you have any objection to telling me what

is behind Roger's sudden interest in Kevin's physical condition?"

"It has nothing to do with his theory," I said honestly.

"All right, if you won't tell me I must respect your reticence. Can I assume you will treat my confidences the same way, and not go blabbing to Roger?"

"Bea, I wish you and Roger wouldn't act like this."

"It is unfair to you," Bea said, more mildly. "The one in the middle is in an uncomfortable spot."

"I don't mind that; I just wish you weren't at odds."

"You are passing the parsonage," Bea said. "Again."

Father Stephen was pounding away at his typewriter when his housekeeper showed us in. He put his work aside and offered us chairs.

"I apologize for being so mysterious over the telephone," he said to Bea. "But I wanted to talk to you in person."

Bea waved his apologies aside. The gesture verged on brusqueness, and proved to me that she was much more nervous about the interview than she had pretended to be. I braced myself for another argument, with me in the middle, as usual.

"First," Father Stephen began, "I must tell you, Anne, that I was able after all to obtain an answer to your question."

I had almost forgotten my interest in Ethelfleda. Roger's theory and my own modification had replaced her. "Ethelfleda's ashes?" I asked.

"We don't know what remains," Father Stephen said, "and I hope we never will. However, the contents of the house removed to Pennsylvania by Mr. Karnovsky included three lead coffins. Presumably the other occupants of the crypt had possessed less durable caskets, of which nothing solid remained."

He waited for a comment. None was forthcoming, so he went on, in a more casual voice, "It was pure luck that I was able to learn so much. The relevant papers are, as we surmised, now in the possession of Mr. Blacklock. Presumably they were deposited with his lawyer, or man of business. They included an inventory of the objects in the house, based on the shipping lists drawn up for Mr. Karnovsky. I might add that this filled a thick folio volume.

"After Jack had told me this, I was about to give up when an idea occurred to me." He sighed and shook his head, but there was a suspicion of a smile on his mouth. "I discovered I have a regrettable gift for duplicity. Without actually lying to Jack, I told him that my friend, Mrs. Blacklock's sister, was somewhat disturbed to think that people were actually buried in the house. We chuckled over your fear of ghosts, Bea—I hope you'll forgive me. At any rate, Jack admitted he had looked through the inventory. Naturally he had been amused and intrigued by the bizarre transaction. He distinctly remembers the coffins, because they struck an even more bizarre note. I believe we can depend on his memory."

"Bizarre is not strong enough," I said. "What kind of people were the Mandevilles, to sell their ancestors? That's really despicable."

"They were not Mandeville ancestors," Father Stephen said. "And some people, my dear, will sell anything. What surprises me is how Mr. Karnovsky obtained permission to transport human remains. But I suppose anything can be done with money."

"Yeah," I said.

"Now that your curiosity is satisfied, we can forget that matter. I really wanted to see you, Bea, to ask if you have reconsidered my suggestion. Wait—before you answer, I must tell you something I neglected to mention the other day, when I described my conversation with Miss Marion. Her—er—delusion had a name. She referred to it as 'Edmund.'"

Again he waited expectantly. Again he got nothing from us but blank stares.

"Think what that could mean," he said urgently. "I spent an hour this morning talking—no, let me use the right word—gossiping with Frances, my housekeeper. If there is anything she doesn't know about the residents of these parts, living and dead, I would be surprised. She assures me that no one of that name had even been connected with Miss Marion."

"Even neighborhood gossips miss things," I said. "Maybe he was someone she met when she was away at school, or on vacation. It could even be a character in a book or movie. When I was twelve I had a terrible crush on D'Artagnan."

"Possibly. But I seem to recall that one of the Mandeville sons was named Edmund."

"That is correct," Bea said reluctantly. "He was shot. A hunting accident."

"Oh? One is entitled, I think, to wonder about that convenient verdict."

"Father," I said, "I hope you'll excuse me for saying this, but don't you think we have a superfluity of ghosts?"

"I couldn't agree more." He treated me to one of those charming smiles that relieved the austerity of his features. "I won't press the point, but I do suggest that steps be taken to eliminate whatever influence is at work."

Bea shook her head. "I can't give permission for an exorcism."

"My dear Bea, I've no intention of charging into the house with bell, book, and candle. I couldn't if I wanted to; an exorcism cannot be performed without the Bishop's permission, and believe me, that is not lightly granted. All I am suggesting is a small private service of prayer and meditation."

"Well, I suppose it couldn't do any harm."

"Excellent." Father Stephen pounced on this equivocal permission. "Then shall we say tomorrow afternoon? Or would evening be better?"

"You don't want Kevin to attend, do you?" I asked. "He's usually around during the day."

"Yes, it had better be evening," Bea agreed. "Kevin is taking that young woman somewhere tomorrow night. A dinner theater, I believe he said. *She* invited *him.*"

The stress she placed on the pronouns demonstrated her opinion of forward young women who pursued reluctant young men. She might be right at that. Kevin appeared to have cooled toward Debbie recently.

"Fine," Father Stephen said. "When may I come?"

"Come for dinner," Bea said. "We'll eat early—as soon as Kevin leaves. I'll call you."

A few lurid streaks of dying sun broke the blackness of the clouds in the western sky when we emerged from the parsonage. The breeze had died and the air was breathlessly hot.

"You don't approve of Father Stephen's suggestion," I said, since it was clear that Bea didn't intend to initiate a conversation. "Why not?"

"All I can refer to are my feelings, my instincts," Bea said. "But you won't think that they are important."

I was strangely hurt when she said that. I hunched down over the wheel and stared straight ahead. After a few moments Bea said, "I'm used to working out problems alone, Anne. I haven't had people to talk to. Will you promise not to tell Roger?"

"If you want it that way."

"It has to be that way. If you won't give me your word, I won't tell you. But I confess I would like someone with me when I do what I mean to do."

I felt like the White Rabbit in *Alice*. Oh, dear, oh, dear—oh, my fur and whiskers! What was the nice, silly woman up to now? I had a nasty suspicion. And if I was right, it was imperative that I be allowed to take part.

"All right, I promise," I said, with a sigh. "What is it, a séance? That's Roger's bag, Bea, not yours. Remember Saul and the Witch of Endor. Remember—"

"I have no intention of engaging in any such irreverent performance," Bea said coldly. Then, with a sudden change of tone, she exclaimed, "All I want to do is reach out to her, to reassure and comfort. I shall be armed with prayer and love."

"You must expect some danger, or you wouldn't want my company," I grumbled.

"I'm aware of the possibility of self-hypnosis, even of hysteria. I want you for two reasons, Anne. First as a witness. Second, to interfere if anything goes wrong.

You'll be in charge. I'll stop the minute you tell me to."

I rolled my eyes despairingly. Never would I cease to be amazed at people. Bea's project was the oddest blend of mysticism and common sense, of childish Sunday-school Christianity and practical precaution. At least she had wits enough to acknowledge some of the perils. Obviously I couldn't let her tackle something like that alone. My sensible, down-to-earth mother substitute had some weak streaks that might, under stress, start a landslide.

"All right," I said gruffly.

"And you won't tell Roger?"

"No." He would beat me to a pulp if he knew I was letting her do this.

"I can't tell you how much I appreciate it," Bea said, as if she were thanking me for helping with the dishes. "It will have to be late, after midnight, to avoid interruption. The question is, where? Kevin's room would be ideal, but how are we to get him out of it?"

I hesitated. Then I thought disgustedly, what the hell; in for a penny, in for a pound. I said, "Kevin was entertaining the idea of changing rooms when I talked to him earlier. His is too hot."

"Perfect. I wonder why I didn't think of that. He should not be sleeping in that room anyway."

But she was quite ready to have us sit there and invite someone—or some thing—to drop in on us. I began to think everybody was crazy but me—and I wasn't all that sure about myself.

Chapter Eleven

I HAD BEEN a little uneasy about how Kevin and Roger would get along without us. They weren't exactly bosom buddies. We found them in companionable tête-à-tête in our usual corner of the library. A chessboard lay on the table between them, but it had been pushed aside. The space was filled with a familiar jumble of books and papers.

"Back so soon?" Roger said.

"Obviously," I said, craning my neck to get a look at the books.

Roger anticipated me. "We've been talking about the prehistoric remains in the house. Kevin agrees that there is strong evidence for the existence of some ancient cult."

I heard Bea catch her breath. I was so angry that for a minute I literally saw red. Kevin gave me an uncertain smile. He sensed I was furious and didn't know why. I felt an overwhelming rush of sympathy and protectiveness. They were using him, both of them—oh, sure, with the best intentions in the world, but quite selfishly, for their own ends and their own private duel.

Roger was making odd little grimaces meant to

assure me that I needn't worry—he had been the soul of tact, Kevin was fine, no damage had been done. From Bea's expression I knew she shared my anger. But she was just as bad; it hadn't occurred to her that Kevin might profit from a change in rooms until she needed the room herself.

It hadn't occurred to me, either.

So I swallowed my gorge and took a seat, and tried to talk about the chess game. The others weren't having any of that. Even Bea was curious to hear Kevin's views on ancient religion.

"I like the idea of Ethelfleda being a priestess of the mother goddess," he said with a smile. "No, Roger, I'll buy your taurobolium—I never heard of it, but I'll take your word for it. The rest is a little farfetched, don't you think?"

"Exactly," Bea said, before Roger could answer. "I'm glad you agree with me, Kevin."

"Wait a minute," Kevin said. "I don't disagree with Roger, I'm simply not convinced. It's an interesting idea. I read Murray's books years ago, and I would say she makes a reasonable case for the survival of some elements of a prehistoric cult."

After that the conversation became technical and dull, to me, anyway. Kevin had done more reading than I, and proved a good foil for Roger, who, as I might have expected, lost sight of the main point of the discussion. They rambled on about druidism and nature gods and vegetation spirits for some time. It was almost eleven when Bea, who was as bored as I, made her move.

"Goodness, it's hot tonight! I wish the storm would break. My room will be cool, though—those nice big windows."

"Uh-huh," said Roger. "It has been suggested that

the Roman intolerance toward the druids was more political than religious. The archdruid—"

"What about something cold to drink?" Bea said. Now *she* was making gestures at me. I interpreted them correctly.

"That sounds good," I cried. "Hey, Kevin, didn't you say something about changing rooms? This would be a good night to do it. I'll bet your bedroom is like an oven."

My rotten acting got through to Roger, who stopped babbling about the archdruid. Kevin looked at me in mild surprise. "Maybe I will," he said.

"I'll give you a hand," said Roger, who had had time to think the idea over.

"What do you mean, give me a hand? I'm not going to move my stuff, I'll just sleep elsewhere till the weather breaks."

"The tower room at the end of my corridor has windows all around," Bea said eagerly. "I could put sheets on the bed in five minutes."

Kevin was looking at us oddly, so I reverted to the burning question of cold drinks, and offered to help Bea. She refused, but Roger took the hint and the subject of where Kevin would sleep that night was dropped. We had our drinks and a snack. Then Bea rolled up her needlework.

"I'll make that bed for you, Kevin," she said.

"We'll do it together." Stifling a yawn, Kevin got lazily to his feet. "I feel as if I could sleep tonight. Must be the heat that makes me so groggy."

After they had gone I lingered long enough to ask Roger about his plans for the night. Instead of answering he gave me a suspicious look. "Who had the bright idea of suggesting that Kevin change rooms?"

"I'm surprised we didn't think of it before," I said glibly. "We ought to find out whether the—the thing follows Kevin or is confined to his room."

"I thought you were concerned about someone human getting to him."

"The accesses to his new room are a lot easier to watch. The corridor is brighter and more populated, and there is only one stair."

"What about stairs in the tower?"

"I don't know. The tower room on that level is a bedroom, obviously; but I don't remember what is underneath, or whether there is a separate stair. That's a little job for you."

"I'll have to go outside, and look for a door," Roger grumbled; but I could see the prospect rather interested him.

"Watch out for the burglar alarm."

"I'll take care of it. Let's see, if I put one camera in the hall and another one—"

"Good night," I said.

I hadn't been in my room five minutes before Bea slipped in. She was wearing a nightgown and robe, and suggested I follow her example. "In case we are caught out of our rooms," she explained.

"You make this sound like a boarding-school frolic," I muttered, pulling my shirt over my head. "Are you sure you want to go through with this? Maybe Kevin will stop . . . dreaming when he's sleeping somewhere else."

"You don't believe that, and neither do I."

We crept down the hall like a pair of burglars, pausing at the head of the stair to listen, and then tiptoeing on. Kevin's room looked harmless enough. A couple of shirts tossed carelessly over the back of a chair and a pile of books on the bedside table suggested that the occupant had just stepped out for a minute.

"I hope he doesn't come back for a book or something," I said uneasily, as Bea drew a table out into the middle of the floor and pulled up a couple of chairs.

"He won't come back."

"What makes you so— Bea! You didn't!"

"I couldn't risk his walking in on us. Sit here, Anne."

"You drugged him!"

"What a terrible thing to say! I just gave him the sleeping pills the doctor prescribed for me when I was having a bad time. I didn't take many of them. I don't like drugs."

"You don't like . . . My God."

"They are very mild."

"But you don't know what else . . . How many did you give him? The same dosage that was prescribed for you?"

Bea's eyes shifted. "It's by body weight. He's larger than I am. Anne, stop fussing. A good night's sleep will do him good. Now if you sit here, and I sit across from you, we can watch both the windows and the door."

I dropped into the chair she indicated and watched her incredulously as she moved around the room, drawing the heavy draperies over the French doors and arranging a silk scarf around the bedside lamp, which she carried to the table. Then she pressed the light switch. I heard her footsteps move toward me, and a dim glow appeared, garishly crimsoned by the scarf she had placed over the lamp. Her face looked like something out of a horror movie, all red skin and black shadows and a gleam of eyeballs.

"Sit still and don't talk." she said quietly. "I think we had better hold hands. Would you like to take notes?"

"What with, my toes?"

Bea sighed patiently. "Make jokes if it helps you feel more comfortable. We'll hold one hand—one hand each—goodness, you know what I mean. It's impossible to form a circle with only two people, but contact may help."

For someone who scorned the shoddy devices of spiritualism, she was awfully well informed about the techniques. I thought of pointing out that holding hands—two hands each—would ensure that neither of us was playing tricks, but decided that was the least of my worries. She was right; I had to make smart remarks, if only to myself, in order to keep from howling. I was scared.

We sat in silence for a long time. My eyes gradually adjusted to the dim light. Bea held a pencil in her free hand; her head was bowed. I had heard of automatic writing; I told myself that if the pencil started to move I would put an end to the proceedings. Her hand in mine was soft and cool and relaxed. Her breathing was even. So far, so good, I assured myself.

There were all kinds of weird noises in the room. Though the windows were closed, the approaching storm brought a breeze that slid slyly through various cracks and made the draperies rustle. It was extremely hot, and the red light increased the impression that I had landed in one of the less popular regions of the universe. My physical discomfort increased to a point where I forgot about being frightened. Surreptitiously I wiped perspiration from my streaming face with my free hand.

After a while I realized I wasn't perspiring as

heavily. The temperature in the room was almost comfortable—cool, in fact. Cool and steadily growing colder. Bea lifted her head. The fingers of the hand I was holding tightened on mine.

I felt as if I were going to die, and that is not a figure of speech. My lungs deflated, and the blood started roaring along my veins.

The figure was dim and utterly transparent, like a painting on a thin sheet of plastic. Either it shone with a faint light of its own making, or I saw it with some other sense than vision, for though it wavered slightly, as if a breeze stirred the surface on which it was painted, I could make out every detail—the long robe of rich forest green bordered with fur, the jeweled belt, fastened high under the breasts, the sparkle of tiny gems netting the hair. The face was not so clear. But I think the eyes were blue.

Bea was muttering in a low, quick voice. I couldn't hear all she said, there was still a roaring in my head, like the sound you get when you press a seashell to your ear, but I caught a few phrases.

". . . many mansions . . . in him is no darkness at all . . . commend to thy fatherly goodness all those who are in any way afflicted . . . when two or three are gathered together in thy Name . . ."

Then she pulled her hand from mine, folded hers, and bowed her head. Her voice came stronger. "O God the Creator and Preserver of all mankind, we humbly beseech thee for all sorts and conditions of men . . ."

She went from that, whatever it was, to the Apostles' Creed and the Lord's Prayer; and the transparent shape wavered and swayed more strongly. With the last "Amen" it was gone. It didn't fade, it just vanished. A long, shaken sigh died into silence.

After a moment, Bea took the scarf from the lamp. Her eyes were shining. Shimmering trails of dampness streaked her cheeks. It might have been perspiration. Once again the room was as hot as a pizza oven.

I tried to think of something to say that would not be banal or anticlimactic. I couldn't. So I cleared my throat and inquired, "Can we go now?"

"If you like," Bea said quietly. "It's done—finished."

"It is?"

"Can't you feel it? It was wonderful—the sense of peace, of rest." She wiped her eyes with a handkerchief; Bea would, of course, have a clean handkerchief. "I shouldn't cry," she went on. "It was so beautiful. I'm so happy."

"I'm glad to hear that."

"But my poor Anne." She gave me a quick hug. "I suppose you were frightened. I'm sorry, darling. But I'm glad you were here, to help me and to bear witness. Come along and I'll tuck you into bed. Would you like a cup of tea?"

The combination of tea and spiritual comfort was almost too much for my nerves. "No tea," I said, swallowing. "Thanks just the same."

Bea refused to tiptoe on the way back. She swept down the hall like a saint on her way to glory. She wouldn't have minded meeting Roger; she was dying to tell him of her triumph. We didn't see him, though. I refused another offer of tea and finally saw her door close behind her.

I stood in my own doorway listening to the silence. I felt the same relief that follows recovery from the flu; I knew the worst was over, but every muscle in my body was limp.

Of all the things I had seen thus far, the ghost lady

was the most easily explicable. I could even visualize how it might have been produced. What I couldn't understand was how anyone could have known of our plans. The only time we had discussed them was when we were alone in the car.

But that was not what kept me hovering uneasily in my open doorway, unwilling to collapse into bed. I had been frightened during the performance, I had to admit that. Now I was still frightened—of Bea. Terms like "Jesus freak" and "religious fanatic" came to my mind, together with fear of the spiritual arrogance that dared to fight the devil for the salvation of a damned soul. Oh, I was overreacting, and I knew it even then; but I couldn't forget her calm admission that she had slipped Kevin a Mickey. She had not heard my theory about drugs and hypnotism, but she was well aware that he might be unstable. How could she have done such a thing?

I knew I couldn't go to bed until I made sure Kevin was all right.

I think I closed my door, but I'm not sure. The tower room was beyond Bea's at the end of the hall. My feet were bare. They made no sound.

I opened his door without knocking. The windows were wide open, and the curtains were lashing in the wind. The temperature had dropped. The cool air felt good on my damp skin. The bed was one of the big, high-postered affairs with a heavy canopy. In its shadow I could see the outlines of Kevin's body. I could not hear him breathe.

I called his name, and when I got no response I started shaking him. His head flopped around on the pillow like the head of a rag doll. I put my ear against his bare chest. It moved up and down with his breathing. His heart was beating. I was so relieved I stayed there, listening to that lovely, regular throb, feeling the smooth warm skin against my cheek.

After a while he stirred. He made a funny, sleepy little sound, and then he said "Anne." Just that, just my name, not even questioning. His arms went around me and pulled me down against him.

II

Kevin was still asleep when I left next morning. I stood looking down at him, thinking the thoughts loving and tender women are supposed to think at such times—how young he looked, how defenseless and innocent. Actually, he did. His lips were sweetly curved and his face was calm.

I pulled the sheet over him. The air was brisk and fresh. Apparently it had rained during the night. I hadn't heard it. I wouldn't have heard a tornado.

Roger and Bea were in the kitchen when I went downstairs. I could hear raised voices some distance away; and when I caught the phrase "painted on thin plastic" from Roger, I knew what they were talking about. When I entered, he turned on me, happy to have some other object on which to vent his spleen.

"Damn it, Anne, why didn't you tell me about this harebrained scheme of Bea's? You had no right—"

"I'm tired of being Watson," I said, getting a cup and saucer from the cupboard. "I resign."

"Don't take it out on her," Bea said. "I insisted that she give me her word before I told her of my plans. You ought to thank her, Roger. If you want to scream at someone, scream at me."

"My darling girl, I don't want to scream at you. I was worried, that's all. It was a damned risky thing to do."

"According to you, the apparition was only a cheap trick," Bea said. "What was the risk in that? Not that I agree," she added.

"You had to be there," I said vaguely.

"All right," Roger said, cultivating self-control with such effort that the veins on his forehead bulged. "Let's hear your version, Anne."

So I obliged; but I was sufficiently annoyed with his masterful manner to conclude with an analysis that anticipated his objections.

"It could have been faked—paint on some flimsy, transparent substance, or even a film projection. I noticed a distinct drop in temperature." Roger's lips parted, and I hastened to add, "But shock and fear can make people feel colder, can't they? I was certainly frightened, but there was no aura of frightfulness about the apparition itself."

"Quite the opposite," Bea said in a low voice. "It was gentle and troubled."

"A totally subjective reaction," Roger said.

I threw up my hands. "Every damned reaction is subjective, Roger. We haven't got a thing, except a few fuzzy snapshots, that could be regarded as objective. Unless you got something last night?"

Roger shook his head. "In deference to your theory I strung trip threads across the top of the stairs when I came up, high enough to avoid the animals. They were unbroken this morning. The tape recorder I set up on the balcony outside Kevin's former room got nothing. There is a door into the tower, on the ground level, but

I checked it, and if it has been opened in the last twenty years I'll retire from the ghost-hunting business. The hinges are rusted solid and the cracks are stuffed with dust. If something got to Kevin last night—"

"Nothing got to Kevin last night," I said. I thought for a minute. "At least, nothing you need to know about."

Bea flushed. She might have been shocked. I hoped she was ashamed, remembering the sleeping pills.

"It would have saved me some effort if you had condescended to tell me you planned to spend the night with Kevin," Roger said irritably. "All that time I spent stringing threads—"

"I didn't plan to."

"Well, in the future kindly let me know."

"I'll be damned if I will. I'm not mounting a rescue expedition, Roger."

"You ought to. If—"

"Roger." Bea's voice was very quiet, but it shut Roger up. The look he gave me promised I hadn't heard the last of the subject, though.

"What would you like for breakfast, Anne?" Bea asked. "You need something more solid than coffee, after—" Then she blushed again as she realized that her reference could be misinterpreted—and probably would be, by Roger. Her expression was so sheepish I had a hard time holding my anger. Hadn't Roger said, in reference to Father Stephen, that he was sound on all subjects save one? Bea was sound too, until her religious beliefs got mixed up with her emotions. Nobody is perfect.

But I refused her offer of breakfast, saying I wanted

to get some work done that morning. There was no future in sitting around listening to the two of them bicker; we were still where we had been all along, entwined in nets of conflicting belief, with nothing solid to stand on. My main reason for escaping, however, was that I wasn't ready to face Kevin, especially in the presence of those two. I was shy. It sounds ridiculous, but it's true.

So I had my desk and a pile of books as a barricade when he came into the library. We stared at one another. Then Kevin said, "'Morning."

"Good morning."

"Nice day."

"It rained last night," I said.

"Did it?"

The corners of my mouth started to twitch. We both laughed.

"I didn't dream it, then," Kevin said. He added hastily, "That's a stupid thing to say. I just mean . . . it was an outstanding dream."

I didn't mind. It was a personal tribute to me that I had managed to keep him awake as long as I had. Bea must have given him a handful of those damned pills. Before and after he had slept as if hit over the head with a hammer.

"It was outstanding for me too," I said.

"I'm glad. I don't seem to remember much about it." Kevin slapped his forehead. "Wow. I am really not at my best this morning."

"You're doing all right. Feel like getting some work done?"

Kevin slumped into a chair. He took my hand and ran his fingernail lightly down the back of it, tracing the lines of the tendons. "I'd rather review last night.

Maybe we ought to practice it again, to make sure I got it right the first time."

"Show-off."

"The trouble is . . ." Kevin glanced over his shoulder and lowered his voice. "I feel as if I'm living in a commune. How long is Roger going to hang around?"

"Why don't you ask him?"

"I don't want Aunt Bea to think her friends aren't welcome."

"You don't like him, do you?"

"Oh, I don't know." Kevin continued to stroke my hand. "There's something about him. I guess he's not my type."

"I hope not."

Kevin grinned. "Want to go out someplace tonight? A drive-in movie, maybe, or . . . Oh, hell, I forgot. I'm supposed to go to some stupid dinner theater with that stupid blonde."

I tried not to look smug, but I probably did not succeed. Kevin said, "I'll get out of it. Tell her I've got the plague or something."

"You can't do that at the last minute. It would be rude. Besides, she's liable to rush over here bearing flowers and chicken soup."

"She might at that. Oh, hell. What am I going to do?"

"Go, of course."

"You don't mind?"

I only hesitated for a second. "Of course I mind. I'd like to scratch her eyes out. I'd like to choke her with her own ruffled panties. I'd like—"

"This?" His long hard fingers curved around the back of my head and pulled my face to meet his.

If Roger had been three seconds later, I wouldn't

have been aware of his arrival. As it was, I had time to slide back in my chair and pick up a book before he walked in. Roger's matter-of-fact acceptance of Kevin's and my new relationship was easier to take than Bea's embarrassment, but I was in no mood for wisecracks or knowing looks.

"Oh, there you are, Kevin," Roger said briskly. "Do you mind if I look through those cupboards upstairs, at the end of the gallery? You could give me a hand if you have nothing better to do."

"We're trying to work," I said.

"Oh, sorry. Go right ahead; I won't make any noise."

Whereupon he proceeded to thunder up the iron staircase. Kevin grimaced at me. "Later?" he muttered.

"Later." I knew what was bugging him, and it wasn't the irresistible lure of my beautiful self. Poor boy, he really had been zonked out the night before; he had a vague feeling that perhaps his performance had been substandard, and he was anxious to show me what he could do when he was up to par. I was a little curious myself.

We worked conscientiously and sedately for the rest of the morning, and there was pleasure in that, too, for our minds fit together as excellently as our bodies had. There was a constant background noise from Roger up above—a series of bumps and rustles, enlivened by an occasional crash and a vehement "Damn!" when Roger dropped something. Then Bea called us to lunch, and afterward Kevin suggested a swim. Roger said that was a great idea. He went upstairs to change, and Kevin made a series of hideous faces at me behind Bea's back.

"You were the one who told him he needed exercise," I pointed out.

He didn't have much stamina, though; it was not long before he retired, announcing loudly that he had lots of work to do in the library. I need not say that neither of us responded to the hint. We spent the next few hours in one of the most romantic spots I've ever seen—certainly it was the most romantic spot in which I have ever been made love to. (Churchill was right; when you have something important to say, don't worry about prepositions.) It was a little glade in a remote part of the grounds, with weeping-willow and cherry trees curtaining a tiny artificial pool. The shaded ground was carpeted with thick green moss, and the sifted sunlight quivered like quicksilver. The naked marble nymph in the pool might have been the innocent Eve of that little paradise. That afternoon was the best, the high point. Sometimes I think it is a mistake to achieve perfection. Everything else is necessarily an anticlimax.

We went back to the house hand in hand. It was like walking from sunlight into evening; all the petty worries and concerns of ordinary living piled up on my shoulders. I actually caught myself wondering what Bea would say. She had once hinted that she wouldn't mind having me as a niece-in-law, but she might not approve of this development.

We had whiled away more hours in dalliance than we had supposed. By tacit consent we entered the house through the courtyard, avoiding the kitchen where Bea was likely to be found. In the library, being entertained by Roger, was Debbie. Her shining waterfall of golden hair rippled as she turned to greet us.

"Good God," Kevin exclaimed. "Is it that late?"

"I'm a little early," Debbie said. Her eyes were furious, but her face and voice were sweetly apologetic.

"I'll be ready in ten minutes," Kevin promised. "Have a drink—think up names to call me—I'll be right back."

He crossed the room at a run, moving lightly. Debbie's eyes followed him. You could see she couldn't help herself. I felt a twinge of unwilling sympathy. But I felt awkward, too; I suspected that the back of my shirt was stained green.

"Want something to drink, Annie?" Roger asked.

"I've got to change. Nice to have seen you, Debbie. Have a fun evening."

I can be sweet and conventional too—when I'm winning.

Kevin was occupying the bathroom on our corridor, so I went down the hall and bathed in the Roman sarcophagus. I took my time. I wanted them to be gone when I came down. I don't really enjoy sadism.

I had, believe it or not, forgotten what was planned for that evening. When I found Bea setting the table in the small dining room, using delicate china and crystal that rang when she touched it, I started to ask why we weren't eating in the kitchen as usual.

"Give me a hand, will you, Anne?" she said, without looking at me. "Father Stephen will be here soon. We're running a little late."

I don't think she meant the last sentence as a reproach. But she was stiff and ill at ease. I fetched the silver she wanted from a little mahogany chest, and folded damask napkins. When the table was done to her satisfaction, I asked if I could help in the kitchen.

"It's all done," Bea said, with that same hint of underlying criticism. "You run along. You might answer the door when he rings; we're having cocktails in the courtyard."

I looked back as I left the room. She was unfolding the napkins I had fixed and doing them again.

Father Stephen had already arrived. Roger had let him in and taken him to the library. I found them deep in one of their friendly arguments, with Roger waving documents at his adversary.

"I tell you, we are missing some vital papers," he insisted. "I found a footnote in the Mandeville genealogy mentioning material that concerned the early history of the house. The pompous ass didn't use it; he was only interested in his own smug, stupid family. But it must be somewhere here."

"Keep still for a minute, Roger," Father Stephen interrupted. "I want to say hello to Anne. You look very nice this evening, my dear. Not that you don't always look nice."

We were still exchanging compliments when Bea came in. Another round of civilities followed, and Bea herded us out to the courtyard. Belle was already there, sprawled on her side in a patch of sunlight. She opened an interested eye when Bea brought out a tray of cheese.

"How she can lie in that hot sun I don't know," Bea said, with the air of one determinedly making polite conversation.

Father Stephen smiled at the old dog as she ambled toward him, her tail wagging. "Old people and animals appreciate warmth. She probably has arthritis. Do you mind?" He held up a piece of cheese.

"Everyone slips her snacks," I said. "Even Roger."

"I resent the implication," Roger said. "I like dogs. Shows what a nice fellow I am. Is that enough small talk, Bea? We had better get down to business, or we won't finish before Kevin gets back. I suppose he'll be home early, won't he, Anne?"

"He didn't say."

"Have you two had a fight already? This business with Debbie—"

"Really, Roger!"

"Oh, come on, Bea, this is important. Kevin is our main concern, isn't he? I don't give a damn about what he and Anne are doing—except that I hope they are enjoying it."

He grinned at me, and I was tempted to stick out my tongue at him and his damned patronizing amusement, but of course I didn't. After a quick glance at Bea's pink face, Father Stephen said, "Wait a minute, Roger, you're getting me confused. Let someone else talk for a change. Anne, have there been any new developments that I ought to know about?"

That beautiful display of tact was primarily for Bea's benefit. Father Stephen must have known I had no intention of suppressing anything; in fact he may have assumed all along that Kevin and I were sleeping together.

"Kevin changed rooms last night," I said.

"An excellent idea. I should have suggested it myself."

"Yes, we all wondered why it hadn't occurred to us before," I said grimly. "We keep talking about our concern for Kevin, but we've been sickeningly negligent; we should have kept watch every night." I hesitated, but only for a moment. "I was with Kevin from about two o'clock on. I can't swear that nothing happened before I got there, but I don't believe it did."

"I see." Father Stephen nodded coolly. "So he may indeed have benefited from the change to another room. We can't be sure, however; there are too many other—er—factors involved. You are absolutely correct, Anne; we have not been sufficiently concerned with Kevin's well-being. Is there anything else?"

Again I hesitated, cursing myself for failing to arrange my thoughts in advance. I didn't want them to think I was ashamed of having been with Kevin, but there were so many things I couldn't mention without betraying Bea's confidence. She was not going to help me. Her eyes avoided mine; her hands were tightly clasped. She had told Roger about the séance, but not about the sleeping pills. Father Stephen didn't know about either. Well, I thought, it's up to her.

"There is something else," I said. "Did Roger explain his idea about a prehistoric cult?"

"Yes, he told me about it before you came in. He also mentioned your suggestion." From the gleam of amusement in his eyes I knew Roger had not omitted my suspicions of various people. I gave Roger a hard stare.

"I hope Roger also mentioned that I was just tossing ideas around. I didn't really believe—"

"No apologies are necessary, Anne. I don't know whose ingenuity to admire more, yours or Roger's. In fact, your neatly woven plot makes better sense than his."

"Do you mean—"

"Good heavens, no. I would be the last to deny that such groups do exist, but I'm sure nothing of the sort is happening here." He glanced at Roger and added, in the blandest possible voice, "If I thought our quiet little community harbored a witchcult, I'd assume Roger must be the head of the coven."

Grinning, Roger raised his glass in salute.

"Witch cult? What are you talking about?" Bea asked.

"Just one of Annie's harebrained ideas," Roger said. "I had a chance to talk to that little blond nitwit before you and Kevin came in, Anne. She hasn't a thought in her mind except to drag Kevin to the altar. I understand she will be graduating next year, and at her college a girl who hasn't got a ring on her finger by June is a failure."

"Kevin is quite a catch," I said. "Young, good-looking, rich, intelligent, gentle, kind—"

My voice cracked. It surprised me as much as it did the others. I turned my head away.

"It's all right, Anne," Bea said. "Really it is. Let me speak now. I was going to tell him anyway."

The offer sounded nobler than it really was. She must have known Roger would spill the beans if she didn't; and she did not mention the sleeping pills.

I thought Father Stephen would be horrified. He just looked tired. The lines on his face deepened as Bea spoke, and when she had finished he shook his head wearily.

"I wish you had not done that. I warned you."

"I can't see that it did any harm," Bea said.

I said bitterly, " 'The last temptation is the greatest treason: To do the right deed for the wrong reason.' "

Father Stephen glanced at me with a slight smile. "That's Eliot, isn't it? He's always pithy. But this was not the right deed. Never mind, Bea; we'll discuss it another time."

"You still want to go ahead with your ceremony?" Roger asked.

"I cannot accept Bea's story as conclusive evidence."

"We agree on that, anyhow," Roger said. "But exorcism—"

"Confound it, Roger; how many times must I repeat this? I cannot conduct an exorcism without a license from the Bishop, and I can't apply for that without Bea's permission."

"It might be interesting at that," Roger murmured. "I've read about the procedure, but I've never seen it done. I can't see why Christian ritual and symbolism would affect something that never respected them in the first place."

"You're missing the point, Roger." Father Stephen leaned forward, intent on the argument. "Did you read about the church in Mildenhall, England, which was closed recently because it was possessed by the spirits of pre-Christian devil worshipers?"

Roger laughed. "Yes, I saw the article in the paper. The vicar believed the church was built on the site of a pagan temple, where virgins were sacrificed. You people get so uptight about virgins—"

"But isn't that precisely what you claim happened here?"

"I don't know about the virgins. In that particular case exorcism didn't help, did it?"

They went on sniping at one another all through

dinner, and my annoyance continued to mount. They were old friends, they enjoyed their debates, but they had no right to discuss the subject as if it were another exercise in rhetoric.

Bea said very little. We exchanged only a few words as we cleared the table, leaving the men to continue their discussion. Then we all went to the chapel.

III

The window over the altar faced west. That evening it glowed as gloriously as the finest modern stained glass, a blend of bright copper and gold. Framed within its wide rectangle, a towering mass of pearly clouds might have been an impressionist rendering of the celestial city.

Bea closed the heavy oak doors. Even Roger seemed subdued, though it may have been regard for Bea rather than the golden silence that affected him. Father Stephen was . . . taller. Larger in every way. He didn't look at us, or speak; he started slowly down the aisle. Bea slipped into a nearby pew. We sat in a row, like children in an old-fashioned school. Bea bowed her head and folded her hands. Roger sat bolt upright, his arms at his sides. I fell into the uneasy slump that is my stupid compromise when I'm forced to attend a church service—head down, eyes fixed on my knees.

Father Stephen stood with his back to us, his head raised. He was contemplating the sunset, or the carved relief on the wall under the window, I couldn't tell which.

When he began to speak his voice was so soft I could not hear all the words. I guess it was one of the conventional prayers. Bea's voice joined his in an equally inaudible murmur.

After the initial prayer he spoke more clearly, and I recognized much of the substance—it was almost all from the Bible, various Psalms and quotations from the Gospels, especially Luke. He had turned to face us. The setting sun gave his silvery hair a glowing nimbus. His voice was even more impressive than his appearance—low but distinct, investing the beautiful old phrases with a deeper meaning and a melodic music. As his quiet voice went on, I started to feel sleepy—not surprising, after my eventful night and busy day. Calmed and at peace, my mind wandered, remembering the moss-carpeted glade with its veils of green boughs. The memories didn't seem irreverent; they were in perfect harmony with the soft voice that spoke of love and mercy and kindness.

The light went out, as suddenly as if a curtain had been drawn or a switch pressed down. Startled, I looked up and saw that the western window was black with storm clouds. The room was so dark I could hardly see. Father Stephen had changed from a silver-haloed saint to a dark, featureless shadow, identifiable only by his voice. He finished the sentence he had begun in the same calm tone, and then fell silent. After a moment a point of light sprang up and multiplied. He was lighting the candles on the altar table. The flames were like tiny folded hands; but the illumination seemed weak and frail compared to the tempest-darkened skies. When Father Stephen turned, his long black shadow leaped and quivered, a mocking distortion of the human form. Lightning bisected the high windows. For an instant every object in the chapel shone with a lurid glow.

A thunderstorm at that time of year was not unusual. Sometimes they came on with astonishing suddenness. But in this case my normal dislike of such phenomena was intensified by the uncanny impression of struggle between the great impersonal Forces without and the single small human figure whose quiet voice was increasingly drowned out by the roll of heavenly kettledrums. Between thunderclaps the rain provided a pounding, persistent counterpoint.

When the storm was at its loudest, Father Stephen got down to cases. He began to pray for all the dwellers in this house, for all those who had suffered and were troubled in spirit. In a brief—very brief—lull in the thunder, I caught the name of Edmund Mandeville.

Participating in Bea's séance had not been fun, but this was worse. I felt as if I were on a battlefield, right next to the commanding general, and that all the enemy cannon were trained on him. A hit, or a near miss, would blow me to smithereens. Yet after a time I began to think that maybe our side was winning. The rain slowed to a drizzle, the thunder died; the western window paled to a lighter gray. Father Stephen's voice rose in triumph. "As smoke is driven away, so drive them away; as wax—"

The next clap of thunder bellowed like a bomb going off. The candle flames, which had burned steadily in that solidly insulated room, danced wildly. A second crash, like an echo, literally shook the floor. And this one, unlike the first, had come from within the room.

I leaped to my feet and banged into Roger, who was trying to push past me. Before we could untangle ourselves, Bea snapped, "Sit down, both of you!"

Her command was repeated, in an equally forceful tone, by Father Stephen. "Be calm; there's nothing to be afraid of. Pray with me—yes, Roger, you too. 'The Lord is my Shepherd. . . .'"

I suppose he picked that one because he hoped even the heathen among us would know it. Which we did. If there is anything in the Bible, aside from the Lord's Prayer, that is part of our universal heritage, it is the Twenty-third Psalm. Psychologically the choice was sound. There are no more reassuring words. Except for that part about the Valley of Death.

And as his voice rolled smoothly on, the storm passed. "Surely goodness and mercy . . ." brought light to the western window; and "the house of the Lord forever" called out a ray of pale sunshine.

The Psalm concluded, Father Stephen made a final sotto-voce appeal to the altar. I glanced at Roger. He looked like a gargoyle, his lower lip protruding, his cheeks bulging with repressed exclamation. Finally he could hold them in no longer.

"I'll be damned! Look at that."

Bea's breath hissed out between her teeth. Father Stephen paid no attention, but I think he cut his final prayer short, knowing Roger wouldn't keep quiet much longer. As soon as he turned, Roger bounced up, shoved past my knees, and erupted into the aisle. I had never imagined that Bea's pretty features could look so malevolent. The look she threw at Roger's retreating back should have burned a hole between his shoulder blades.

Father Stephen met his old friend/enemy in front of

the altar. It was not until then that I realized what had prompted Roger's impious exclamation. The relief of the mother and son—whichever mother and son—was no longer on the wall.

I joined the men, who were staring at something behind the altar. The slab of stone with the relief leaned against the wall at a slight angle, with the sculptured face still visible. Apparently it had slid straight down, striking with a force that produced the second crash, but had not fallen face down because the edge of the altar table had tilted it backward. I looked up at the wall. The stone had been supported by four metal brackets, two above and two below. The two lower supports had snapped. The jagged pieces remaining were red with rust. No doubt—oh, no doubt at all—the vibration of the last clap of thunder had finally broken the worn metal.

Roger was the first to speak. "Not bad, Steve, not bad at all. I don't know how you conjured up the storm, but it couldn't have been more suitable."

"Oh, I don't know," Father Stephen said calmly. "If I ever preached on hellfire and damnation—which I don't—such an accompaniment would be perfect. I'd have preferred something a little less theatrical on this occasion."

"Anyhow, you prayed the heathen image out of its socket," Roger said, with genuine admiration. "Who the hell is Edmund Mandeville?"

The last was too much for Bea. Rigid with fury, she rose to her feet. "Thank you, Father," she said. "Won't you come to my sitting room? I'm sure you could use a cup of tea."

"We'll be right there," said Roger, to her retreating form. "Come on, Steve, who was Edmund?"

Father Stephen explained as we walked toward the door. Roger kept making gruff sounds indicating incredulity. Not that Father Stephen claimed he had gotten to the root of the trouble; in fact, he scoffed at the suggestion that the fall of the carving had anything to do with his service. "That's childish," he said. "God may work in mysterious ways, but He doesn't throw pieces of scenery around for effect."

I had to agree with that. In fact, we were getting too damned many effects. The someone, or something, in the house seemed almost too willing to oblige our ignorant efforts.

Chapter Twelve

DURING THE FOLLOWING DAYS I began to think that I had underestimated Father Stephen's spiritual influence, or Bea's much-maligned séance. Something appeared to have done the trick, for one day followed another in peaceful sequence, without the slightest disturbance. They were halcyon days, days of wine and roses, heavenly days that cannot die, salad days (for I *was* green in judgment), red-letter days, a time full of sweet days and roses.

There is a special tang in hours spent with someone who shares not only your emotions but your interests —someone you love *and* like. Obscure references and professional jokes don't have to be explained, they are caught and tossed back, weaving an ever-strengthening web of closeness. When Kevin was moved to quote "My mistress' eyes are nothing like the sun; Coral is far more red than her lips' red; If snow be white, why then her breasts are dun. . . ." I could cap it with "Everything that grows, Holds in perfection but a little moment." When he came up with a juicy suggestion from his beloved Restoration dramatists, I could dredge up something equally licentious and literary from Donne. Kevin enjoyed it too.

Not all women melt when they are wooed with Shakespearean sonnets.

The other relationship didn't develop so well. The day after the ceremony in the chapel, Roger told Kevin he was leaving.

"Was it something I said?" Kevin asked, trying not to smile too broadly.

"I didn't mean to impose so long," Roger said. "Thanks for everything."

"I trust this is not farewell forever," I said—for of course I was with Kevin. I usually was.

"Oh, right," Kevin said. "Drop in anytime."

"I would like to use the library now and then, if you don't mind. I could start on the cataloging."

Kevin said sure, and offered to help Roger carry his stuff to the car. Roger refused. I guess even Kevin would have wondered if he had lifted those suitcases, with their load of cameras and equipment.

It was not hard to figure that Roger had been given his congé by Bea. She wasn't happy with me and Kevin either. She had had a long session with Father Stephen at the parsonage, and had returned looking as if she had been crying. I assumed she had confessed to him about giving Kevin sleeping pills. Undoubtedly he had scolded her for that, and no doubt spiritual arrogance and materialism had also been mentioned. For all his gentleness, I wouldn't have wanted to be on the receiving end of one of Father Stephen's lectures. She went moping around the house for several days, and finally I decided to take steps. I was so happy I wanted everybody else to be happy too. Except perhaps Debbie.

I ran Bea down in the kitchen while she was getting dinner. She had been cooking huge elaborate meals that nobody wanted; some women do that, I am told, when they are feeling sorry for themselves. She refused my offer of help, so I sat myself firmly in a chair and asked straight out what was the matter.

"Something has gone wrong between you and Roger. I know it's none of my business, but I can't keep my nose out of the affairs of people I care about."

Once again, by instinct, I chose the right words. They pricked her smooth defensive surface as a pin breaks a balloon. She slumped, the knife with which she had been boning chicken dangling from her hand.

"It's easier for you," she muttered.

I had some idea of what her problem was, so her comment made more sense than it might otherwise have done. "Maybe so," I agreed. "But you're an adult, you have no responsibilities to anyone but yourself."

"Those are the only responsibilities that matter." She looked at me. The misery in her face shocked me into silence. "My principles may seem stupid to you, but they are important to me. I can't violate the beliefs of a lifetime without suffering."

I had thought I understood. I realized that I had understood only with my mind. My heart and my gut couldn't understand, couldn't agree. At least I had sense enough not to argue with her. Logic never convinces the heart. I tried to find a way out, one she could accept.

"If you are going to be married—"

I hit the wrong note that time. Bea jerked back as if I had voiced an obscenity. "Married! I couldn't marry Roger. Oh, he asked me. . . ." And, despite her genuine grief, there was a hint of complacency in the last sentence.

"But I thought—"

"Anne, you don't realize the state I was in when I came here. I hope I hid it successfully; I don't approve of inflicting one's private miseries on others. Those tasteless jokes I made about Harry—that wasn't me, that was a frightened woman whistling in the dark to keep from crying. I—I actually hated Harry, toward the end; yet I felt helpless and terrified without him, as if someone had knocked down the walls of my house and stripped off my clothes and left me shivering in a blizzard. The walls might have been ramshackle and the clothing threadbare; but they were protection of a sort, do you see? Then to come here, to find affection and warmth and comfort—I began to feel I could make something of life after all. Roger gave me something to lean on, his admiration made me bloom. I'll never relish independence, Anne. I need someone. Roger has strength, humor, tenderness."

"It sounds to me as if you're in love with him."

"I love him," Bea said, with a shrug.

"Then what's your problem? Is it—I mean, do you feel as if marrying Roger would be—like adultery?"

"That sounds utter foolishness to you, doesn't it? But I believed the vows I took, Anne. 'What God has joined together . . .' Only," she added, with a faint smile, "I didn't enjoy being joined together with Harry."

"What did Father Stephen say?"

"You're a sly one, aren't you? Yes, I confessed my doubts to him; he told me they were unreasonable. But how can I live with a man who jeers at everything I believe? I know I can't change him; people don't change other people, they can only change themselves. And that's not easy. I do love Roger. But—"

"Isn't love the most important thing?"

The most beautiful look of compassion spread over Bea's face. "My poor child," she said. "Of course it isn't."

II

We talked for a while longer. Bea thanked me for encouraging her to let it all hang out—she put the phrase in verbal quotation marks. The conversation cleared the air between us, but it brought home to me the fact that we couldn't ever really understand one another. She had thrown Roger out of her life because he didn't believe in the Trinity or the loving kindness of God. . . . I found myself thinking, "Poor old Roger," which was not a sentiment I had ever expected to feel.

Roger had not given up hope. He turned up from time to time. Occasionally I saw him in the library, but not often; I didn't spend many hours there. Kevin and I were out of doors most of the time. The weather was perfect. The farmers began complaining about the lack of rain; but I didn't care about the farmers. Inside the house matters went as smoothly as they did outside. The nights were as wonderful as the days.

Paradise has no clocks and no calendar. I don't remember how long I enjoyed my personal Eden before the serpent slithered back into it, in the person of Roger. But it wasn't long. Not nearly long enough.

One day I wandered into the library in search of some light reading and heard noises upstairs, in the gallery. I called, "Who's there?" and got a grotesque, upside-down view of Roger's head peering over the rail.

"Annie? Stay there."

I hate being called Annie. I wondered why I had let Roger get away with it so long, and was about to express my sentiments when he came rumbling down the spiral staircase. One look and I forgot my complaints.

I hadn't seen him for several days. He looked terrible. He had lost weight, especially in the face, and his jowls sagged like those of a sick old man.

"I want to talk to you," he said.

"Go ahead."

"Not here." He glanced nervously over his shoulder. "Can you tear yourself away for an hour or so without telling the others where you're going?"

"Certainly." I resented the implication. "That is, if you can give me one good reason why I should."

"You think it's all over, don't you? Well, it's not. I could tell you things. . . ." He broke off, with a repetition of that hunted look. Stains of sleeplessness circled his eyes. His rapid, muttering voice and his changed manner alarmed me. I took a step back. His hand shot out and clamped over my wrist. "No, don't go. Promise you'll meet me."

"All right. When and where?"

"This afternoon."

"I can't. Kevin and I are—"

"Kevin and you. That's what I was afraid of." Then the tight lines around his mouth relaxed, and he produced a fair imitation of a smile. "You look terrified, Annie. Don't worry, I'm not cracking up. When can you get away?"

"Tomorrow morning? I'm not sure what time. I'll come to your place if you're going to be home."

"I'll make a point of it." Only then did he release

his hold on my arm. "Don't let me down, Annie. It's important."

Without waiting for an answer, he trotted back up the stairs. I picked up my book and left the room. I was trying to think what I could tell Kevin in the morning. A shopping trip? He might offer to come along. I could say I had a headache. . . . Then it struck me as wrong that I should have to invent excuses to get an hour by myself.

III

I solved the problem by getting up and out early, before Kevin was awake. I was tempted to leave him a note, and then I got mad at myself for considering such a demonstration of servility. I didn't expect him to account to me for the way he spent his time; why should he expect it of me?

The keys to the cars and the doors of the house were kept on a board in the kitchen. I snagged the keys of Kevin's car, the old Vega he had been driving as long as I had known him. For some reason the Mercedes struck a wrong note.

Early as it was, Roger was expecting me. The door opened before I could knock. I was about to commend his habits when I realized, from his haggard face, that he had not been to bed at all.

"What did you tell him?" was his first question.

"I didn't tell him anything. Why should I?"

"Okay, okay. Come in the dining room. I've been working in there."

"I want some coffee," I said. "And you'd better have some too. You look like hell, Roger."

"Charming as always." He passed his hand over his unshaven chin. "I feel like hell, if you want to know."

"You might try eating now and then, and sleeping a few hours every night."

It wasn't hard to find the kitchen; the house was tiny, with only two rooms on the ground floor, separated by a minuscule hall. The kitchen and pantry had been stuck on to the house behind the dining room. It would have been a cute little place, furnished tastefully with antiques, if it had not been in such a state of neglect. The furniture was dull with dust, and the floor had not been swept for over a week. The kitchen sink was piled with dirty dishes. I had to wash two cups and saucers; there were no clean ones in the cupboard.

Roger's pathetic appearance had aroused the good old maternal instinct, and pity had replaced my vexation. All the world loves a lover. I was more inclined to sympathize with his point of view than with Bea's, anyway. So I ignored his grumpy remarks and made him sit down and eat some toast. The bread was the only thing in the kitchen I would have fed to a dog. Everything in the refrigerator had mold on it, and the egg I broke smelled like a skunk.

"That was a good idea," he admitted, after he had finished the toast.

"You ought to know better. Men have died and the worms have eaten them, but not—"

"For love? Humph. That's part of my complaint, Annie, but not all. If I can settle this business and prove to Bea that she's been wrong from the start—"

"Oh, swell. That's the way to win her heart."

"I don't want any smart advice from you, kid. I've been around a lot longer than you have."

"And you have an experience of women which

extends over many nations and three separate continents."

Roger grinned reluctantly. "I didn't know you read anything as lowbrow as Sherlock Holmes."

"I have been known, on occasion, to sink as low as Agatha Christie. Seriously, Roger, you've changed so much—"

"So have you."

"Me?"

"Look at you." With his thumb and forefinger, fastidiously, as if he touched something dirty, Roger lifted my forearm. "You're getting fat."

He had a knack of saying things in the most insulting way possible. But he wasn't altogether wrong. Fat I would not be for a long time, but the arm we were both examining with such absurd interest was not the bony stick it once had been.

"It isn't just your figure," Roger said. "Your face, your mind, all of you—smug, stupidly sleek and well groomed, like one of those repulsive show cats that's not expected to do anything but lie around and look handsome."

"I take it there is some point to what you are saying—or is this the time for insult practice?" I inquired coldly.

"Most women wouldn't consider that an insult," said Roger, insultingly. "You didn't used to be so damned sensitive. Oh, hell, let's get on with it. Come in the other room."

Bea would have fainted at the sight of the dining room. I took a dirty shirt and a book and a plate off one of the chairs and sat down. "Well?"

Roger sorted through a pile of papers and took out

two photographs, which he tossed at me. "I took these last night."

"You were in the house last night?"

"I have my methods, Watson. And I'll kill you if you tell anybody. Have a look."

He didn't have to tell me where the photos had been taken. I recognized the terrain—the narrow, low-ceilinged corridor, the closed doors, the carved chest. Both photos also showed the luminous column of light with which I was only too familiar.

I threw the pictures onto the table. "You faked them. To give yourself an excuse to come back."

"You'd like to believe that," Roger said. "But you know better. It didn't work, Annie—neither Bea's sweet, stupid exercise nor Steve's prayers. The thing is still there."

"Who cares, so long as it doesn't bother anybody?"

"That's not all," Roger said. "The best is yet to come. Cast your optics over this."

The document he handed me was so charming that for a moment I forgot concern in sheer pleasure. Its age was evident from the tiny cracks that marred the stiff fabric, which was probably vellum or parchment rather than paper. The sheet was of considerable size, a foot wide by some eighteen inches long. Covering the surface were a series of miniature drawings of human figures, male and female, interspersed with blocks of writing in a neat hand. Pictures and writing were connected by curving lines.

"It's a genealogy," I said.

"They would have called it a pedigree. Can you read the names?"

"No. It must be in Latin; I can't make any of it out.

Aren't they cute? This little man is wearing armor. And look at the headdress on the woman next to him, it—"

Roger made an emphatic sound of disgust. "Cute! Pay attention. The writing isn't Latin, but I admit the script is difficult. Look here." His finger jabbed the page. "'The said Anne, daughter and heir to Lord Richard de Cotehaye, married Henry Lovell.' The drawings are presumably portraits of Anne and Henry. Underneath are their two daughters and their son."

"Lovell. Wasn't that one of the names—"

"They owned the house from about thirteen hundred—when Richard Lovell married the daughter of the previous owner—to 1485, when their descendant was killed at Bosworth. Here he is, at the bottom."

The small, delicately drawn face looked mournful, as if it had a premonition of its fate.

"Look at the names." Again Roger's forefinger stabbed the sheet. "Anne, Katherine, Elizabeth, Margaret. Typical of the times, named after popular saints and reigning monarchs. Now . . ." He jerked the parchment from my hand. I let out a cry of protest.

"Roger, that must be valuable. You'll tear it. Does Kevin know you made off with this?"

"He doesn't even know it exists. I found it in a box at the back of one of the cupboards. Here."

This time the sheet of paper he shoved under my nose was more legible, though Roger's handwriting was not at its best in this transcription.

"This is the genealogy of the Romers, who acquired the house in 1485. I had a devil of a time putting it together, from various documents and books, but it's accurate. Again, note the names of the women. Elizabeth, Mary, Frances . . ."

"Why don't you just tell me what you're getting at? It will save time."

"And you have so little of that to spare," Roger said, a curious twist disfiguring his mouth. "All right. I am now an expert on a number of subjects I never expected to give a damn about, including ornamental brasses. That type of incised metal work on tombs started around the end of the thirteenth century and continued into the early sixteen hundreds. The name aroused my suspicion from the first; it's a Saxon name, and has no business on a stone which, on stylistic grounds, probably dates from the fifteenth century."

"Name? What name?"

"Ethelfleda. Damn it, Anne, concentrate on what I'm saying. You've seen the list of women who lived in that house between thirteen hundred and sixteen hundred. None of them had that name. There never was any such person."

IV

Maybe Roger had been right about my brain being stupid and sleek. The gears had rusted; it took a while to get them started.

"Then Bea's ghost—"

"You can't have a ghost without first having had a body. I took another look at that brass the other night. There is no mistake about the name. Why would the

Lovells put up a monument to someone who never existed?"

"A remote ancestress," I hazarded wildly. "A saint or holy woman—"

"There may have been a Saint Ethelfleda," Roger conceded. "The calendar of saints is excessively over-loaded, and some of the English saints have weird names. But this is a funerary monument we're talking about, not a memorial. It won't wash, Anne. If—"

I pushed my chair back and stood up. "If, always if! You and your stupid theories! Drop it, Roger. And stop breaking into the house. One of these fine nights Kevin will catch you in the act and beat you to a pulp."

"Are you going to tell him?" Roger asked. His voice was almost disinterested.

"Well . . ."

"I'd rather you didn't."

If he had demanded or threatened, or even pleaded. . . . But that dead, flat voice got to me.

"Just don't do it again."

"Hmm," said Roger.

Which was about as firm a nonpromise as anyone could make.

It's no wonder I was on edge that night. I kept starting at imagined noises, and finally Kevin said in mingled amusement and exasperation, "What's bugging you? You look like a bird, cocking its head and listening for cats."

So I turned my attention to the matter at hand. I ought to have known Roger wouldn't risk anything so soon after talking to me; he couldn't be sure I would not squeal to Kevin. He waited until the next night before making his move—and it was almost the last one he ever made.

V

A couple of mildly ironic incidents marked the day—the ghosts of our pasts, Kevin's and mine, coming back to haunt us.

The first was a call from Debbie. I happened to be in the hall when the telephone rang, and I almost dropped the instrument when I recognized her voice. I said I would fetch Kevin. She said no, that was all right; she would just as soon talk to me.

That had an ominous ring to it, and I braced myself for a little auditory scene—reproaches, tears, accusations. Instead the small, polite voice said, "I'm leaving tomorrow; I just wanted to thank Mrs. Jones for her hospitality and say good-bye to all of you."

"Oh—well—that's nice. I'll tell Bea you called. I'm sure she would join me in saying good luck next year and all that sort of thing."

"I suppose you'll be going back to teaching soon."

I didn't answer at first. I was trying to calculate. How long had it been since I looked at a calendar or read a newspaper? Classes started around the end of August. Faculty was supposed to be there a few days early, especially the serfs like me.

"I suppose I will," I said slowly.

"Have a good year."

"Thanks. Are you sure you don't want to talk to Kevin?"

"That won't be necessary." Her laugh had a tinny,

mechanical quality; voices over the telephone often do. "Say good-bye for me, and thank him."

After I had hung up I stood motionless, thinking about the conversation. There is something to be said for good breeding and good manners, I guess. The girl was in love with Kevin. I had seen the way her eyes followed him, with that blank stupid expression that is the surest sign of infatuation. But she had class enough to retreat without a fight when she knew she had lost.

But the worst shock had been her reminder of the passage of time. I had no idea of the date, but it had to be around the end of July—maybe even August. I ought to go home for a few days before classes started. I had arranged to have my apartment back on August 15, so I could finish cleaning and settling in before I took up the academic load. One more week—two, at the most.

The thought was like a heavy, dark blanket dropped over my mind. I was almost as perturbed at my perturbation as at the idea itself. I had known from the first that I would only be here a few months. It had been a heavenly summer—with one or two exceptions—much better than I had expected or deserved. Kevin would be going back too; our relationship would continue. So why did I feel as if my dog had died?

The answer wasn't hard to find. I was afraid of losing Kevin. We had made no commitments. Once he was back among the adoring English majors, he might not be interested in Little Orphan Annie, even if she had put on a few pounds and gotten a haircut. So I went in search of him. I wasn't going to try to pin him down, or anything like that. I just wanted to see him.

He had been looking for me—or so he said. We went for a walk. Usually we ended up in the glade, but not always; sometimes it was enough just being together, talking and touching.

I stopped now and then as we walked through the rose garden to knock Japanese beetles off the flowers. They were bad this year; Mr. Marsden was barely holding his own, for all his sprays and dusts and traps.

Kevin picked a rose for me, one of the dark crimson ones that deepen into black at the base of the petals, and started to make a pretty speech, but he stuck himself on a thorn and the compliment turned into a curse. I tucked the rose behind my ear—my dress had no buttonholes—and reflected that only love could present a crimson rose to a redheaded woman.

"What's the date?" I asked.

Kevin removed his wounded thumb from his mouth and looked thoughtful. "August first?"

"That sounds like a wild guess."

"August second, then. Why, do you have bills due?"

"Probably. I usually do. Do you realize that we have to be back in a few weeks? I am going to hate to leave."

Kevin took my hand. We walked on in silence for a while.

"You don't have to leave, Anne."

"Maybe your mother would hire me as a scullery maid."

"I'm not joking."

He stopped in front of a carved stone bench. A Japanese maple shaded it, the delicate sharp leaves as precisely cut as carvings in jade and carnelian.

"I've been wanting to talk to you," Kevin went on. "Let's sit down."

"Oh, is it going to be that kind of a talk?" The light

tone I had intended didn't come off. My breath was too fast, and my heart had picked up its beat.

"Why do you do that?" Kevin asked.

"What?"

"Oh, you know—always some flip remark, always a stinger after everything you say. What are you afraid of?"

"People. The world. I suppose that's how I protect myself."

Kevin's eyes held the grave, sweet concentration I loved to see. He leaned forward, his elbows on his knees, his hands loosely clasped.

"I've almost decided not to go back to teaching this fall, Anne."

"But you've got a contract."

"It's not very ethical to notify them at this late date," Kevin admitted. "But you know as well as I do that there are fifty applicants for every academic job these days; they won't have any trouble filling my slot. I have responsibilities here too, and this slot isn't so easily filled. Mother and Dad aren't getting any younger. I want them to have the things they deserve, while they can enjoy them—peace of mind, leisure, the companionship of the people they love."

"It's a noble sentiment."

Kevin laughed. "There you go again," he said affectionately. "You can't insult me, darling; I know my decision is partly selfish. Why the hell should I kill myself when I don't have to? Slogging through the mud and sleet to class, grading papers for a bunch of low-grade morons who don't know how to write their own language. I'd have time to do the kind of research I've always wanted to do, without the pressure of schedules and academic demands. It's the best of all possible worlds for everyone concerned, and I'd be a fool to throw it away."

In the silence that followed there was no sound except the musical rustle of leaves overhead. The warm breeze, heavy with the scent of roses, caressed my skin. The stone walls of the house were golden in the sunlight. Leaving this place would be like tearing out part of my body.

"I can't disagree with you," I said at last. "You would be a fool to go back."

"And so would you." Kevin turned and took my hands in his. "You love this place, and you've given me the impression that your feelings for me—"

"I have for you certain sentiments of the most profound respect and approbation."

Kevin's eyes danced. "You're a panic. We'd have to get married, I suppose. Mother is a little sticky about things like that—"

"Wait. Don't." I pulled my hands from his grasp and blundered to my feet, putting one hand on the tree trunk to steady myself. The wood was warm and textured under my fingers.

"Don't pull a Jane Eyre on me," said Kevin. "You can't be altogether taken by surprise."

"Nobody ever proposed *marriage* to me before," I blurted.

As always, Kevin understood. "It scares me too, Anne. I don't believe in all that claptrap about marriage being made in heaven—"

"But divorce is messy and very expensive."

This time Kevin's laugh held a jarring note. He had a right to expect his honorable offer to be received, if not with a cry of rapture, at least without sarcasm. I don't know what held me back. I still don't know.

Instead of turning, instead of going into his arms, instead of saying any of the right things—I stood still, my back stubbornly turned.

"I don't feel I can quit without giving them some notice."

"If you told them now, you could quit after one semester without feeling guilty, couldn't you?"

I loved him for accepting what I said, for not trying to talk me out of it. I almost turned and shouted, "Take me, I'm yours!" The same indefinable, illogical reluctance stopped me.

"If I do decide to teach another semester—what will you do?"

"Is that a test question, Anne?"

"'Not love, quoth she, but vanity, Sets love a task like that.' I hope I'm not that cheap, Kevin. I just wondered."

"I honestly don't know," Kevin said. "I would rather not be separated from you, even for a short time."

Then I turned. He sat relaxed and quiet, his clàsped hands dangling, smiling up at me. There had been more conviction in his calm statement than in an embrace or passionate protestation.

"I would rather not be separated from you," I said, just as quietly.

"Then . . ."

"Let me think about it. My God," I added in disgust. "I've got to stop reading the Victorians. Not only am I talking like them, I'm starting to think that way."

We left it at that, but it wasn't satisfactory, and I knew it. Over and over during the day I asked myself what the hell was the matter with me. If I wasn't in love with Kevin my feelings were so close to love that only a pedant would have quibbled over definitions. I thought he would probably wear well, which was even more important. Passion passes into fondness, even indifference, but congeniality endures. Compared to Joe, for instance . . .

Naturally I thought of Joe, if only to make invidious comparisons. Arrogant, boorish, chauvinist, and he hadn't even pretended to care about my work. Since he was on my mind, I was not surprised to recognize his handwriting on a letter that came that afternoon. Things work that way sometimes.

Arrogant Joe might be, but he could take a hint. I suppose the fact that I had not written for six weeks might be considered a hint.

He assumed—he wrote—that since he had heard nothing from me, even in response to his last letter, any arrangements we might have had for fall were canceled. That was okay by him. I was a free agent, there were no strings, et cetera. (The "et cetera" represented two pages of griping.) However, he did feel that I owed him a statement of intent, since he had to find someplace to live. As I well knew, housing in that part of the city wasn't easy to find. If I was planning to give up my apartment, he would like to take it. What was the name of the rental agent?

Up to that point my only emotion was one of amusement at Joe's attempt to sound stiffly detached. But the letter ended with a comment about Kevin that was so hateful I threw it on the floor and stepped on it, as I would have crushed a poisonous insect.

After I had calmed down, by inventing all the names I would have called Joe if he had been there to hear them, I became aware that under my anger ran a tiny current of remorse. Joe must be feeling very hurt to descend to such malice. I ought to have written him weeks ago, as soon as I knew I didn't want him to move in with me again. I ought to write the university, immediately, if I decided not to go back.

That night I was not listening for strange noises. If there was a quality of desperation in my caresses Kevin didn't recognize it as such, but welcomed it as a demonstration of ultimate commitment.

I was in a deep, dreamless sleep when something woke me. I sat up in bed, fully awake and abnormally alert, like someone who expects an urgent call. But there had been no sound.

Moonlight filled the room like silvery water. I heard nothing except Kevin's deep, regular breathing. He slept neatly, lying on his side with his knees slightly flexed and his arms folded.

Then the sound came. I have never heard anything like it. Hollow, reverberant; a remote brazen clanging; its vibrations seemed to strike into the core of the walls and go on echoing. Muffled as it was, it had a piercing quality that was loud enough to wake Kevin. He sat up, shaking his head.

"Anne?"

"Yes, I heard it." I got out of bed and slipped into my robe, and reached for my glasses.

"Hold on," Kevin said, as I headed for the door. "I didn't hire you to catch burglars. Wait for me. Where are my clothes?"

"Probably on the floor, where you always throw them. Did you set the burglar alarm?"

"I think so. What the hell *was* that?"

"It sounded like a big bronze gong."

"We don't have one."

"We'd better check. Hurry up."

Bea's door opened as we approached it. Her eyebrows lifted slightly when she saw us together, but she only said, "Did I hear something?"

"Burglars banging a gong to announce their arrival," Kevin said. "Stand back, ladies, and let me be the first to rush headlong into danger."

At the top of the stairs we were greeted by Amy, who was delighted to have company. She could never understand why we wasted eight hours a day sleeping. She threw herself at Kevin, who staggered.

"What we need around here is a watchdog," he said. "It can't be a burglar; Amy would be with him, showing him where we keep the silver."

The dog continued to make playful rushes at him as he descended the stairs. A quick tour of the first floor showed nothing amiss. The rusting shields and weapons adorning the walls of the Great Hall, any one of which falling from a loosened peg might have caused such a sound, were all in place. Nothing else seemed to have been disturbed, and when Kevin checked the alarm, it was fully functional.

"I might as well have a look at the cellar while I'm at it," he said, yawning. "You girls go back to bed, why don't you?"

Bea's eyes sought mine. The nightmare had been half forgotten; but, like her, I knew we should not let Kevin go into the cellar alone.

Armed with flashlights, we made a thorough search and again found nothing out of place until we reached the small chamber that had been part of the old crypt. By that time we had all decided the whole business had been a false alarm. Kevin didn't enter the room, he just stood in the doorway and flashed his light around. There was nowhere anyone could have hidden, only the bare floor with its uneven stones. Only that, and . . . something more.

We almost missed it. We were looking for something the size of a man, not a small object less than a foot square. It sat on four little carved feet near the bottom of the brass which, I reminded myself, was not that of a Lady Ethelfleda.

"How did that get here?" Kevin asked in a puzzled voice. "I don't remember seeing it before."

I picked it up. It was surprisingly heavy—or maybe not so surprising, for it was made of stone, a translucent marblelike substance that had once been white. Stains of lichen and rust streaked its sides.

Kevin didn't expect an answer, so I did not give him one; but as we inspected the remaining rooms of the substructure I swore at myself for not thinking of the obvious cause of the disturbance. I also swore at Roger. If I had not had so many other things on my mind, I would have figured the clumsy oaf had sneaked into the house again. Had I but known, I would have tried to persuade Kevin to go back to sleep, and avoided what might be a bloody confrontation. However, Roger had probably escaped by now; we had taken a long time to get this far.

It wasn't hard to spot his means of entry. The others didn't notice anything; they didn't know what I knew. I remembered Roger's mentioning the tower door. I should have realized at the time that he had protested too much about its rusty, dusty appearance. The bare little room into which it opened was empty. Kevin gave it no more than a quick flash of light before turning away. I was the only one who noticed the dangling wire beside the door. It had been cut.

Kevin was ready for bed by that time, if not for

sleep, but Bea insisted we have a little snack of something first. She was always trying to feed people, but that night I knew she had something else on her mind. I was carrying the box we had found. When I put it down on the kitchen table Bea was the first to examine it.

"I could swear that wasn't there the last time I was in that room," Kevin muttered.

"Roger . . ." Bea swallowed something that had caught in her throat before she went on. "Roger would say it was Greek or Roman, wouldn't he?"

I would have said so too. The fabric was alabaster, carved with garlands and flowers. In the center of one of the long sides was a shape that looked like a shallow bowl or saucer, with two handles.

Kevin picked the box up and shook it. Something inside responded with a bony rattle.

"Ha," Kevin said. "Treasure? The moldy ribs of a saint?" He selected a knife from the rack over the sink.

Bea took a quick step away from the table as Kevin inserted the tip of the knife into the crack that separated the casket from its lid. I stood still. Something was nibbling at the back of my mind. Something seen, something heard, something vaguely remembered. Something wrong.

"Feels like glue," Kevin grumbled, scraping and jabbing.

"Be careful," I said absently. "Don't cut yourself."

Something seen. A shadow, in the wrong place. Where?

Kevin let out a grunt of satisfaction as the lid gave way. "Well, I'll be damned," he said. "I was right the second time."

Two of the objects in the box did appear to be

bones, brown with extreme age and so hard they were virtually petrified. Kevin lifted them out, and as the light bathed them I saw that my appraisal had been incorrect.

"Not bones." Kevin was equally as quick. "Horns. Sorry, Aunt Bea, no saint. Unless he . . . What does that make me think of?"

"The Minotaur," I said. "Half man, half bull. They aren't very big. Is that gold around the base of each?"

"Looks like it. Let's see what else is in here."

There wasn't much. Fragments of broken pottery that fit together into a shape resembling the shallow bowl carved on the outside of the casket, and a thick layer of brittle fragments that fell to dust when Kevin touched them. Once they might have been flowers. That was all. But it was enough for me, and for Kevin, who was now deeply interested and using his considerable intelligence.

"That's a patera," he said, indicating the fragments of the bowl. "Used in Roman sacrifices and offerings. Roger's antique cult is looking pretty good, isn't it?"

The bits and pieces of memory I had been trying to fit together suddenly clicked into place. I shoved my chair back. It hit the floor with a crash.

"Oh, my God. Maybe it's not too late. Quick— hurry—"

Kevin caught up with me as I wrestled with the cellar door. My hands were slippery with sweat; I couldn't get a firm grip on the knob. When he started to ask me what was wrong I shrieked at him. "Hurry—quick. . . ." They might have been the only words of English I knew.

I kept repeating them as I plunged down the steep narrow stairs, with Kevin close behind, making futile snatches at me. He thought I was going to fall, and it's a wonder I didn't. I was going to look like a perfect fool if my wild hunch proved wrong. I prayed it would. But the pieces fit together too neatly. The marble box—Roger wouldn't have forgotten it or abandoned it voluntarily. That was one of the things that had troubled me. And the sound—"a hollow, metallic and clangorous, yet apparently muffled reverberation . . ." Edgar Allan Poe, *The Fall of the House of Usher*. How did it go? *They laid her living within the tomb.*

And the last piece of the puzzle—the long shadow, half concealed by the low rim of the slab in which the brass was set.

I snatched up the crowbar and inserted the tip into the crack between the brass and the stone—a crack now cleared of the old mortar that had once sealed it.

Kevin stood staring at me, his arms limp at his sides.

"Damn it, help me!" I shouted. "It's too heavy; I can't do it alone."

He might have argued with me—I'm sure I looked wild enough to justify a suspicion of instant insanity —if it had not been for Bea. Some flash of insight or premonition must have touched her. She made a horrible deathrattle noise, deep in her throat, and sprang forward to place her hands beside mine on the lever.

By then Kevin had figured out what we were trying to do, if not why. He thought we were crazy, but he knew better than to discuss it.

"You'll never get it up that way," he said. "Hold on a minute."

He went out of the room, and I will admit he moved

fast. He returned with an armload of logs of varying sizes.

We used them as wedges to brace the brass as it gradually lifted free of the stone ledge that supported it underneath. The process was agonizingly slow. I had plenty of time to wonder how it had been managed the first time.

Finally the brass stood on its edge, like a metal door. The space underneath was about three feet deep and four feet square. It was lined with stones, gray, monolithic, unadorned. The bottom was littered with fragments of splintered wood and debris. Lying among them was the body of a man, his knees drawn up at an awkward angle. On the back of his gray head was a shape that looked like a big black spider, its hairy legs embracing his skull.

Chapter Thirteen

THE GOTHIC ATMOSPHERE was so thick I half expected Bea to jump into the tomb with her lover. Of course she had better sense, though her face was as ghastly as one of the exhibits in a wax museum's Chamber of Horrors. Kevin went down while Bea and I stood with our backs against the brass to keep it from slipping again. At least I assumed that was what had happened to Roger; in his excitement he had neglected to take precautions and had paid dearly for his carelessness.

"Is he alive?" Bea asked tonelessly.

Kevin was quick to reassure her. "Alive and snoring. He got a bad bump on the head, but nothing seems to be broken. He must have been bent over when the brass fell. Should we try to move him, or call a doctor first?"

Roger answered the question by groaning and trying to sit up. When Kevin asked him how he felt his reply was worthy of the occasion. He refused to stay where he was until we could summon medical assistance, so Kevin boosted him out. He promptly subsided face down on the floor.

"Anne," Bea whispered. "Can you hold this alone?"

"No. Kevin, get the hell up here."

"Son of a gun," said Kevin, rooting among the scraps at the bottom of the hole. "So that's how he did it. Block and tackle—yep, there's the hook, in that ceiling beam. Roger, you damned fool, why did you let the apparatus fall down in there with you? We might never have known you were there if Anne hadn't . . ."

He broke off. Slowly his head and shoulder rose up out of the pit. The effect was quite gruesome; and the cold, accusing stare he directed at me increased the impression of a modern Dracula inspecting his next victim.

"Goddamn it," he said. "What's going on around here? How *did* you know? What's Roger up to, sneaking around my house and—"

"If you say one more word, Kevin, I am going to slap you," Bea interrupted. "Come here this minute and help me. You can ask questions later."

His lips tightly set, Kevin obeyed. As soon as he relieved her, Bea went to Roger. She crouched on the floor beside him, holding his hand, while Kevin and I piled logs under the ends of the brass and tipped it back into a safe position. As we worked, I examined the odds and ends that covered the bottom of the pit. I thought I knew why Roger had hidden the ropes and pulleys; he was tidying up, so Kevin wouldn't find the evidence of his activities. Or perhaps the falling brass had pulled the ropes from their support and dragged them down. What I couldn't understand was the absence of the lead coffin I had expected to see. I could only assume that the coffins mentioned in the inventory had belonged to three other people, and that the pieces of broken wood in the pit were the remnants of the container that had once been there. Apparently it had contained only the marble casket; I saw no bones—or teeth.

When the brass finally fell into place, it gave off a sonorous ringing murmur.

"Metallic and clangorous," I said, shivering. "Thank God for E. A. Poe."

"What?" Kevin glanced at me, his expression still hostile.

"You remember. They buried her alive, and when she fought her way out of the coffin and the crypt—"

"Oh." The effect of this somewhat incoherent statement on Kevin was little short of miraculous. Admiration, affection, relief—all pleasant positive emotions —replaced the angry suspicion on his face. He put his arm around my shoulders. "Was that what alerted you? You're a sharp one, darling."

"That and a few other things. The little marble box—"

Roger let out a croak. "The box. Where is it?"

"In the kitchen." Kevin's voice was harsh. He no longer suspected me of complicity, but he was understandably vexed with Roger. "Far be it from me to be inhospitable, Roger, but what the hell—"

"Shut up, Kevin," Bea said. "Help me get him upstairs."

II

It was dawn before Dr. Garst left. I don't suppose anyone but a personal friend would have made a house call at that ungodly hour—or at any hour. He was efficient and reassuring, but his bedside manner left something to be desired. He told Roger he was lucky to have such a damned thick Irish skull, and made a few leering references to silly old goats who went out on late dates.

Kevin was boiling over with embarrassing questions. No use trying to convince him that Roger had had a tête-à-tête with Bea that night; gentlemen don't meet ladies in crypts, much less under them. Bea wouldn't let him interrogate the patient. She shooed us both out. I suggested Kevin get a few more hours sleep.

"I have the feeling everybody knows what's going on but me," he muttered, and wandered off.

I went to my room but I didn't go to bed. I was standing behind my door, peeking through a crack, when Bea emerged from the sickroom. Her eyes were red, but she was smiling mistily. "Of all the paths lead to a woman's love, Pity's the straightest." At least that's what the poets say, and it appeared that in this case they might be right for a change.

After her door had closed I continued my vigil and, sure enough, about ten minutes later Roger's door cautiously opened. He had put on his pants, but I guess the effort of bending over to locate his shoes had been too much for his aching head. His feet were bare. The white cap of bandage gave him a rakish look, and his wary expression was that of a prisoner of war watching for enemy guards.

I waited till he had shuffled some way down the hall before I followed. He kept putting his hand to his head; no doubt the pounding inside prevented him from hearing me. He didn't see me till he reached the stairs and turned to go down.

I put my finger to my lips. "They'll hear you if you yell."

"And vice versa. Don't try to wrestle me back to bed, Florence Nightingale."

"It's on the kitchen table."

"What is?"

"You're wasting your time playing coy with me, Roger. I'll tell you what is in the box if you go back to bed; but I don't suppose that will satisfy you."

It didn't satisfy him. He started down the stairs, holding the handrail firmly. I followed, prepared to break his fall if he started to buckle at the knees, but he made it without a mishap and headed purposefully for the kitchen.

The contents of the box revived him remarkably. His eyes shone with satisfaction as he fitted the scraps of pottery together.

"Time to eat a little crow, Annie. Who was right?"

"You, O pearl of wisdom. I take it these are the sacred relics of the worship of the Great Whoever, hidden away by a devotee when things got too hot for honest pagans."

"Wiseacre," Roger said absently. "One of these days you're going to let your guard down and turn into a human being; you'll be surprised how good it feels. You know what this is, don't you? It's a patera— probably a couple of thousand years old. One of the symbols of the Mother. The bull's horns—"

"They don't look big enough to be a bull's."

"So it was a little bull," said Roger, with no intention of being funny. "The horns are often found in connection with the double ax. I wonder where— ah, here we are."

From under the crumbling leaves he drew a scrap of metal, black and oxidized. "Silver," he muttered. "The wooden handle would be long gone."

"Okay, now you've had your gloat. How about getting back to bed?"

"You think I dragged my battered bones down here just to look at this junk? Hell, no, Annie. We've got to get rid of it—right now, before Kevin adds it to the family treasures."

My head didn't feel too good. I rubbed it, but that did not help. Oh, I knew what he was thinking, and I couldn't prove he was wrong. Perhaps these tattered remnants of a cult that had once boasted marble temples and statues of ivory and gold were the ultimate cause of the disturbances in the house. Perhaps they were just another blind alley, like the other leads we had followed. But one thing was sure—Roger wouldn't rest until they were disposed of—rendered harmless, as he would say.

"What do you propose doing with them?" I asked.

"They ought to be burned," Roger said, with fanatic intensity.

"I can't burn a couple of petrified horns!"

"I guess not. Water, then. Running water is an ancient defense against evil spirits." He looked as if he were starting a fever. Two bright circles of red spotted his sagging cheeks. "That's it. The stream. We'll throw them into the stream, as far from the house as we can get."

"You won't get far," I said, catching his arm as he swayed. "Go back to bed and let me take care of this. I'll do as you suggested."

"Promise?"

"I promise."

He needed all my strength on the return trip, but he stayed on his feet, and I blew out a sigh of relief when he was finally back in bed.

"I'm all right now," he mumbled. "Need a little sleep . . ." His eyelids popped open and he fixed me with a penetrating glare. "You promised."

"I'll do it, I'll do it. What about the casket? It won't be carried down to the cleansing sea, it will sink like a stone. Which it is."

"Harmless," Roger said. "Leave it."

I didn't ask how he knew. "But what am I going to tell Kevin when he sees the things are gone?"

"Tell him the dog ate them." Roger closed his eyes. "Tell him the cleaners threw them out. Tell him . . . crumbled into dust . . . air . . ."

I watched him anxiously until his breathing settled into a steady pattern. If I had erred in letting him get up, the damage was done; the only thing I could do for him now was carry out my promise. I went to my room to get my sneakers and some clothes. I suppose I could have dumped the relics into the trash can, or hidden them; but I have this funny obsession about keeping my word.

It was a beautiful morning, bright and clear and cool. I set out briskly, wanting to finish the job and get back to bed. But when I reached the stream there wasn't enough water in it to float a paper boat. I had to follow the feeble trickle for a mile before another stream joined it. The combined flow was not what anyone would term voluminous, but by then I was so tired I didn't care. I tossed the relics into the water and left, without looking to see whether they had been carried away or were just lying there, waiting for another victim.

The cleaners' van was pulling up when I got back, so I knew it was nine o'clock. I let them in, warning them about being extra quiet, and went to the kitchen to make coffee. The alabaster box was sitting on the table, looking innocent and harmless; but it was going to blow up like a stick of dynamite unless I could think of a good story to tell Bea and Kevin. The latter, especially; he had been tickled pink to find some ancient relics. I sat at the table drinking coffee and staring stupidly at the box while I tried to come up with a brilliant idea. Eventually I went outside and looked for dust. I had a terrible time finding any. The surfaces that weren't covered with rich green grass were mulched or graveled or covered with rich black soil. But I managed to scrape some up, from a corner where Amy had been digging, and I dumped a couple of handfuls into the casket and dragged my weary body up the stairs. Another day was upon me and I still couldn't make up my mind what to do about Kevin and my job. I only had a couple of weeks before I had to act, one way or the other.

I didn't know it then, but I didn't have two weeks. I only had three days.

III

If I have not mentioned that quintessence of modern culture, the television set, it is not because the house lacked such amenities. There were several of them, but we seldom turned them on. It might have been sheer coincidence that prompted Kevin to listen to the evening news, the day after Roger's adventure in the cellar. Or it might have been something else.

The house was positively saccharine with old-fashioned romance. I don't know how Bea had come to terms with what had once seemed an insoluble problem. Maybe she had decided that love was the most important thing. Maybe Roger had stopped crowing about his superior intelligence. Why try to find reasons? They were reconciled, and it appeared that Roger would be in residence indefinitely. She had driven him home to get his clothes, and then brought him back with her. If she had not been convinced that he needed her constant attention, the sight of his filthy house would have done the trick. She went around with a starry-eyed look, and Roger resembled the Cheshire cat, all one smug grin.

While their love affair bloomed, mine began to show signs of whitefly. Kevin did not refer again to the choice I had yet to make. He was as fond and considerate as ever, but there was a little crack between us, nothing so deep that it couldn't be crossed with one long step, but I was the one who had to take that step, and I didn't.

Kevin was also put out by the disappearance of the relics. I had to admit that the dust in the casket was unconvincing, but search as he might for a suspect, Kevin couldn't think of any other explanation. Roger —bandaged, feeble, and afflicted with the grandfather of all headaches—was obviously incapable of making off with the things, and no one else would want them. Kevin finally decided that Amy must be the culprit. Amy wagged her tail and grinned when she was accused.

Roger joined us in the library that evening, hovered over by Bea and visibly enjoying his new status. It might have been his undesired presence that prompted Kevin to switch on the television set.

The news was the usual grim collection of disasters, local and national. I concentrated on my needlepoint and tried not to listen. Then Kevin leaned forward alertly, and I caught the word "hurricane."

At least they were naming them after men now. This was Martin. Winds up to one hundred miles an hour. It had already killed sixty-eight people in various Caribbean islands, and it was heading northwest.

We are becoming inured to manmade horrors—murders, muggings, rapes, one per minute every minute of every day. Large-scale natural disasters still grip the imagination, perhaps because they are beyond any hope of control. We listened unwillingly to the ghastly totals—so many dead, so many injured, so many millions of dollars' worth of damage.

Kevin jumped to his feet. "The east front is the most exposed. I'll pick up some sheets of heavy plywood—"

"What, now?" Roger asked in surprise. "Cool it, Kevin, it's just a storm. Probably won't touch this area."

Kevin gestured toward the set, where the weatherman was sketching broad sweeping lines indicating the hurricane's possible path. "It could change direction."

"We'll have plenty of warning if it does." Roger's voice made it clear that the subject did not interest him. "I can't think of a safer place to be; this house is built like the Rock of Gibraltar, and it's sitting in a natural basin. Bea, how about a walk?"

Kevin continued to monitor the set all evening. The eleven-o'clock report was equivocal. It was not until the next morning that we learned Martin was definitely heading in our direction. If it hit the Carolina coast and went inland, the force of its winds would be broken over land. If, as was now expected, it made landfall farther north, the eastern portions of Virginia, Maryland, and Pennsylvania were in for trouble.

Kevin drove the truck into town, and came back with sheets of plywood, tape, and rolls of heavy plastic. By that time even Roger was forced to admit some action might be advisable. I went to the village with him to help him secure his house. It didn't take long. Like many Georgian houses, his had functional shutters. After he had turned off everything that could be turned off and yanked out the plugs on the appliances, we went back to find Kevin balancing on a high ladder boarding up the east windows. By midafternoon the skies were dark and the wind was strong enough to make the trees bow and dance.

I had never been in, or through, a hurricane. Even an electrical storm makes my stomach ache. I wanted to spend the next twenty-four hours under my bed, preferably dead drunk. I couldn't voice my feelings because everyone else was so nonchalant. No, nonchalant is not the word to describe Kevin, but the grim-faced intensity with which he went about his tasks convinced me he would have neither the time nor the patience to comfort me. Bea's coolness shamed me. She was concerned about water damage to rugs and furniture, so we moved some of the more valuable pieces away from the windows, sealed cracks with tape, and covered other objects with plastic.

Late in the afternoon the telephone rang. I picked it up before I remembered that telephones are dangerous in thunderstorms. I didn't know whether the same applied to hurricanes, so I juggled the instrument nervously for a while before I got courage enough to say "Hello."

It was Father Stephen, calling to make sure we were

ready for the big blow. (His words, not mine.) I told him Kevin had practically wrapped the house in plastic and plywood, and he laughed.

"It's as solid as a fortress, Anne. You're perfectly safe there."

So he had sensed my state of nerves. I stopped pretending. "I hate storms," I whined.

"Some people are sensitive to changes in barometric pressure, and electricity in the air—if that is the right way of describing it, which it probably isn't. I barely scraped through physics in college."

I appreciated his efforts to restore my morale. It is less humiliating to be sensitive to barometric pressure than to be a yellow-bellied coward. "Why don't you come here?" I suggested.

"I'm on call," was the calm reply.

"You mean you'll be going out in it?"

"No more than I must, believe me. There's nothing to worry about, Anne. Roger is there, isn't he? Well then, you've two able-bodied men on hand; I'm sure Roger and Bea know what to do."

He stopped speaking. I didn't reply; a big lump was blocking my throat. After a moment he said, "Anne, is it the storm that bothers you? Is there anything else?"

I shook my head before I remembered he couldn't see me.

"No," I squeaked.

"You're sure? Please be honest. I'll come in a moment if—"

"No, really. Everything is fine." It was the truth. And even if it had not been true, I couldn't have begged for his company. There would be people injured, women having babies, houses damaged, fires.

He would be needed for more serious matters than one neurotic woman's fear of storms.

"Good," he said. "Don't worry, Anne. You couldn't be in a safer place."

After he had hung up I held on to the phone, trying idiotically to maintain the contact. I couldn't be in a safer place. A place where phantoms walked the hall by night and tomb markers fell on people's heads. But, I told myself, that was all over. Roger's clumsiness had brought the brass down on his head; the rest had been hallucination or a harmless psychic outburst, now ended.

By evening it was as dark as midnight, and the gale-force wind produced an uncouth symphony of cacophonous sounds. We settled down around the big trestle table in the kitchen. It was undoubtedly the safest room in that secure house. Kevin had boarded up the small windows, and the three-foot-thick walls muffled most of the sounds. But I heard the rain begin. Within minutes it had risen to a steady roar. Bea was at the stove when the lights flickered and went out.

"Better crank up the generator, Kevin," said Roger's voice, from the dark.

"We've been on our own power for several hours," was the reply. "The cable between the house and the shed must have gone down."

A spark flared as his match caught one of the candles on the table. He lighted the whole batch, a dozen or more, remarking, "We'll have a romantic dinner by candlelight. Did anyone feed the animals?"

No one had, so Kevin took care of that chore. All the pets were with us in the kitchen. They were fairly calm except for Amy, who had retired under the table when the rain began and was nervously licking my shoe. She came out long enough to eat, and retreated again.

I couldn't eat. My stomach was tied in knots. I kept telling myself my apprehension was senseless. This wasn't an atomic bomb, or even a tornado, which strikes with concentrated fury on a single spot. It was just a bad windstorm. It was making plenty of noise, but that was about all it could do here. Even if the windows broke or a tree fell on part of the house, we were perfectly safe. The kitchen was like a large warm cave lighted by mellow natural light instead of the glare of electricity. The cats had curled up and gone to sleep; Annabelle was a furry uncouth puddle at Kevin's feet; Bea and Roger were sitting side by side on the settle in front of the fireplace, hands entwined, talking in low voices.

The house was secure, safe. The trouble wasn't with the house, it was with me. As I sat with my hands tightly clenched to keep them from trembling, I knew that part of the trouble was my sense of helplessness. I wanted to be in control of what happened to me. If I made the wrong decision I was willing to pay the price, but I had to have the right to choose. One cannot decide whether or not to have a volcano erupt, or direct a hurricane's path.

Which was big talk from a woman who couldn't even make up her mind whether to marry a man she was crazy in love with.

Kevin wouldn't go back with me if I decided to teach next semester. I knew that as surely as if he had told me. But three months wasn't very long, three months should not commit me unalterably to that way of life. If Kevin wouldn't wait three months, he didn't want me. I could fulfill my obligations and come back—to Kevin, to the house, to a life of leisure and luxury and peace.

If Kevin still wanted me.

When Bea said sleepily, "We might as well go to bed," I could have shouted with relief. That was what I wanted to do—go to bed, with Kevin, his arms tight around me.

"Go ahead," Kevin said. "No reason why we should all lose a night's sleep."

"Aren't you going to bed?" I asked.

"No, I want to keep an eye on things. You go, Anne. You look bushed."

Bea murmured something to Roger. Then she said aloud, "Why don't we move into the library? There are two couches there, and the chairs are comfortable; we can nap."

I could have kissed her. At the same time I resented the offer. Was my state of nerves that obvious?

At first the change of scene was a relief, but before long I wished we had not moved. These walls, though thicker than normal, were not as massive as the ones in the kitchen. The sound of the storm was much more audible, and Kevin had not boarded up the long French doors, since they opened onto a sheltered courtyard. Solid and shielded as they were, they creaked under the assault of the wind.

Roger consented to recline on one of the couches, and Bea sat with him. I didn't have to be persuaded to lie down. Irrational terror is the most tiring thing I know. From where I lay I could see the whole length of the gracious room, like a stage set or a painting. In fact, it reminded me of one of the Flemish genre paintings—a family interior, a story painting. It was exaggeratedly chiaroscuro, great spaces of darkness broken by pools of soft light that shed strange shadows. A small battery-powered electric lamp illumined the faces of the older pair. Bea's eyes were closed, her face sagging in half-sleep. The deeply etched lines in her cheeks and forehead made her look old, but it was peaceful old age, resigned and fulfilled. Roger's eyes were steady on her face; his lips were curved in a quiet smile.

Another lamp made a circle of brightness around Kevin's lean brown hands and the book they held. They were beautiful hands, scarred by the labors of that long day, but shapely and sensitive. His face was in shadow, but I could see the alert lift of his head as he listened. Yes, it was a story painting—the two generations, one resting after a lifetime of labor, the next virile and strong, ready to take up the burden. I was the only one not in the picture. I was the spectator, looking on.

As I continued to look, more and more I had the feeling that I was missing something. The scene was a puzzle picture, like the ones they invent to amuse children, but more complex—find the heads of ten United States Presidents, or twenty animals. The shape of the hidden object was there, masked by other lines and shapes—glaringly conspicuous once it has been found, invisible until the eyes isolate its outlines.

Kevin was only pretending to read. He hadn't turned a page in ten minutes. Finally he closed the book and got to his feet. Bea's eyes opened. She was not as relaxed as she appeared to be. We all watched Kevin walk to the window and pull back the draperies.

He leaned forward as if trying to see—an impossibility in that howling chaos of darkness, with rain pouring down like a twenty-mile wide waterfall.

"See anything?" Bea asked. I was glad she was the one to voice that silly question. If she hadn't I would have.

"The big maple at the northwest corner," Kevin said.

Roger grunted irritably. "You can't see anything from here. Sit down, Kevin, you make me nervous."

"It's going to fall," Kevin said.

"If it goes, it goes," Roger said. "Nothing we can do. Unless you're planning to swim out there and hold it up."

Kevin's pose had unquestionably sparked that attempt at a witticism. He strained forward, as if prepared to support a heavy weight. He was wearing white painter's pants and an old shirt, the sleeves rolled above his elbows; his ruffled brown hair curled over his ears and the back of his neck. A sudden stab of anguish pierced me, as if I knew I was seeing him for the last time.

"It's going," he said quietly. "Now."

The crash caused scarcely a tremor in the solid fabric of the house. Only an echo shook the air, like a high, distant wailing.

And then I knew. I felt neither fear nor horror, only the solemn satisfaction of finally working out the solution to a long equation. But without conscious thought, without even knowing I had moved, I found myself at the front door pushing at the bolts, trying to turn the massive key. Kevin was beside me, his face distorted, his hands attempting to trap mine; he was shouting. "What the hell are you doing? Have you gone crazy?" and something about "letting in the wind." I understood why he said that. It made me redouble my frantic efforts. Kevin had to hit me. I didn't blame him. It was the only sensible thing for him to do.

When I came to, I was lying on the couch in the library. I could hear them talking in low, concerned voices. ". . . always been afraid of storms. . . ." "You didn't have to hit her." ". . . tranquilizers or something? She needs . . ."

The last comment scared me. Little white pills to dull my fears were the last thing I needed.

"I'm all right," I said. "I don't . . . need anything."

My voice was steady, but I didn't open my eyes. I knew they were standing around the couch looking down at me, like the learned doctors in that awful painting of Rembrandt, and I was the naked corpse on the dissecting table, with one arm already opened to bare the bloody bones and tendons. A dead man cannot protect himself from being flayed. I had the same helpless feeling—that their questions, their ignorant concern would tear off the skin and muscle and show the dark places I had to keep hidden. There was so much I still did not understand. Until I did, the safest course was to hide my knowledge. My first reaction had been pure panic, stupid as panic always is. I wanted to lie still, in the darkness behind my closed eyelids, until it was safe to act. But I couldn't risk it. They might try to give me something—for my own good. Drugged, I would really be helpless. I opened my eyes and moved the muscles of my face.

"I don't know what came over me," I said. "Storms. You know how I'm afraid of storms."

There were the faces I had envisioned, and the expressions of fond concern. I had not realized how

the light would distort them, drawing dark shadows in
the wrong places and hiding the eyes in black hollows.
Bea was kneeling; Kevin and Roger stood on either
side of her. Their bodies hedged me in. I could not get
by them. But I had decided I wasn't going to run,
hadn't I? The storm still howled outside in great cries
and gasps, like a living, agonized creature.

"The worst is over now," Bea said gently. "It's
passing now, Anne."

"Honey, I'm sorry." Kevin crouched down, his face
close to mine. "I didn't know how else to stop you. If
you had gone out there, you would have been knocked
off your feet, maybe killed."

And the wind would have come in.

I didn't say that aloud. "It's all right," I muttered.
"You had to do it. I'm fine now."

They helped me sit up. They brought me brandy
and soup and tea, and they chatted brightly to keep
my mind off the howling outside. From time to time
Kevin or Roger would slip out, making the rounds,
checking to make sure the windows were still intact,
the shutters closed, everything in order . . . the house
safe.

Bea had been lying, to make me feel better, when
she said the worst of the storm was over. It rose to new
violence a few hours before dawn, and Kevin came
back from one of his trips of inspection to report that
water was coming in a couple of upstairs windows. He
added, with a reassuring smile at me, that he had
taken care of it. Everything was fine.

"Sure," I echoed. "Everything is fine."

All the while I was thinking, trying to work out the
last remaining pieces of the puzzle. I wasn't sure it was
safe to do this. Maybe thoughts were as perceptible in

that house, and as dangerous, as speech. But I couldn't think of anything else. I had it pretty well figured out by the time a gray troubled dawn lightened the cracks around the draperies and the wind diminished.

The radio had already told us the storm was passing. Nothing of that magnitude had hit the area since 1895, or some such date. Thanks to advance warnings, said the announcer smugly, the damage had not been as bad as it might have been; but most of the utility wires were down, and it would be several days before full power was restored. Everything had been canceled—schools, meetings—and all the businesses in the region were opening late, if at all. There was a long list of emergency numbers for people who needed food, water, transportation, medical attention. It went on and on.

As soon as the rain died down to the strength of a normal storm, Kevin put on boots and mackintosh and went out. He was gone for some time. When he came back he was soaked to the skin, but cheerful.

"It's over," he said. "The sun is beginning to come out."

Roger had fallen into a doze. He awoke with a start and a grumble. We all followed Kevin to the door.

The wind was still brisk up on the heights, but in our hollow it was now scarcely more than a stiff breeze. Gray clouds rushed westward, with streaks of brilliant blue already showing in between. Bea let out a cry of distress at the sight of the flower beds; buds, leaves, and twigs had been stripped. The lawn was littered with debris, and the big maple had seen its last summer. It had fallen straight toward the house, struck, and slid sideways, taking a few shingles with it but doing surprisingly little damage. Indeed, as Kevin pointed out, we had gotten off lightly. If some Good Samaritan would cook him a hearty breakfast on the camping stove he had been clever enough to buy, he would start clearing the drive of fallen branches and taking down the makeshift shutters.

It should have been an occasion warm with camaraderie and shared congratulations—the relief of survival, the triumph of having defeated nature red in tooth and claw. We sat with our elbows on the table; Kevin and Roger wolfed down the food Bea prepared. Everybody talked and laughed and compared notes. Yes, everybody. I played my part quite well, I think. I even joked about my panic, and Kevin's "brutal attack." I joined Kevin and Roger in their clean-up efforts. It took our combined strength to drag one big limb off the drive. Little did they know how anxious I was to accomplish that particular chore.

After a few hours Roger wiped his perspiring brow and announced that he personally had had it. The sun was beaming down out of a bright-blue sky and the ground steamed with moisture. We had done the essential chores; the rest could wait till we got help. It was useless to expect anyone to come that day; the gardeners were probably busy cleaning up their own property.

I followed Roger to the house, leaving Kevin still raking and cleaning. He had promised to quit soon and get some sleep. Bea had already gone to bed. I figured they would sleep until evening.

I had to wait till Kevin was out of the way, but there was plenty to do before I left. I packed one bag and shoved it under the bed, in case he came to my room before he hit the sack. Then I sat down at the table and started writing. I couldn't leave without an explanation. I owed them that, even though I knew it wouldn't do any good.

I had not been writing long when I heard Kevin's footsteps. He stopped outside my door for a moment, but didn't come in.

After I finished my letter I folded the sheets and put them on the bedside table, with the lamp on one corner to anchor them. I got my suitcase out from under the bed and slung my purse over my shoulder.

The house was very quiet. The silence was particularly noticeable in the kitchen, without the normal humming of the refrigerator, freezer, and other appliances. I took the car keys from the board by the door. Annabelle was lying on the hearthrug. She lifted her head to look at me. I leaned over and scratched her gently behind the ears. Her tail moved lazily, a furry flutter.

"Good-bye," I whispered. That was the only time I had to say it.

Chapter Fourteen

THE BUS was two hours late leaving Pittsfield. Not bad, the driver pointed out, when you considered. I got a window seat.

The ravages of the storm were apparent everywhere —flattened crops, shattered trees, flooded roads. Crews were already at work along the highway replacing telephone poles and power lines. We had to make several detours because bridges were out or parts of the road were under water. The bus was full. Everybody was talking about the storm, telling of their own experiences and asking for news. My seatmate, an elderly woman, tried to chat with me, but I closed my eyes and pretended to be asleep.

I was remembering what I had written and wondering whether I should have said more—or less. Not that it mattered.

"We were all wrong. And we were all partly right. It wasn't someone in the house. It wasn't some thing in the house. It was the house itself.

"The manifestations we saw and heard were part of

it—the cause or the effect, I don't know which. And of course everything was colored, for each of us, by our personal needs and fears. It tried to give us what we wanted. Does that sound absurd? Think about it. Remember what happened, in the light of that interpretation, and see if it doesn't fit. Remember the feeling of warmth and of welcome that endured incomprehensibly through all the horrors, reassuring us, forcing us to accept the unacceptable? The whole place is permeated by that atmosphere. It's like a colorless, odorless gas; the more you struggle, the more you breathe in, and the more it dulls your senses.

"Oh, it made some mistakes. It must have been out of practice after so many years of inactivity. Miss Marion was happy with her 'companion'; Kevin's parents didn't need artificial encouragement, they had everything they wanted. They plan to end their days there, tending their lovely old home with the fond attention, and the money, it requires. Kevin was the problem. He had to stay and carry on the loving, the tending. He had to want to stay.

"So the house tried to make him happy. It experimented. It didn't mind when he found a flesh-and-blood lover; the other one was only designed to fill a gap. Or maybe it was a test; some people prefer phantoms to reality. Faust was ready to sell his soul for the privilege of embracing the shade of Trojan Helen.

"It never meant to frighten me. I caught it by surprise, that was all, and it didn't know how to react. There is something horrifyingly human about its reaction; but it is not surprising that after all these centuries it should have developed qualities we think of as human, or at least animal. Self-preservation is one of the strongest of such qualities.

"That's what it's all about—the house wanting to survive. It endures repairs and restorations and additions the way a person accepts necessary surgery, even amputation, so long as the essential core can continue. With the help of its attendants, its lovers, it survived flood and storm and siege. And when Armageddon threatened, when the bombs were about to fall, it found a safer place.

"Perhaps the essential core is, or was, human—the sum total of all the people who have lived in the house and loved it. Caught, while living, in the web of that love, and dying, adding their strength to the total. Perhaps it started with Roger's ancient priests and the principle of Life they worshiped. That doesn't matter. What matters is that now it's too strong to be defeated. No one will ever get rid of the spirit, the psychic energy, without destroying the physical house all the way down to the deepest foundations. And even then something may survive—some seed, some root, that will gain strength over the years.

"All that is academic because no one will ever want to destroy it. No such hostile, hating thought could ever enter the mind of anyone who lived there. If it did . . . Well, I don't know what would happen. I think the house would find a way of protecting itself, by one means or another.

"Not by violence, if it could find any other way. It is not malevolent. It's not a hell house, or a house of evil or a house of blood. *It wants people to be happy.* That was what I found unbearable.

"I don't think you'll have any more trouble. Not unless you continue playing games with it—summoning up troubled spirits, or trying to photograph the invisible. And don't worry about Kevin. He'll be all right. That's exactly what the house wants—that Kevin should be all right.

"I'm sorry I couldn't stay. I can't explain why. I love you all. I'm sorry."

The woman sitting next to me got up and changed seats. I didn't blame her. I wasn't enjoying my own company.

The last paragraph of my letter had given me a lot of trouble. I wanted to say more, to explain, to justify myself. But I couldn't without making myself sound conceited or condemnatory, or just plain touched in the head. I couldn't hurt Kevin by telling him what I suspected—that his feelings for me were just another contrivance. I was admirably suited for the position in so many ways, and at first it must have appeared that I was adjusting nicely—taking up needlepoint and flower-arranging and all the other lady-of-the-manor hobbies. Yes, I was ideally suited—in every way but one. Call it stubbornness, call it independence of mind, call it a neurotic rejection of happiness—there was some rock-hard nugget of will that would not succumb to a manufactured content. I would like to think that quality was unique and wonderful, yet I doubt that it was; there must have been others, Mandevilles and Weekeses and Romers, who never sensed the glamour. But how could I say this without seeming to gloat over my superior strength of mind? How could I tell Kevin he never cared about me, not really—that it was all part of a pattern, a role he played under the guidance of an unseen director?

I wasn't playing a role. At least I don't think I was.

And that was why I ran away—because I couldn't be sure.

II

The airport was teeming with people who had priority because of flights canceled the day before. I couldn't get a seat on a plane. I spent the night in a cheap hotel in the city; I was afraid that if I stayed at the airport Kevin would, somehow, manage to find me. I mailed the keys of the Vega to him, with a brief note telling him where I had left the car. On my way back from the mailbox I stuffed my pretty lime-green dress in a garbage can.

Late the next afternoon I walked into my apartment. My tenant was a relatively imperturbable lady; she looked up from her book and said calmly, "I wasn't expecting you till next week. Didn't you have a good time?"

"No," I said. "Not very."

Chapter Fifteen

I SAW ROGER and Bea last month in Chicago. They stopped over on their way back from their honeymoon in Denver just to meet me. It was Bea who suggested I "write it out." She thought it would be therapeutic. She may be right—though not in the way she meant. She told me, not once but several times, that I looked just fine.

One of the reasons why they made a special effort to see me was to break the news gently. Kevin is engaged. He and Debbie plan to be married in June, after she graduates. All very formal and proper. There was an announcement in the paper, and an engagement party, and a diamond—not big enough to be flashy, just big enough to brag about. I smiled and said I hoped they would be very happy. They will. Of that I have no doubt.

Roger asked about my plans. I told him of the grant I'm hoping to get, which will mean a year's work in England, and about my students. Bea's big brown eyes were so imploring I hated to tell her that, no, I had no romantic plans. I see Joe now and then in the cafeteria. His department doesn't have much to do with the English people.

They invited me to come for a visit, and I said I would, sometime. I lied. They knew I lied, but they didn't know why. I wouldn't go back. I'd be afraid. Even at this distance, after so many months, the attraction is too strong. Sometimes it's all I can do to resist it. If I were only a few miles away, if I saw Kevin again . . .

We didn't talk about it, at least not much. What would be the use? They're part of the pattern now, moving smoothly along the appointed paths. All the snarls and rough spots have been rubbed away. Everything seems to be working fine.

I'm fine too. Oh, there are moments—on those endless gray afternoons when the sleet raps sharply at the windows and the one-room apartment seems as big and empty as a warehouse. Or in the early morning hours, before it's light, when I wake up for no reason and can't go back to sleep. Then for the hundredth time I go through the long list of unanswerable questions. What was it, really? Was my final explanation as incomplete as the ones that satisfied Bea and Roger? Did four seemingly normal people simultaneously and coincidentally reach critical breaking points in their emotional lives, and imagine the whole thing? Was there some simple, factual explanation none of us discovered? And the last, the worst question of all, the one that keeps me sleepless sometimes until the sun rises—did I deliberately throw away love, happiness, comfort, because of some mental distortion that will keep me lonely all my life?

I have dreamed, not once but several times, of going

back. The dream is always the same. I am walking along the curving avenue beyond the gateposts, but instead of tall trees the road is lined with the statue-stiff forms I saw in other nightmares. This time I am moving in the opposite direction, from the beginning forward in time. The shapeless masses of protoplasm take shape, reptilian, then four-footed and finally human. Priest and soldier, lord and lady, robed and kirtled and armored. And at the end I see Kevin, the last of that dreadful company, but not yet one of them; for he is aware of me as I approach. His lips shape words, his hands reach out. I cannot hear the words; I cannot tell whether the gesture is one of appeal or rejection.

I will never know. "I have heard the key turn in the door once, and turn once only . . ." I got out the door. It won't open again.

Sometimes it's cold out here in the big wide world.